'*First Name Second Name* is the quintessential Australian novel – a stunningly complex and intelligent portrait of who we are now and who we are destined to become. MinOn is a critical, insightful and compassionate new voice. Absolutely a name to remember.'

Michael Mohammed Ahmad

'*First Name Second Name* is a glorious, inventive novel about the experiences of a Chinese–Scottish family, from the goldfields in North Queensland to 1980s Brisbane to the present day. You will be both entertained and moved by this wonderful novel.'

Mirandi Riwoe

'*First Name Second Name* is exhilaratingly brilliant. Steve MinOn's voice is wry, wise and utterly original. Here, MinOn delivers a spellbinding odyssey through the past of a migrant family from Far North Queensland.'

Lech Blaine

'Ambitious and inventive … *First Name Second Name* takes themes of racial, familial and sexual identity and explores them in an entirely original way.'

Judges' comments, Queensland Literary Awards

Steve MinOn was an internationally awarded advertising copywriter and a restaurateur before becoming a writer of fiction. He grew up in North Queensland and he now lives in Meanjin/Brisbane. Steve has written often about outsiders and his family's mixed-race ancestral history, and his articles and short stories have been published in *SBS Voices*, *Mamamia* and various anthologies. He won the Glendower Award for an Emerging Queensland Writer in the 2023 Queensland Literary Awards for *First Name Second Name.*

First Name Second Name

Steve MinOn

First published 2025 by University of Queensland Press
PO Box 6042, St Lucia, Queensland 4067 Australia

The University of Queensland Press (UQP) acknowledges the Traditional Owners and their custodianship of the lands on which UQP operates. We pay our respects to their Ancestors and their descendants, who continue cultural and spiritual connections to Country. We recognise their valuable contributions to Australian and global society.

uqp.com.au
reception@uqp.com.au

Cover design by Josh Durham, Design by Committee
Cover images by Alamy Stock Photo and Josh Durham
Author photograph by Chris Crawford
Typeset in 12/17 pt Bembo Std by Post Pre-press Group, Brisbane
Printed in Australia by McPherson's Printing Group

Epigraph on p. vii taken from *The Shadow Book of Ji Yun*, edited and translated by Yi Izzy Yu and John Yu Branscum (Empress Wu Books, 2021). Reproduced by kind permission of Yi Izzy Yu and John Yu Branscum.

This manuscript won the 2023 Glendower Award for an Emerging Queensland Writer, which is generously supported by Jenny Summerson. UQP launched the Emerging Queensland Writer Award in 1999. Presented as part of the Queensland Literary Awards, in partnership with State Library of Queensland, UQP is proud to publish the annual award-winning manuscript, and is committed to building the profile of, and access to, emerging writers in Australia and internationally.

University of Queensland Press is assisted by the Australian Government through Creative Australia, its principal arts investment and advisory body.

A catalogue record for this book is available from the National Library of Australia.

ISBN 978 0 7022 6880 9 (pbk)
ISBN 978 0 7022 7020 8 (epdf)
ISBN 978 0 7022 7021 5 (epub)

University of Queensland Press uses papers that are natural, renewable and recyclable products made from wood grown in well-managed forests and other controlled sources. The logging and manufacturing processes conform to the environmental regulations of the country of origin.

Sometimes, when a Taoist is exhumed or digs himself out of the grave, he has no skin.

– Ji Yun (纪昀), Special Advisor to the Emperor of China, Imperial Librarian

The Bolin Family

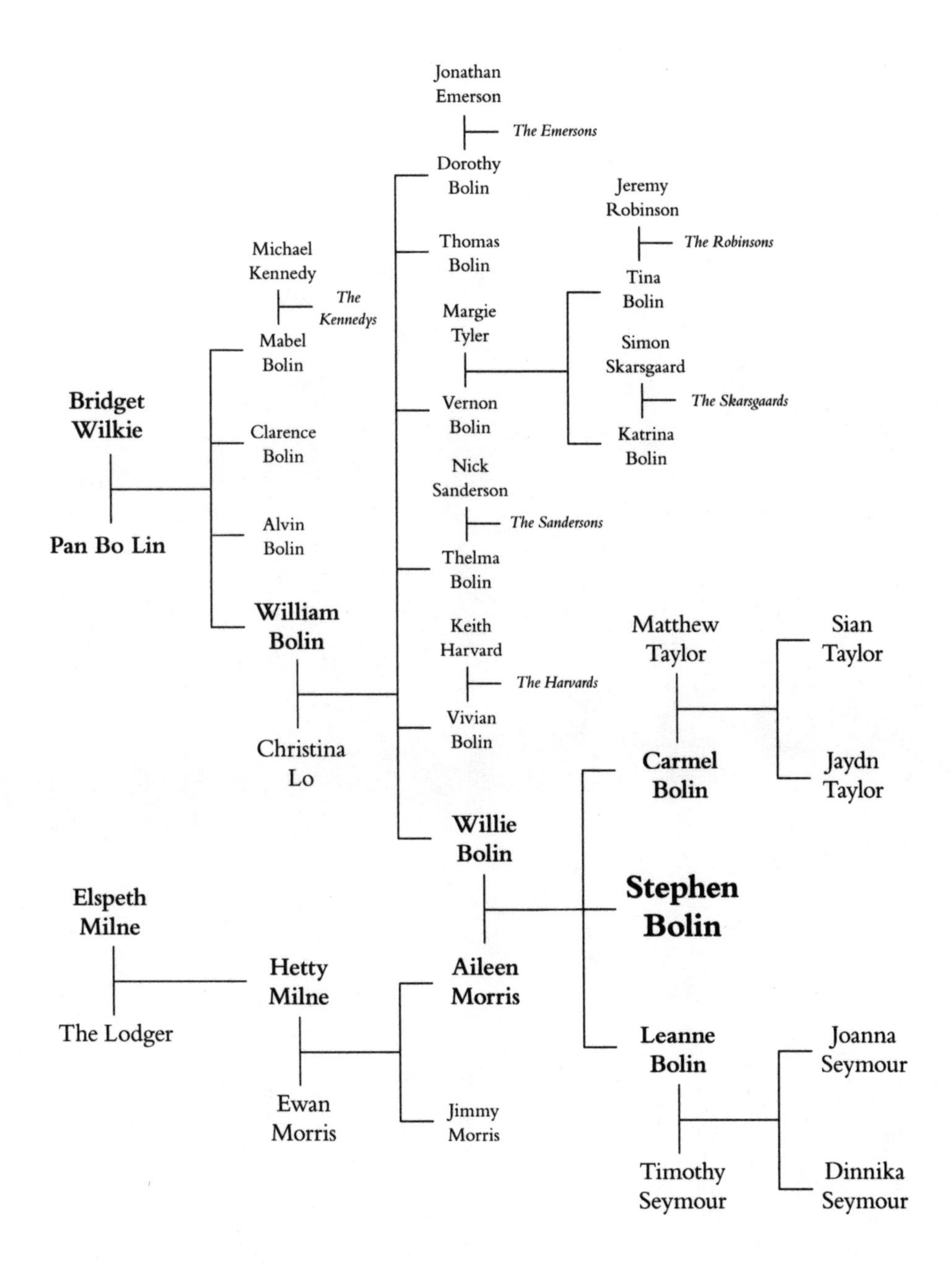

Jiāngshī

In the watershed between life and death, Stephen Bolin conjured a notepad and a pen to map out a task for his sisters. He was cold with practicalities. He gave instructions for the repatriation of his corpse: back to the town of his birth, back to Innisfail. Poles of bamboo should be cut thick enough to support his weight and approximately three metres in length. The felled poles should be run in parallel beneath his arms. His elbows and wrists should be strapped tightly with leather or vine. In the order of their birth, his sisters should arrange themselves at either end: Carmel at the front, Leanne at the back, his corpse in the centre. *The journey*, he wrote, *will be long and difficult, one thousand miles.* He instructed his sisters not to make a spectacle of themselves. *Try not to be too obvious. Stick to the backroads. Walk at night and avoid the heat of the day. You'll know you've arrived when you get there.*

2002

It was fair weather in contrast to the events. Optimistic light bled in through the blinds. The hospital called Carmel's phone just as her alarm went off at six. Stephen's nurse broke the bad news, in between the buzzing that kept interrupting.

'He … passed … five-thirty … I'm sorry, do you need to … okay … Can you? … See you then.'

Carmel thanked the nurse and hung up. Woken by the alarm and the call, her husband, Matthew, had listened in on the conversation, but he kept his eyes closed to give her space. He understood his wife, how she liked to stay in control. His sympathy would trigger tears.

Thinking Matthew was still asleep, Carmel slipped out of their bed and moved to the kitchen to call her sister. She wanted to ask if Leanne could come with her to collect Stephen's things.

'Honey, he's gone.'

Carmel could only hear Leanne sucking short breaths in through her mouth, nothing coming out. 'Darling … Take your time.'

There was a pause, still no words from Leanne, so Carmel

filled the space. 'It's okay. I can do it alone if you don't feel you can come.'

'I can come,' Leanne said, but her tone was argumentative.

Carmel knew her sister well enough to know that Leanne was only mad at herself. At her emotions. 'There is honestly nothing you can do that I can't do alone,' she said. 'There aren't many of his things to collect.'

'I just don't want to see him ... like that.' Leanne set herself off with the image of their brother, of her sister grieving over his body. She tried to mask the liquid sounds of her sobbing.

'Darling, it's alright. It's been a very long seventy-two hours for all of us. We've all seen enough of hospitals. Rest up. I'll bring Mum. I'll call you when we get back. Come to ours tonight. If you feel like it.'

'Thanks. I'll be alright.'

Next Carmel called their mother, Aileen. 'Mum, can you come with me to the hospital?'

'Is someone sick?'

Carmel realised that she had raced ahead. That her mother hadn't been given the news. 'Mum ...' Carmel took a steadying moment. 'Stephen.'

'Yes?'

'Mum, Stephen passed. I need to go to the hospital to sort things out. Can you come with me?'

'Oh.' Aileen sounded hesitant. 'Should we take flowers?' She was processing the shock, or perhaps she thought it was someone else who had died. Carmel wasn't sure.

'We don't have to take flowers, Mum. I'll pick you up on the way. Bring a cardigan.'

Carmel put the phone down and returned to check on Matthew, who was now sitting up. He said he was sorry and sad to hear the news, but it was probably for the best that Stephen hadn't hung on for very long. They held hands and he gave hers a squeeze. Then he offered to drive her and Aileen in, and Carmel felt grateful to have someone to do that for her.

The nurses had done an excellent job of making Stephen look composed and neat. They'd removed the drips and the ventilator and freshly dressed his bed. Seeing their grieving mother rush to Stephen's side finally broke something inside Carmel, and she wept and gobbed against Matthew's shirt. It always annoyed her how her mother's emotions weakened hers. Eventually she felt her decorum return. She attempted to tidy up her face and then she went with Matthew to collect the few things Stephen had come in with.

While Carmel did that, Aileen remained bedside, stroking Stephen's hand. She looked closely at her son's face, as if she was trying to remember him alive, and then she frowned as if she had failed.

When the nurse brought Stephen's things out of safekeeping, Carmel was told her brother had left a note. It read like a prank to Carmel – bamboo poles, a thousand-mile journey, travelling at night – but the nurse made her sign for it anyway. He must have returned to semi-consciousness, momentarily. It was the only explanation. Sometimes they did this, the nurse said, people with catastrophic brain injuries. Sometimes they broke through the fog of their condition and could communicate. Their words might seem intentional, she said, but they were mostly just tricks of the dying person's brain, failing physiology causing synapses to fire randomly, activating fantasies. Stephen's last words were idiotic, Carmel thought. A wasted opportunity to say something useful to them. She folded the note and took it with his belongings.

Now the note lay on the coffee table in Carmel's living room. Leanne could read it from the couch where she sat. She was still having trouble controlling her emotions. Carmel couldn't stand her sister's sobbing, so she rose to make them both a cup of fenugreek tea, which she usually drank for the statins, to stave off her high cholesterol. Perhaps the tea would also soothe her stomach, which was lurching and cramping with suppressed grief.

Aileen sat apart from them, staring at the television, which had been turned on to kill the silence. She was waiting for her daughters to decide what to do next. To decide for her.

The handwriting on Stephen's note was unsteady but familiar to all of them. As children, Carmel and Leanne had worked hard at developing their handwriting. Stephen had not. Carmel and Leanne had designed theirs to look beautiful. Stephen couldn't care less about his. It just came out the way it did: forward-leaning, sharp and efficient, similar to that of their father, Willie. So, while the content of Stephen's note was strange, unlike anything he'd ever said, they were all certain that these were his words, flowing from his dying hand.

Leanne, a balled-up tissue in her fist, eventually noticed Stephen had signed the note *Jiāngshī*. The word vibrated through her tears, and she wondered what it meant.

Carmel watched her, expecting Leanne to write the note off as she had. Their brother had been delusional in the end. That's what the nurse said. There was nothing in the note they could act sensibly on. What he was asking them to do was impossible, ridiculous, and probably illegal. He was asking them to carry his body on foot to where? Innisfail? The brain was strange.

'It's very him to do this to us,' Leanne said, finally.

'Do what?'

'Leave us all guessing.'

'At the time I'm sure he thought he was making it quite obvious,' Carmel said, and pointed to the last line on the note. 'What is Jiāngshī?'

'Who the hell would know,' Leanne said, picking up the note by its corner as if it was toxic. She turned it over, but the back was blank. 'Poor Stephen.' And then came the tears again. And then the sobbing.

'His brain wasn't working, darling,' Carmel said, moving in to sit with her disintegrating sister.

'Is it a Chinese word?' Leanne asked.

'If Dad was alive, he might have known …'

'Did your father speak Chinese?' Aileen asked, breaking from the television.

'Mum,' grizzled Carmel.

'No, he didn't speak Chinese,' Aileen said with renewed certainty. Then she seemed to waver as she remembered something: 'Gong hei fat choy.'

Leanne laughed but midway coughed up a sob.

'That's what you say at Chinese New Year,' Carmel said. 'Everybody knows that one.'

'I can picture him somewhere up there, annoyed at us,' Leanne said.

'Who? Dad?'

'No, Stephen. Or maybe he'd be laughing at his stupid sisters.'

Carmel folded the note so the offending words were hidden. It was opening old family resentments. She straightened up.

Before long, Leanne had pulled herself together as well. She and Carmel had always been aligned that way. There was a synergy between them that their brother was left out of – a sisters' language, not a sibling language.

There were things to be done – but done right. They couldn't help that they were more conventional than their brother. A simple memorial would have to do for Stephen, just like the one their father had. And just like his, Stephen's body would be donated to science. They were defying his instructions, but his instructions were absurd. Someone should benefit from the whole stupid tragedy of their brother's death.

Leanne made the call to Stephen's housemate in London to let her know. She asked Shelley if she knew how to contact Stephen's other friends. Did he have any others? Aileen watched her daughters. She could hear their husbands talking in the kitchen. Where was Stephen?

Jiāngshī

The emptiness of his death was interrupted by a sound. The hum of something mechanical, like an electric motor. Like a fridge – an industrial fridge. Or a cold room.

Why am I hearing?

Stephen wondered if this was normal. If this was what death was meant to be like. Occasional vibrations echoing through from the living world. The molecules of his eardrums being pushed around by sound waves.

I'm in my body still?

Was he meant to register these sensations? He wasn't sure. Concentrating, he was able to understand that the vibrations were coming from beneath him. He was lying on a hard, metallic surface.

How could he still be conscious and part of him still functioning? His nerves were coordinating. His synapses were communicating. He was making a certain connection between the sensations and himself. He knew he was dead but maybe he wasn't completely dead or completely inert. He was sentient and that was not what he had expected.

Why am I still here?

He wondered how long he would exist like that. It was horrible to be thinking it. Awful to have awareness of himself in that state. He tried to let the thoughts go. That's what they say, don't they? *Let go. It's time to let go.* But the vibrations were tenacious, demanding. They pulled his attention back to the physical, away from the ethereal. Away from the question of where he was going to next. Away from the glorious acceptance of nothingness that death was meant to bring.

I wonder if I can move my toes.

He felt a sensation of tightness around one of them. Meanwhile, his face felt weighed down by something slick, like vinyl or rubber. Once again, his thoughts combined to orient him and, once again, they combined to devastate him. He tried to open his eyes but either they were determinedly dead or it was too dark to see. He tried moving his toes again, hoping to feel nothing at all and then bliss or departure. But there was movement and a distinct sensation of constraint. There was something tied around his big toe that was cutting off its circulation. Or it would have, if he had any blood at all moving through his body.

Fear gripped his heart and he was overcome by a violent wave of panic that rattled his legs like a pair of crumpled jeans being shaken out. His body jerked up and down. Through the involuntary spasms, he felt the impact of his head on metal. He was certain then that he was in a freezer in a morgue.

His legs and arms were stiff with cold, despite the unholy undulations. His head banged on what must have been the ceiling of his compartment, and his shoulders pushed forward and back, juddering against the metal tray he was laid out on. He was like a live fish that had been tossed in an empty esky. He had inexplicably come alive in the ice.

With all the shaking, the latch burst open, and the tray slid out from the wall of freezer drawers before coming to an abrupt stop, which caused Stephen's body to concertina in its bag. The zip split open, and light flooded in across Stephen's saline-encrusted eyelids. They cracked open and his eyes took in a grid of ceiling tiles, a dirty air-conditioning vent and a fluorescent tube. Two fluorescent tubes. His eyes were still focusing.

Stephen sat up suddenly on the fulcrum of his hips. But the motion flipped him forward, throwing him off the drawer. He torpedoed towards the floor. He tried to use his arms to cushion his fall, but they were awkward and slow.

He lay there for a while in shock, face down, wondering if he'd damaged himself – though what did it matter if he was dead? He rolled over onto his back and attempted to stand up. His arms shot out and his legs stiffened as if on pneumatic pistons. Rigor mortis disrupted his joints. They hinged tyrannically. It was miraculous and hideous and ridiculous.

He looked down along his nose to his chest and below: he was naked. The constriction around his big toe was caused by a small manila tag. It gave his name, his case number, his date of birth, his time and date of death, his height, his weight, his sex and his race, which was listed as mixed.

A habit from his former life compelled him to close the freezer door. As it sealed, a gust of vapour, dry and icy, blew out towards his torso, passing around his body and between his legs, playing pizzicato on every body hair it touched. The sensation was relayed with a slight delay like a voice on a long-distance call.

Stephen's eyes searched for something to cover his nakedness. On one wall, there were shelves stacked with translucent plastic boxes, perhaps a dozen or so, each labelled with a name.

Other people's things. He went looking for his own, but in the box marked Stephen Bolin there was nothing.

In its nearest neighbour, he found a pair of tracksuit pants. His fingers, stiff and ugly as ginger root, stretched the waistband as he fed his legs through. They were heavy as lopped logs. He tangled his arms in the sleeves of an oversized t-shirt. On the back of the shirt were the words *YAY GIR MY STIR* – a reference to the German herbal liqueur Jägermeister, a phonetic guide for drunks. Pushing his feet with their tag still attached into a pair of busted shoes, Stephen turned and fled.

1878

It's not gold in the stream you're panning for, it's just pyrite that's been coloured yellow by piss.

That's what Pan Bo Lin wanted to say to that treacherous dog, Yung Jam. That fart. That rotten egg in the basket. But he held his tongue. He let Mr Marsland, his counsel, speak for him. The Charters Towers courthouse was full of Chinese busybodies who were only there for the gossip. Mr Marsland approached the bench.

'The Crown has no case,' he said. 'Ah Gee and his gambling house are strangers to Pan Bo Lin. He is not who Yung Jam has accused him of being; that other person, Pan Lin, the name that was written on the summons to appear here.' He lifted his hand to point at the dock. 'This is Pan *Bo* Lin. A different Han. He is not the banker of Ah Gee's fan-tan place. He was not there when Ah Nam, Gin War, Yick Sing Tong, Num Char and Hop Lee were putting down their five pounds on the game. He did not take their money. They did not promise their Qing coins to him to hold for cash either. Qing coins are worthless. Those that were allegedly found in Pan Bo Lin's bedroll were worthless brass.'

Qing coins are just old rubbish? thought Pan Bo Lin. He had heard the translation but wondered if the court interpreter could be trusted. Was he a Sze Yap spy too?

Mr Marsland continued, 'They are not being held for Ah Gee in lieu of pounds. They are not Yung Jam's coins or Ah Nam's or Gin War's or Yick Sing Tong's or Num Char's or Hop Lee's. Pan Bo Lin, my client, does not know what Ah Gee does with his own coins. Perhaps he spends them on tobacco or opium.'

Or, if your name is Yung Jam, your coins would pay Ah Nam to play a song on the dizi in your pants, Pan Bo Lin thought. He wished he could have said that to that dog's face, right then and there. Yung Jam, the big-mouth dog. He would curse him later but here in the court he was trying to be smart, and he kept quiet. Because he knew Mr Marsland would apply to the bench on his behalf.

'As well, a man,' Mr Marsland said, 'regardless of his name, whether he be the accused Pan Lin or even my client Pan *Bo* Lin, cannot be convicted under the Gaming Act where and if and especially if the Crown has entered Ah Gee's fan-tan place without the possession of a warrant!'

Ha! How does that feel, Yung Jam?

'The bench upholds Mr Marsland's objection,' said the magistrate. 'The case is dismissed. Professional costs of two pounds, five shillings and nine pence are to be paid to Mr Marsland by the Crown.'

So much for you and your Sze Yap lies, Yung Jam.

Pan Bo Lin walked quick and free from the courthouse, past the tents and timber mining towers of the new settlement. He took Gill Street, a snake street, a highway of robbers. Dust rose to his mouth. He sifted it with his teeth while he swore again at Yung Jam for reporting him to the police and almost having him in chains. And then he was back to his pile, back to the tailings in the outer claims. He squatted angrily by his bark-walled hut down by Millchester Creek under the pissing runoff of the Hope and Wonder shit-pile that poisoned the skin of his feet.

The Hope and Wonder owners paid no attention to the problems of celestials like Pan Bo Lin. They kept their eyes on the big fortune being taken by the big miners, not the crumbs being found by the troubled Chinese. So, as Pan Bo Lin said 'fuck you' to his Sze Yap masters and 'fuck you' to all the Sze Yap who frequented the fan-tan place, like Yung Jam, Ah Gee, Ah Nam, Gin War, Yick Sing Tong, Num Char and Hop Lee, nobody listened. Pan Bo Lin had even said 'fuck you' to Gold Commissioner WSEM Charters once, when he saw him marching through the Towers in his pristine boots. Pan Bo Lin had added, quietly, 'Fuck your mother too.' But again, nobody listened.

The owners of Hope and Wonder didn't notice Pan Bo Lin down there as he quietly swirled his pan in the water. When Pan Bo Lin crouched to the creek and reached for his knife, they didn't notice him do that either. And when he sliced through to the roots of the braid that he and his countrymen called their biànzi, they didn't care what he had severed. But Pan Bo Lin knew what he had done. It was an act of spite. He had cut himself off from his country. Now he couldn't go back. If he did, he would be a Han without his biànzi and that amounted to a Han without his head.

Still, he had his debts, the money he owed to the Sze Yap for his passage to Australia. And he had his wife in Chikan, to whom he owed a promise, that he would send her living money for the life of loneliness she endured. He couldn't be the banker for the fan-tan place that Ah Gee ran anymore. That Sze Yap fucker. He couldn't find his fortune by pawing through the pathetic golden dribble that ran like incontinent piss from the Hope and Wonder claim either. The few specks of gold Pan Bo Lin found were all going into Mr Marsland's pocket to protect Pan Bo Lin from those Sze Yap.

The next day, Pan Bo Lin took the last gold crumbs he had combed from the gravel. He rescued them from their hiding spot – the dusty hole he had dug in the floor of his bark hut, three hand-widths out from the corner. In a small packet, he stashed them against his body, wedged behind his cotton dùdōu, the bellyband his wife gave to him on their wedding day, which reminded him of his promise to bring her money. He hoped she still wore hers, the one he gave in return to remind her of her obligation to care for his mother. He and his wife were bound by their dùdōu. He hoped she fulfilled her role well as daughter-in-law.

But how would he get her money now? Not through the Sze Yap channels. Of that he was certain. Perhaps it would be easier in the port of Maryborough. There would be fewer Sze Yap there to report him. There would also be other countrymen who were happy to say 'fuck you' to the Sze Yap and to help him smuggle money out.

Behind the courthouse, Mr Marsland accepted Pan Bo Lin's payment for the fan-tan case, with a cursory wave of his hand. He represented him out of astuteness. His colleagues hadn't seen the opportunities he had seen with the celestials. They paid him in gold. They were always in trouble. Many gold specks came his way. Bit by bit he was amassing his fortune.

Pan Bo Lin followed Mr Marsland and his possibly Sze Yap interpreter back to the Charters Towers hotel, where Mr Marsland had a room. He wouldn't leave without saying what he wanted from him next.

'Citizenship!' Mr Marsland laughed into his shirt buttons, tipping back in his chair. He noticed a stain on his waistcoat and tried to brush it away, but it was set there in grease from the sandwich of dripping he had eaten for lunch. He asked Pan Bo Lin why on earth he would wish to be a citizen, why he wouldn't return to his own country, a country more natural to him. Amid the transactions of his profession, Mr Marsland had learned enough about the hardships and inequity endured by his celestial clients to wonder why they did it to themselves. Why they even came.

He asked Pan Bo Lin, 'What do you know of the Aliens Act?'

Pan Bo Lin smiled. He was always offended by Mr Marsland but he didn't show it. He didn't want to put him off. He needed the counsel's advice, and he was willing to pay for it. He pushed another tiny crumb that he had panned from the runoff of the Hope and Wonder claim across the grease-stained surface of Mr Marsland's desk.

The counsel scooped it up, dropped it quickly into the watch pocket of his waistcoat and began to write a note. In the dim light of the hotel room, it was difficult for Pan Bo Lin to see what he was writing: not words but symbols. A woman and … and a man. Mr Marsland told Pan Bo Lin that he must be settled locally with a wife to be considered worthy of naturalisation. That he must demonstrate a commitment to stay and not be the type to ship money offshore to China. This was the essence of the Aliens Act, to ban outsiders from undermining the country's wealth, to ban the uncommitted from sending money home.

Pan Bo Lin lifted his shirt to show Mr Marsland the dùdōu: this was his wife's commitment to him and surely Mr Marsland would understand that if it was there on his body, then this was all the proof he needed. He motioned to the interpreter to look.

He was already married, and so, already qualified. Mr Marsland understood. But he pointed to the woman on his diagram.

'You need to bring her here,' he said, now pointing to the floor, as if he was pointing through the floor to the dirt of the Towers.

Pan Bo Lin wanted to tell Mr Marsland that he was unable to do that. He knew that for sure. The cost was prohibitive. He already had one Sze Yap debt. And what about his mother? Without his wife there to look after her, how would she live?

Fuck you to the Sze Yap.

Pan Bo Lin stared at Mr Marsland's note. His legal options were reduced to bad sketches on a scrap of paper. Was that all the assistance that weeks of panning in the toxic runoff could buy him?

'Let me know if you wish to proceed,' Mr Marsland said, wanting to get on with his day, 'and I will be happy to help.'

Fuck you, Mr Marsland.

Three years later:

Not tranquil and clear anymore, the Mary River was brown and angry. The water surged and swirled across low-lying banks.

Pan Bo Lin was told by the Scottish foreman to let the wharf horses through. Onto what was left of Pan Bo Lin's crop, on the sliver of unused land he'd cultivated for himself. 'That way,' the foreman said, 'they won't eat the specimen plants, the valuable plants the curator has gathered from New Zealand and from Polynesia and from America. And from Ballarat.'

The foreman made curious sounds but Pan Bo Lin had learned enough of his body language to understand. The horses would eat Pan Bo Lin's ong choy. His cabbages. His tomatoes. They would eat his peanuts to the ground. They were not important to the curator's world of science. They were not valuable to him, though they were to Pan Bo Lin. He traded them for salt and soap and pig meat. They reminded him of Chikan. He grew them here when he was not tending the lawns and pulling weeds and sawing back the rampant vines and gathering the fallen bunya nuts and chasing the kangaroos away from the exotic sausage tree that the curator had planted.

The Mary River wharf was running deeper and deeper in flood and the horses would only move if they were let into Pan Bo Lin's garden.

'We need to move the horses. Fence them in!'

Fuck you, Mary River. Fuck you, Scottish foreman. Fuck you, horses.

Pan Bo Lin looked at the plot of his own labour, his own sweat, his own enterprise. The one he started when he arrived in Maryborough, after the long walk from Charters Towers. It would be reduced to hoof marks and horse shit. There would be just a brown mess where his market garden once stood. But he did what was asked of him. He made temporary fencing out of rope and brigalow sticks. He slapped his hands and shouted insults in his own language so the Scottish foreman wouldn't make out what was said about him. It sounded like he was cursing the rain, shouting at the horses, but he was describing the foreman in detail.

Fat-pink-fuck-in-a-rich-woman's-hat.

The temper of his mother was Pan Bo Lin's only inheritance.

One more horse contained, and he would be done. After that he left them to his peanuts and his tomatoes and his ong choy and made his way through the slop on the road, down through the teeming rain to Bazaar Street, to the corner where John Hunter Boots and Shoes had an awning that offered some shelter from the endless storm. The rain kept coming down. His plot was doomed. He would have to wait it out under cover.

Pan Bo Lin was not the only one on the corner of John Hunter Boots and Shoes. There were gold diggers in town from the mines at the Towers. He avoided them like the stink. They had already proven themselves no friends of his and it was easy to avoid their gaze. They looked past him anyway, like he was not there, just as they had done for the three years he spent on the Hope and Wonder tailings.

Pan Bo Lin squatted with his back against the store window and waited. There were timber workers under the awning also, jostling with the miners for dry space. Pan Bo Lin knew their type too. He traded with them. They wouldn't have bothered with him except that he had something they needed. His talent with compost and seeds and cultivation meant he could grow things. They could only cut things down. Pan Bo Lin sold them vegetables to keep them healthy and regular. Otherwise, they sat in agony, pushing their salted-beef bowels to exhaustion over the pits in their stinking outhouse latrines.

They only knew to buy things they recognised, like peanuts and tomatoes and cabbage to boil. They left him to keep the ong choy, the water spinach that he grew in the boggy part of the plot. They left him with the bitter melon too, so ugly to their eyes. Those were the best foods. And yet they were left for Pan Bo Lin to eat himself.

On the other side of the street was a furniture store, and the awning there was wide and stormproof. But the distance across was made interminable by the sheeting rain and wind. Anyone who attempted it was drenched. Through the legs of the milling men on the veranda of John Hunter Boots and Shoes, Pan Bo Lin saw that there was someone stupid enough to try to leave the furniture store. A woman in a pale blue dress was struggling with her broken parasol. Not a small woman. Not a fragile belle. She was as broad as the men she stood beside. They cowered from the swinging arc of her umbrella. Pan Bo Lin craned his neck to watch her as she stepped out into the rain. She'd given up on the malfunctioning umbrella and strode out, uncovered, into the brutal weather.

Her first steps dropped deeper than she was expecting. She stumbled briefly in the mud. The men under the awning gave her a mighty cheer and made their bets that she would surely fall. In the rain, her petticoats were soaked through. Transfixed, the men in front of Pan Bo Lin hooted with delight as she made her way across to them, wet now to the skin. They formed a leering welcoming committee, a rank, damp, woollen wall. There was something animal bristling under their sweat-stained gear and it almost pushed her back out into the rain with its odour and its threat.

Pan Bo Lin recognised that smell and he saw its effect on the woman: her fear, but also her determination. She didn't have a husband or a helper. There was a sense of make-do about her. By the cut of her clothing, she was a woman of ordinary means to go with her equally ordinary looks. But she was still a rare thing in a colony, a woman alone.

Pan Bo Lin waited to see how she would handle the men who lined the step to the shelter under the awning outside the John Hunter Boots and Shoes Wholesale and Retail store on the corner of Bazaar and Alice Streets in Maryborough. He waited and he watched.

While the Mary River rose to the border of his plot, swallowing much of Queens Park in its flooding current, and while the wharf horses dined in the rain on Pan Bo Lin's ong choy and his peanuts and his tomatoes, the woman held out her hand to the nearest man, the biggest man under the awning, hoping he would oblige her. And, of course, he did. He was flattered by her attention. He was cheered on and he was slapped on his wet, buffalo-wide back by his mates.

But she had chosen him for a reason. And she had braced against his weight. And because he didn't expect it, he was pulled like a fruit off a tree by the strong right arm of the woman. He landed on his barrel chest in the mud. Having made room for herself under the awning, she stepped around him up onto the veranda and into a widening circle of men. She wiped her hands on the hips of her dress, stomped the mud off her boots and made her way to the first man who refused to leer at her, refused to laugh, refused to look up any higher than her boots.

Pan Bo Lin was that man, a man who was soon to be married to her, to Bridget Wilkie, single woman, free woman, recently arrived from Ireland.

Bridget Wilkie's attitude had been hardened through childhood fights in a boys' orphanage. As the daughter of the supervising chaplain, she had learned an important lesson – the law of a stronger arm. If you didn't have one, then act as if you did. If you feared violence, you'd be easily beaten. If you needed friendship, befriend the smallest boy. Because even your friends would one day want to better you. One day they'd steal your share. These were things every smart boy at the orphanage picked up, and so did Bridget, pushed into the arena by her father, an egalitarian by politics and a survivalist by creed. Only later, long after her father died, did she realise his lessons made her ineligible for marriage. She was too much for men to handle.

With no father and no Irish husband to support her, and with the English taking more and more of the Irish share in her county, she decided to leave for a country with more freedom and more hope. In the Australian colony, she was told, a woman with strength would be no threat to a man. An asset, even. And there was money to be made with jobs for the willing. Over there she might free herself from her inequity, and from her feuds with expectation.

During her voyage, she was cornered and nearly raped on deck in the night, except that she was unafraid of violence and she broke the stupid sod's nose. As soon as she arrived in the colony, however, she could see that the same rules that had held her down still applied, even in a new hemisphere. What was yours was not likely to stay yours for long. Even the Irish men were willing to take Bridget Wilkie for a fool and expect her to yield like a woman.

On the docks, she noticed men of a type she hadn't seen before in Ireland. They were lightly built, with beardless complexions, ignored by other men. Bridget realised she didn't fear these men when she saw them – these celestials, as they were called. The Chinamen she saw had an order to them. Their clothes were laundered and repaired. Their huts were neat. Their muddy shoes were kept at the door, even if their floors were dirt.

Bridget knew in this colony she could not make it on her own. She needed and wanted a husband. But she needed and wanted one she didn't fear. One she could control physically, perhaps, if she had to. One who couldn't hold her down.

There was no ceremony for them. There was no wedding night or honeymoon. There were no vows spoken beyond the acknowledgement of the question asked by Mr Marsland, who had made it by some perfect coincidence that week into Maryborough; he had been brought to the registrar's office by Bridget Wilkie herself, and was surprised to find his old client Pan Bo Lin waiting.

'Do you take this woman to be your lawfully wedded wife in holy matrimony?' he asked.

Pan Bo Lin had practised his answer under the tutelage of his fiancée, by candlelight, the previous night. She coaxed it from him with a soap-softened hand.

'I do.'

The words were foreign to him, though he knew they had a role in the ritual. When Bridget taught him the words, she had massaged her hand through a gap in Pan Bo Lin's pants. The dùdōu that was still around his waist shifted imperceptibly under her attention, as if it was loosening its grip but not enough to fall away. Bridget believed that he was wearing a garment of modesty, part of his underwear. Perhaps a version of a corset, though he was thin and not needing to be cinched.

With conviction at the ceremony, Pan Bo Lin spoke as he'd been asked, for the benefit of Mr Marsland and Bridget Wilkie, his wife-to-be. And then he waited like a cat with a sardine moustache for Bridget to say the same.

Afterwards, Mr Marsland dipped his pen in the inkwell on his rented desk and began to draw up the marriage certificate for the unlikely couple. A Chinese man and an Irish woman, drawn together by the legal loops of his professional handwriting. The marks were unreadable to Pan Bo Lin, who watched over Mr Marsland's shoulder. The words spanned the document left to right and seemed to be painted by spiders. These characters made no sense. Why were they grouped the way they were? But

Mr Marsland had served him well and had kept him on the right side of the law before.

Bridget made more of the letters than Pan Bo Lin. She was familiar with their form, though not with their formality.

Marriages solemnised in the district of Wide Bay in the colony of Queensland …

Mr Marsland wrote it in flourishes and Bridget gripped her handkerchief tightly.

Married in the office of the District Registrar at Maryborough, according to the Act of Parliament 28 Victoria No. 75.

Bridget saw for the first time how her husband's name was spelled out.

Pan Bo Lin, wrote Mr Marsland. And then he added, *Bachelor.*

Bridget knew nothing of the wife that Pan Bo Lin already had, nor the reason for the dùdōu under his shirt. And Pan Bo Lin was determined not to tell her why he wore it. She had her reasons to marry him. He had his reasons to marry her. He could barely afford one wife, yet here he was, marrying a second. But he could see that their union was useful and that he could outwit the Sze Yap with her at his side. There would be none of their taxes. He would be free to make his own fortune; Bridget would be his ticket to citizenship and all the riches that belonging would offer.

As Mr Marsland wrote *Canton, China* under the section for her husband's birthplace, and *Cork, Ireland* under hers, Bridget sighed. The words spelled out the vast distance between them. The distance she had drifted from her old life and the distance he had drifted from his.

'What would be your profession?' Mr Marsland asked Bridget, peering over the rim of his smudged spectacles.

'Write down dressmaker,' she told him.

'And your age?' asked Mr Marsland.

'Write down nineteen years,' replied Bridget.

Mr Marsland was surprised. He didn't believe her. He didn't ask anything of Pan Bo Lin. He already knew the answer to his age. He wrote *30 years.*

Bridget was taken aback. She looked critically at her husband, at his stature and his slim, hairless body and the shy way he had with his hands. She had thought for certain he was younger than her. She suddenly felt monstrous beside him in her white dress, with her petticoat flared like the buttress of the fig that grew in the flood mud of Queens Park, where Pan Bo Lin had been repairing his garden.

Mr Marsland inserted the word *Gardener* as Pan Bo Lin's profession.

Bridget eyeballed Pan Bo Lin's clothes. Her first impression had been they were well maintained, but on closer inspection they were old. She wasn't watching when Mr Marsland wrote the names of the people she hadn't met and never would. *Que Fook*, the father of the groom, deceased. *Sin Chow*, the mother's maiden name. Pan Bo Lin thought about his wife and how he might continue to send her money.

Bridget had a question: what would her name be, as the wife of this Chinaman? She didn't care that asking such a question might reveal how little she knew of her husband. She was a woman marrying a stranger in a colony. What did it matter that the strangeness extended to the language he spoke, which she didn't speak, and to the customs he followed, which she didn't follow? She was a practical woman who understood the sacrifices that needed to be made and how she must put all comforts aside. For in this colony there were greater dangers than illiteracy. And for now, at least, Pan Bo Lin had shown only deference. She felt safe with him, and he seemed smart enough to see her for what she was: respectability. But first she had to be his wife by law and what would that sound like exactly?

'What will my married name be?' Bridget asked Mr Marsland, who sat back to consider her question.

'That is a choice for you,' he said at last. 'Pan is his family name. Bo Lin are his given names.' With his index finger he jabbed at the words on the marriage certificate, speaking to Bridget as if her husband wasn't in the room. 'Do you want to be called Mrs Pan?' Mr Marsland raised a palm to stop Bridget before she could reply. 'You'll find he has been addressed more often as Mr Bo Lin and has become quite used to it. It's a misunderstanding, of course. A miscarriage of translation. First name, second name, round the wrong way.'

Bridget didn't need any complications. Getting married was the sensible thing to do; her married name should be sensible too. She pointed to Pan Bo Lin's name on the document, jabbing her finger just as Mr Marsland had, but eyeballing her husband, who watched her with awe, a little turned on by her assertiveness.

'First name, second name,' she said, as if she could reverse the order that had developed over thousands of years of Chinese tradition, just by the force of her finger.

Bridget snatched up the pen that rested in Mr Marsland's ink well. On a piece of paper that Marsland handed her, Bridget wrote *Bridget Bo Lin*, three times in quick succession. She was practising how it would look. The letters looped comfortably from her hand, and each time the words Bo and Lin came closer together – until they merged like two vines.

Bridget Bolin

'When you write it like that, it doesn't look Chinese at all,' said Bridget for Mr Marsland's benefit.

'Bridget Bolin it is then,' cried Mr Marsland. 'First name,

second name,' he said, echoing the new order determined by the new wife. He called Pan Bo Lin over with an impatient gesture.

'Mr Pan Bolin,' Mr Marsland said, rolling the words together as Bridget had done.

'Mrs Bridget Bolin,' Bridget repeated to her husband. She tapped her finger on the paper where Mr Marsland had indicated their signatures were needed as a couple. But Pan Bo Lin just nodded, and pointed to where Bridget should sign on his behalf.

There was a great distance, Bridget thought as she signed the certificate, between her and the man she had married. It was a distance she was willing to cross but only with the full confidence of the law behind her and with the strength she still retained in her arm.

Jiāngshī

Stephen experienced few reactions from people as he searched for an exit from the hospital, aware that his gait was more a hop than a walk. But the politeness of the hospital was inherent. It was a place of healing, with all kinds of ailments being suffered and treated. Everyone looked unwell. Everyone looked as poorly as Stephen.

An odour of clinic and rot seemed to follow him, while the oversized t-shirt he'd chosen to wear swayed and flicked and danced with his every step. He felt compelled to hurry but was afraid to run, unsure of his legs. Afraid to draw attention to himself. He didn't just want to fit in, he wanted to disappear. He was forced to wade through a small crowd that had gathered near the glass exit doors, but managed to pass unnoticed.

At least it was night. The ambulance driveway was busy with light but there were margins of darkness, hedged gardens that he could escape into, as if he was slipping away for a smoke. At the road, he avoided the pedestrian crossing, jaywalking in the wake of a passing vehicle. There was a McDonald's on the corner that he skirted around. But as he did, he noticed a figure at the nearby bus stop.

If Stephen had been breathing, his breath would have caught in his throat. If he hadn't still been desiccated from the effects of his refrigeration, tears might have welled in his eyes. The man at the bus stop triggered a memory. Stephen heard his mother's voice speaking down a phone line – a lifetime ago, but less than a year ago. She was telling him that his father's diagnosis was terminal. She was pleading with Stephen to come home.

In the dark of the McDonald's carpark, Stephen saw his father in that old man. His own father, in the numbing aftermath of a terminal cancer diagnosis, sitting at that exact bus stop, eating some fries. Had the old man gone into the McDonald's to buy some fries to distract himself from the thought that he was dying?

Stephen's mother's voice came to him again. *Help him. Be a better son.*

He imagined how it would have gone if he'd come in his car to collect his father, pulling into the bus stop from the left-hand lane. The tide of impatient drivers would have glowered as he slowed. His father would have looked up, but Stephen's car would have been out of context. It wouldn't have made sense to his father to see Stephen there. How would he have driven from London to pick him up?

'Dad, get in!' he would have had to shout.

It would have been an awful drive home: Stephen trying to hold it together, to put a positive slant on what he knew; his father rattled, his voice weakened, sapped. The McDonald's fries going cold in his father's hands while he stared out through the windscreen, trying to form his words. He would have looked defeated.

'You're the man of the house now,' he might have said to Stephen. 'I want you to look after your mother and your sisters.'

The old guy at the bus stop came back into focus. His grey hair was thin and so transparent it offered no cover to his brown and shiny scalp. His shoulders were narrow, and his old hands hung lightly in his lap. He wore a sloppy joe over a pair of comfortable jeans. Beside him was a bag that might have been filled with shopping, although the shops were long closed. His shoes were discount runners. He was out of place at that hour. Someone's grandfather who should be in bed.

Stephen hopped behind the bus stop to peer at him through the glass panel. The old man seemed to be watching the traffic carefully, like he was waiting for a ride. *Waiting for me?* There would be very few buses running at this hour.

Trying not to alarm him, Stephen shuffled around to his side of the stop. The old man didn't look at Stephen. Without invitation, Stephen sat down, or to be more accurate, he folded down beside the man. All he wanted was an opportunity to sit with him. And if the old man was waiting for the bus after all, Stephen wanted to see him get on, arrive safely and be welcomed home. With no drama. Especially no diagnosis of terminal cancer, just a sleepy hello and then life would be good, uninterrupted by grief and disappointment about a retirement terminated prematurely.

The headlights of a bus approached from a distance and the old man stirred. Feeling an urgency, Stephen tested his voice.

'Here's the bus,' he said, though he noticed that he hadn't moved his mouth and he wondered how he'd spoken at all.

When the old man turned to Stephen, his face drained of colour. He gathered his bag quickly and rushed to the roadside, keen to board the bus, though it hadn't quite pulled in yet. It was as if he was about to leap in front of it. Stephen rushed to the kerb to hold him back, or restrain him, or something more that Stephen couldn't understand.

The old man shrugged him off and refused to look at Stephen in the seconds it took for the bus to settle into the kerb. Finally, Stephen followed the old man onboard, ignored by the driver who must have seen too many drunks, too many drug addicts at that hour to care about hassling for a ticket. He felt guilty about the fare evasion, but he took the seat behind the old man, happy just to be in his presence.

They were the only passengers, an empty voice bubble over their heads. When the bus neared a stop that must have been the old man's, he reached for the buzzer and acknowledged Stephen for the first time.

'Leave me alone,' he said.

Stephen was taken aback by the tension in the old man's voice. He'd practically spat the words.

In the changing inertia of the braking bus, the old man stumbled. Stephen was a good person. Stephen cared about others. Stephen was a responsible citizen in his life. The old man was falling, so Stephen reached out to steady him. But there was a crack in the air like a small firework.

Stephen saw himself and this firework reflected in the window glass, a flash like a passing streetlight or the effect of a retinal detachment. As if magnetised, Stephen's hand snapped onto the old man's wrist and an involuntary spasm contracted in his arm. He pulled the old man towards himself, his dead arm animated by a mad, muscular compulsion.

The old man struggled in rigid horror and the two of them tipped over as the bus driver swerved into the kerb. Stephen experienced a rush of excitement. It came from somewhere at the heart of him. From his solar plexus. It ballooned upwards into his chest, emptying his lungs of the stale dead air inside. Then his body surged towards the fallen man and froze, tilted at an angle, hovering over his face. They were separated by just centimetres. The old man was breathing hard, his head turned away from Stephen, terror in his eyes.

Time passed in a way that was alien to Stephen. It was slow but fast, never-ending but instant. His reactions were focused on the moments in between his breaths. His solar plexus tented again, like the spinnaker on a yacht that had caught a sudden wind and was snapping to its fullness. A vaporisation of something alive and vital hissed out of the old man's skin and straight into Stephen's mouth as the old man passed out. The rancid odour that had followed Stephen from the hospital seemed to waft away for a moment, as if freshened by a breeze.

Shame exerted a greater force on Stephen than the one holding him over the old man, and he regained his corporality and his footing. He bucked and flipped in embarrassment, trying to distance himself, to hold his weight back from the fallen man.

Something else took over for Stephen then. He pushed himself away and spun towards the rear of the bus. The bus driver had been keeping his eyes on the road the whole time. He hadn't seen what had happened. Stephen hopped out the rear doors. As they closed behind him, he looked back through the glass. The face of the old man was watching him. He was lying on the running board, still in the aisle. But Stephen could only see his own father lying there dead. His own father stricken with fear of his son.

1922

In Penicuik, Scotland, in a dwelling of stone and slate held together by moss and lichen and cold weather, the young lass Elspeth Milne was carrying tea to the front room, which her brother shared with a lodger.

The lodger was a shift worker with a complexion of cold granite. But Elspeth was drawn to his blue eyes, pale as the cake of soap she kept for its fragrance in her drawer. She had been testing the extent of her invisibility all that year, convinced she was the family's walking ghost. When she skipped school, nobody noticed. And so she was home as the shift worker was sleeping, and beyond them the house was empty.

She intended to leave the tea outside his door when she noticed that it was open. The lodger was lying on his bed with one naked leg outside his blanket. She stood in the doorway, staring at that leg until she heard him apologise to her as if it was his fault that she had seen him. Elspeth had never had an apology directed to her by an adult before. The lodger invited her in and sat up to drink his tea, telling her how lovely she was for making it. Then time compressed. And things happened. The details were lost between the blue of his eyes and the cake of soap that Elspeth used to wash her body afterwards, to wash the rough feeling of him away.

That night, when the lodger had his dinner with the rest of her family, the atmosphere was different between the two of them. When Elspeth offered to clear his dishes, he didn't answer her. Instead, he took his own plate from the table and left early for his evening shift. Elspeth's mother watched the interaction with quiet distrust.

Three months later, Elspeth had begun to show, though nobody thought to say anything. It was a pregnancy she could never tell them about anyway. When the doctor was finally brought in to make his diagnosis, he had to tell her family twice, once to deliver the shock and a second time to tell them there were two.

In the melee that followed the news, the shift worker made himself scarce, telling Elspeth's brother he'd found a job in Inverness and was leaving straight away. Elspeth watched him move out with no feeling of abandonment, just a sense of things taking their course.

As if keen to get everything over and done with, she went into labour early. She was attended by a local midwife. Elspeth heaved and pushed but hardly complained about the effort that it took. When the first twin emerged, a girl, she was taken from the room in case Elspeth grew attached.

'Try to keep going,' said the midwife. The second baby, another girl, exhibited a more diffident character than the first by wanting to stay where she was. Perhaps she'd already felt the broken connection with her sister. Or perhaps she knew nothing good would come of being born to a mother who herself was still just a child. The whole room was kept waiting until evening, when a blue second baby was delivered onto a torn half sheet. The other half had been used on her sister.

Elspeth looked away from the child while the midwife fussed around, trying to get her breathing. They could have spirited this second daughter away too. Elspeth wouldn't have minded. Elspeth's mother, not exactly revelling in her new status as grandma, took the child by the feet and gave her a slap. It worked. The baby was crying.

'Welcome to Penicuik, Hetty,' she said, using a name she had thought of on the spot. She did this knowing Elspeth would have shilly-shallied around. Nobody had time for Elspeth's rot. Hetty was placed in a wrap on her mother's breast, but Elspeth shrank back from the crying infant, deep into the bed, deeper and deeper into the mattress until she felt she had fallen all the way to the floor.

Ten months later, Elspeth Milne took an unscheduled morning walk past the Flotterstone Inn. The place was empty except for the one barfly who usually occupied the corner table, the one with the window. The beer was his only friend and would usually have occupied his attention, but he was trying to focus through the milky glass at the spectre he saw outside in the snow: a girl, wearing a thin shift of a dress and no shoes. Blinking through the effects of his beer, he watched her pass over Flotterstone Bridge and up the Glencorse Burn. As she crested the hill out of view, he kept staring at the curve of the drystone wall, waiting for her to return.

Elspeth could feel nothing through her feet as she walked. She felt like she was on stilts, like she was walking on jam tins, not touching the ground. It was a beautiful clear day and the

Glencorse Burn was pristine with snow. A ptarmigan fowl with its judgemental scarlet eyebrow took a more easterly path than Elspeth, seeking the sun. The snow that Elspeth broke through with the weight of her feet was hers alone to ruin. She was aware of the rare privilege that the natural world had given her. But it was a bit late to be enjoying that sort of thing.

The untrod path took a winding route through hills that were bare of vegetation. Beyond the frozen heath the hilltops were silvered with even more brilliant snow. Each drift appeared moulded and shaped like marzipan icing on a cake. It was a fairy-tale landscape hosting the coldest of unhappy endings.

Elspeth strode on. *Try to keep going, girl. Just try to keep going,* she thought to herself. Cresting a final rise, she saw the flat, metallic surface of the reservoir making its liquid incursions into the bank. Its fingers poked between the rises and covered the lowest dips and valleys before spreading out between the hills. The water hadn't iced over. It shimmered and lapped as Elspeth drew closer, its curling lip pulling at her toes.

Elspeth's jam tins entered the water. They sank deep into the mud and she was forced to lift her knees with the effort of moving forward. Eventually she was in it up to her waist and the shock of the cold slowed her heart. She pulled her chest high and her stomach in, her navel almost pressed back into her spine, and then she let out a breath that crystallised on the air and floated away as she sank into the reservoir up to her neck.

It was a feeling she knew she should savour. Any feeling was life, after all. But it was surprisingly hot and painful. A final, unwelcome sensation. And then there would be nothingness. Nothing left to worry about. Nothing to grieve. Nothing to bother her, not the past, nor the future. Not the child. Not the mother she should be. Not the grandmother she might have become in a better life.

Those unlikely versions of herself were left behind on the shore, near the dry-stone wall and the road to the Flotterstone Inn. Snowflakes fell on Elspeth's head and her eyelashes drooped as the shock of the cold wore off and her skin felt savagely dry. When her feet dragged through water weed, she worried she might get tangled while she was still only neck-deep. She needed to swim further out.

Soon the movements of her arms that were treading water slowed and the ache in her kicking legs ceased. She felt comfortable as she sank and sleepier still, but not yet ready to breathe in the water. Just a little look first at the vanishing sky. It was blue, like the shift worker's eyes, like the soap from her drawer. And then it was white, like the snow on the Glencorse Burn and the ptarmigan's plumage. And then it was nothing. Elspeth Milne was nothing. Fulfilling all her own expectations.

Jiāngshī

Stephen didn't know how long he'd been moving but the motion woke him. It was night still. Or again. His surroundings were different enough for him to know he'd put some distance between himself and the hospital. And the bus. And the old man who looked like his father, the one he'd accidentally knocked down. Or was it not an accident?

Guilt rose like a backed-up sewer into his throat. He'd returned from oblivion, but what had he become? Was this some kind of stalled reincarnation – one that replayed the traumas of his life?

At least he appeared to be on a back route, a rat run through an outer suburb, just a single lane in either direction. Scrubby acacia trees lurked just shy of the road. Their textured foliage was soaking up the jaundiced glow from a couple of randomly installed streetlights. Their trunks were fringed by recently poisoned grass, yellowed and crazy against the pooling shadows. The humidity suggested a nearby swamp; Stephen could hear frogs chirping and something else doing a buzz roll on a miniature snare drum. A narrow concrete path drew a parallel line with the road, guiding his trudging feet.

The high side of the street was built up with houses set back on the bank of a hill. Their driveways sluiced down between dark pillar-like forms – waiting wheelie-bins. The front yards were generic but behind the houses, architectural ornamentals and exotics raked their fingers across the indigo sky.

Stephen moved along the path, compelled by some undignified urge. The lateness of the hour meant the street was empty and nobody was about. Just the houses watched him through their porch lights. Curtained windows exhaled night breath. Whenever the streetlights conceded to the dark, the moonlight took over.

It was in between those streetlights that Stephen noticed movement in the cabin of a ute that had its nose poking out from under a carport. A light flicked on – the flame of a cigarette lighter – an illuminated face. A man wound down the driver's side window while he reached under the dashboard. There was a frown of intense concentration, then an electrical spark before the vehicle's engine sprang to life. A blinding flare – headlights – stunned Stephen, freezing him in their halogen stare. Stephen lifted one arm to cover his face but both rose at the same time as if they were strung together like a marionette's. The ute leapt from the driveway in a scream of tyres, then fish-tailed down the street and was gone.

In the house attached to the carport, a door opened. Stephen could hear it, but he was still reeling from being blinded. He heard footsteps running across toward him. Small footsteps. Then a girl's voice.

'The ute's gone, Dad! Dad!'

Stephen should have shrunk back into the acacias. But he had always been afraid of insects and snakes. If he left the path, he feared the undergrowth might tangle him, that he would fall into the swamp. In his hesitation, he heard the voice again.

'Dad, there's a man out here!'

'Where?'

'Over there! Can you see?'

More footsteps came running from the house, heavier, and with bigger strides. It took a few moments for them to reach Stephen.

'Hey, mate,' a voice said. It was deep and male and threatening. 'What are you doing out here?'

'Morning run,' Stephen said, surprised at the speed of his wit. Again, his mouth didn't move. How strange it was to speak through closed lips.

'Some arseholes just flogged my ute. Did you see them?'

Stephen turned to face the man, expecting him to recoil like the old man had. But there was no fear in his expression.

'Did you see them?' the man asked again.

'I saw them go past,' Stephen replied.

The guy was shirtless, wearing boxer shorts that hung low on his hips. His feet were bare. His hair was cut in a longer style, a sort of seventies throwback but it draped like chiffon under lights. His moustache was a golden comb. Beneath the hair on his torso, Stephen could see his ribs expanding, the intercostal muscles opening and contracting. Something feathered and powerful landed in the grass behind Stephen. He would have flinched, but he was fixated on the perfection of the man in the moonlight.

'Can I get your number?' the man asked. 'I'll call the police. They might want to speak to you.'

'My number?' Stephen listened for his heartbeat between his ribs but there was nothing. There was no physical reaction to this beautiful young father. He made an audit of the sensations inside his pelvis. There was no rerouting of blood, no surge to his crotch, no warmth flooding in. Those reflexes had caused him confusion in his life and they had driven his entire adulthood into dark corners. He was dead outside and in, yet still he feared those sexual reflexes and how a man like this could make them spark.

The voice of the child rang out through the night again. 'Dad, come back inside. I'm scared.'

'I'll be there in a second,' the guy said. His hair flicked over his powerful shoulders. He was a tradie, Stephen assumed, maybe a carpenter or a roofer who had tanned his skin in the course of his daily work. Or maybe he surfed. Stephen listened for the ocean, wondering if he had arrived at the coast, but he only heard the hiss of the bush and the buzz roll of the frogs.

'Mate, your number?' the man asked again.

Stephen made one up. A random number that came into his head. He wished he could have given this man his real number and been alive to answer his call. But Stephen was no longer alive. The tradie seemed happy with his answer, confident enough to turn his back on Stephen in the night.

That was when Stephen recalled again the old man. Why had he knocked him down? Was he going to do the same to this man? He felt an attraction to the young father as he watched him jog back towards his daughter and shepherd her inside, but he felt no urge to lurch towards him.

In the dark, Stephen felt the sharpness of hard grit beneath his left foot. He'd lost a shoe somewhere. Why had the man not noticed that? Stephen had told him he was running. But with only one shoe? He kicked the remaining shoe off in a graceful arc, deep into the dark where the swamp could lose it for him, beyond the acacias, out there with the frogs.

What good is one without the other? Stephen asked himself. Then he began moving along the path again, answering the urge inside him. *North*, he sensed. He was heading north. Trailing the manila tag still attached to his toe.

1925

Bridget Bolin died at the age of fifty-four in Townsville, in the house she worked hard to buy. The Bolins had six children, all born in that house, all grown now and married. A daughter and two sons still lived in Townsville. Three other sons had moved to Innisfail.

When Bridget was diagnosed with cancer of the cervix, she checked herself out of the Townsville regional hospital rather than wait there to capitulate and die. The cancer had already metastasised, and the diagnosis was certain. She wanted to die at home. She wanted to occupy her house until the end.

Her children admired their mother's strength. Her possession. How she was determined to exert her ownership over that house. Bridget had willed it to her children, not to him. Not to that Chinese grifter. Not to Pan Bo Lin, who had been thrown out three years prior.

A vigil was organised for her body, which meant she could remain there one more day. Bridget had lived like a hoarder since she'd ejected her husband, but there was no energy now to clean the upstairs rooms for mourners. Her children decided to hold the vigil underneath the house instead, between the stumps that were black with creosote, already solemnly dressed.

It was possible that Pan Bo Lin might turn up to pay his respects to his wife, but none of the children had spoken to him about their mother's illness. If he was upset, or even nostalgic, who would know?

There was a cart full of ice delivered to keep Bridget's body cool. It waited under a poinciana tree out the front of her house, draped in sugar bags and packed in salt. A shrouded lump, a maudlin sight, it was a message to the street of her passing. Bridget's daughter had asked her husband, an engineer whom she had met in church, to build a litter for the body. As an American, he didn't understand Irish vigils. Still, he removed the hinges and fixtures from a door and painted it white, ready for his mother-in-law's final journey. He strung makeshift walls – sheets and blankets between the house stumps. He dug gutters in the dirt to direct away the melting runoff from the ice. He'd worked out all the practicalities the way an engineer would.

The Townsville sons were already there with their wives, one English, the other Welsh. They were women who wore their origins on their sleeve, speaking as if they were only roughing it temporarily in Australia. 'Good Lord, it's hot,' they said, as if they had been expecting an English summer.

Of the three Innisfail brothers, only William had married a girl who was born in Australia. Her name was Christina. William wouldn't be bringing Christina to the vigil, and it was just as well. Christina was full Chinese. And in the Bolin family, being full Chinese had turned out to be a problem.

In the twenty-five years of his marriage to Bridget, Pan Bo Lin had kept his other wife, his secret Chinese wife, in Chikan, Kaiping, with money he earned from his gardening work.

He'd been sending this money through a Chinese network of local retailers with freight connections to Guangdong. He'd been propping her up that way from the beginning. Meanwhile the Bolin family could have done with the money he secreted away, and Bridget had always wondered why their savings never stretched as far as she'd liked.

Bridget had always been curious about a box of letters that Pan Bo Lin kept to himself, under their house. At first she thought they were just letters from his friends, written in what Bridget called 'chicken scratch', though their envelopes were addressed in English. But she grew suspicious about the way her husband intercepted them at the letterbox. He had a sixth sense for when the postie was coming, always insisting he'd bring in the mail. When William married Christina in Innisfail, Bridget found she finally had a family member to consult. She asked her new daughter-in-law to translate the letters. Feeling awkward, Christina told Bridget only the gist of their content, keeping some of the words to herself – in particular, the way the writer had cursed Pan Bo Lin's gweilo wife. She told Bridget only the relevant details: that Pan Bo Lin had a Chinese wife predating her mother-in-law and he'd been sending her money. His past had been shadowing the present, and it had finally caught up with him.

'Don't trust people with two languages,' Bridget said to her children the night she threw their father out and made him sleep in the garden shed. Christina felt sorry for Pan Bo Lin but felt wedged. If she'd lied about what was in the letters, her mother-in-law may have found out. She felt blamed for the bad blood in the family. Never again, she thought, would she put herself in that position. Never again would she be a full Chinese for them.

In an act of protest, Pan Bo Lin reverted to speaking only in Cantonese. His English had been quite broken anyway, but he'd been able to communicate with his family. That was no longer the case. From the shame of the garden shed he drove his wife and children crazy with his lurking. They were embarrassed by his reversion to foreigner status. The neighbours were talking and none of them trusted him living so near. Eventually Bridget called the police. Pan Bo Lin fled then to live in the Chinese Joss House in Innisfail.

Bridget's vigil would see a steady parade of family and neighbours coming to watch over her body. They thought Bridget would have been delighted to see them together that way. She would have preferred them all to be forgetting about her death and just enjoying each other's company. What a waste of time, she would have said. What a useless inconvenience dying was for people. It was impractical. Forget about the dead. Get upstairs and look after the living. Feed everyone well.

Earlier, an Irish mortician had helped to prepare her body and would return the next day to take Bridget away for her formal burial. The Townsville brothers were the ones who brought her down from her bedroom, where Bridget had lain in funereal repose. They steeled themselves and tried to ignore the sweat that was pooling under their shirts, under their two layers of flannel, under their waistcoats and jackets. They lifted her depleted body, with one positioned at her head, one at her feet, carrying her in a bundle of linen. On the litter, a single mattress made up like a bed, they shuffled her carefully down the hall, through the kitchen, down the back stairs and around under the house, walking between the creosote-soaked posts while the rest of the siblings stood like a guard of honour.

Afternoon sun came in through the battening, casting zebra patterns on the sheets hanging from the joists. Bridget's litter was balanced gently on the ice. Her daughter had chosen Bridget's dress, and a blanket was pulled up under her chin. Her arms were tucked inside the blanket and her hair was gently brushed and re-pinned so that it was neat and formal and not likely to blow free in the slight breeze that passed through. It was cool there, cooler than inside the house, and more comfortable, less claustrophobic than among Bridget's hoarded things.

Later that evening, from a distance, the little room of gently undulating sheets appeared lit from within like a lantern. At one stage someone thought they saw a solitary shadow moving through the long grass of the empty allotment next door. The children hoped it wasn't their father. None of them went to find out. Instead, they remained watching over the body of their mother, safe within the walls of her bleached Irish linen.

Jiāngshī

When the night ended, and the dawn announced itself as a pink glow, Stephen's body landed face down and he became still as a log. His awareness switched perspective. He was up in the sky as the sunlight hit, in a different kind of dream from the walking one he endured at night.

He'd been told once that people who had flying dreams were looking for escape. They hungered for a life outside the constraints of the one they were in. So they flew, defying the physical laws of their reality. It was an admission of hopelessness to dream like that. A surrender to the situation they were in. Their permanent, inescapable life that couldn't be dreamed away. The flying was merely a reprieve so their brains wouldn't go mad with despair. Was that why Stephen was flying? But hadn't he escaped his life already?

In the east there was a hazy mist, a perfect vignette transitioning from sea to sky. He could see the M1 snaking through sparse brigalow scrub. Service roads split off from the highway, cutting the forest into wedges like a pie. The details of his vision were precise, and he recognised that he was indeed north of Brisbane.

His body, in a drainage ditch to the left of the highway, was shaded by an overhang of *Banksia serrata.* He lay with his arms stiffly at his sides, his legs ramrod straight. On the back of his t-shirt, the words *YAY GIR MY STIR* were a viable excuse for his paralytic state. On his toe, a tag with his details.

This was what he did during the day. His body waited for the light to fade and for the cool of the night to come, for the traffic on the highway to thin out. From the sky, he saw commercial vehicles and trucks lined up on their long-distance commutes. Cars were filled with excited children. Recreational vehicles ferried surfed-out millennials north, and through their windscreens Stephen could see them mouthing their zinc-creamed lips to the songs they played on their sound systems.

In the distance were the eroded volcanic cores of the Glass House Mountains. He was further north than he thought. This was the stretch of forest around Yandina. The road beneath him was straight except for a loop, the get-out-of-jail loop back to Nambour that you could take if you missed the proper turnoff.

All day he floated above his body. Then, as the sun began to set, he returned to his corpse, detecting the glow of headlights through the membrane of his eyelids as if he'd been sleeping and had just woken up. No memory of the day he'd spent detached.

He heard the hiss of a passing vehicle, turned his head in the direction of the sound. Somehow his body bent up from the waist. His corpse hinged the way a living spine wouldn't normally allow. The ugly reverse of a forward bend. Then he stood, concertinaing up in an impossible way. It was nauseating, sickening, but there was no pain from his hyperextended joints, just a hunger to move forward.

From the forest to his left came again the cacophony of rattles, squeaks, buzzes and chirps that he'd heard on his first night. Mother Nature's tinnitus. It became overwhelming in its pulsating constancy the more he listened to it. Millions of voices all tuned to each other's frequency. Wood frogs. Tree frogs. Barking frogs. Crickets, katydids and cicadas. Stephen raised his hands to his ears to block the sound, but his elbows wouldn't bend the way he wanted them to. His arms stood out in front. His hands reached for something unidentified, but ahead. The earth was solid under his feet. Passing headlights lit him from behind and then came darkness again. And then more lights. And then buzzing again. But then something new.

He felt a sense of warning. A nervousness invaded his chest. Up ahead, a stronger light was casting a dome across the indigo sky. He slowed with the traffic. Cars were queuing, their headlights on low beam. Everything crept to a standstill and Stephen passed quietly through, hidden in the darkness as the drivers idled. He scoped an escape to the drainage ditch. The source of the light was becoming obvious. Stephen heard the telltale hum of a generator powering an electric sun. It was an all-night roadwork gang.

'You should get back in your car, mate,' a voice said.

The words came from a short man in high-vis workwear. His accent was foreign: constrained vowels, clipped consonants, a crafted attempt at Strine. Stephen realised he was only being seen in silhouette, backlit by the headlights of the cars behind him, preserving his anonymity. He was compelled to keep moving, but to run would have seemed suspicious.

I'm envious, thought Stephen as he realised the man was the same height as him, with the same body weight, same colouring, even similar facial features. Except Stephen's body had been ruined by death. And this man was in his twenties, an age when everything seemed workable. His body at its genetic peak. If Stephen had his time again, he'd treat his body better.

A second man came to join the first. He was taller and fairer. Older too. His teeth were chipped, and his face was marked with creases, etched by hard living. No longer pretty, yet Stephen could see through all the weathering to the handsome man he'd once been. Eyebrows like sandstone cliffs. His irises, two Corsican grottos. He had his hands on his hips.

As Stephen lined up to walk between the men he was magnetised to the taller man – he'd always been attracted to blondes. But something else forced him to veer back towards the short one with his dark hair and tea-stained skin. He fought to stay away from both, a fight that made him stagger.

'You look a bit wobbly, mate.'

Stephen tried driving his feet harder into the dirt to secure his gait, but the short guy with the accent made a subtle shift in his weight to a different foot and Stephen found himself lurching in his direction. The short guy recoiled just as Stephen landed and for a moment it was comedy. They both tipped over, falling heavily in each other's arms. A nearby truck was dropping a trail of hot bitumen from its tray, and they almost fell into the scalding mass.

In the struggle, Stephen dominated. His arms enveloped the man's body as they lay there, something passing between them. An odour? A spiteful energy? Stephen began to absorb it. He almost inhaled it, except he was grabbed by the taller, older man and lifted clear of the other.

'Chow down! Chow down!' The taller guy giggled, like he was saying 'man down'.

Rough hands from other men pulled the smaller man, the one called Chow, to his feet. As he rose, he gave his coworkers an embarrassed smile and then glanced across at Stephen, perhaps preparing an apology. But he froze. The men who were holding

Stephen by the arms were dusting off his clothes. They too were waiting for Chow to speak. But Chow's smile had faded, his face now discoloured. He stepped back, mouthing a word the others couldn't hear.

'... shìshì ...'

More quickly now, Chow began to back-pedal. The other men watched him, confused. They half-heartedly called out to him, but he couldn't be stopped. He ran to a vehicle that was parked to the side of the work zone. He opened its driver's door and slid into the cabin. Stephen could see him activate the car's lock. He could see Chow's face and his fear through the glass. Stephen realised he had felt that energy before in his solar plexus, the tenting of his diaphragm forming a vacuum, but it was fading now Chow was in his car.

'Don't worry about him,' one of the workmen said. 'He's not hurt. He's just a wuss.'

The hands that were holding Stephen let him go. Some of the cars behind them had begun to be waved on through the worksite. Their engines were revving, and they were rolling forward.

'Just mind your feet. Where's your car?'

'Up ahead,' Stephen said, though his mouth didn't move. 'Just stretching my legs.' Then he hurried off along the line of cars.

Inside his ute, Chow's face went white as Stephen passed by. Stephen should have felt sorry for him, should have felt embarrassed by his own clumsiness. But he wanted to break into the cabin and be near him again. He fought that feeling, pushed himself beyond the ute into the dark, away from the work zone, into the trees. He was answering another call. He had to keep going.

1930

The year that William and Christina Bolin were expecting their first child was marred by three family dramas.

The first was a fight. It happened in the Chinese Joss House, an old place of vapours and foreign mystery, built out of brick and horsehair plaster. The Joss House had stood on Owen Street in Innisfail since before it was even a street. The cheery white picket fence that once surrounded the structure had fallen into disrepair, and rambling weeds were taking it down. The two buildings of the complex were connected by an awning. The larger building was a temple, a moody, windowless room furnished with geometric timber joinery. Moth-eaten fabric adorned with Chinese characters hung in panels along the walls. On every surface, bowls of burning incense catalysed a blueish haze. The red lacquer coating the bowls was chipped and the gold leaf on the joinery had been rubbed thin.

The other building was a dormitory of sorts, housing rows of simple wooden sleeping berths, too short for a tall man to lie straight in. Scattered around were a few pails and the odd box for sitting on. This was the haunt of William Bolin's full Chinese father, the family exile, Pan Bo Lin.

He'd lounged in the Joss House between labouring jobs ever since being caught with another woman. Technically, Bridget Bolin, the woman who threw him out, was the other woman, because she was his second wife, but she didn't care for that argument. So now the Innisfail Joss House was Pan Bo Lin's harbour and also his corruptor. There were several other down-and-outs like him living there. They were all as Chinese as he was. And like Pan Bo Lin, they were hopelessly addicted to opium, caught in the Joss House loop of wanting to be there, needing to be there and having nowhere else to go.

To be fair, Pan Bo Lin didn't start the fight in the Joss House. But he had a tendency to finish a fight once one had begun. He'd been upset after a run-in with his son William, for whom he had been digging up crab grass from the lawn of his house on Ernest Street. He'd been doing the job uninvited at night. He thought his work might heal their rift. He'd spent hours bent at the waist, working over the grass with an iron railway spike that he'd repurposed as a makeshift hoe. But the holes he'd made in the lawn were like bomb craters, and he was soon discovered.

'Get out of here!' William shouted the moment he saw what his father had been doing. 'I thought we had a bandicoot.'

Pan Bo Lin swore at his son in return.

'I can't understand you. Speak English, old man,' William replied.

Frustrated, Pan Bo Lin stormed off back to the Joss House, where he kicked over a box that was lying in front of his bunk.

The owner of the box was See Ann. Pan Bo Lin later told the court at the trial of See Ann that the accused had taken to him with an iron bar and had hit him with it for kicking over his box. As a result, Pan Bo Lin was partially paralysed and had been detained in hospital overnight.

Pan Bo Lin didn't tell his son he'd been assaulted. William had to read about the incident in the local paper, under the headline *Fight Between Aged Chinese in Innisfail Joss House.*

To know his father had been the cause of that kind of trouble at the Joss House was bad enough, but the end of the article was too much for William to bear. It described an exchange between the judge and the prosecutor:

How old is the complainant?

Seventy-six.

And how old is the defendant?

Seventy-two.

The article confirmed to William everything he already believed about his father. That his dysfunction was permanent. That he would always be trouble.

William and two of his brothers had moved to Innisfail for opportunity. William drove taxis and his brothers did farm work. Within a year, William had a down payment on a worker's cottage on Ernest Street. Shortly after, he married Christina Lo. He was drawn to her because she was drawn to him. It was as simple as that. She said he was handsome, and he'd never heard that from any woman before. He felt he didn't have to pretend with her. She didn't care that his father was Chinese, because her parents were too. It was just one of the things that didn't matter to them until Christina was asked by Bridget Bolin to read some letters and became unwittingly embroiled in the Bolin family divorce.

'I only know English from now on,' Christina told her husband, reflecting on her role in exposing her father-in-law's secret. 'One language is enough.'

'And one wife is enough,' William said in reply, shocked at the revelation she'd uncovered.

Their house was an airy colonial structure. Painted white, it had a gabled tin roof with single skin walls of tongue-and-groove boards. It sat on stilts, tall enough to not be flooded by the Johnstone River when it rose on the tail of a cyclone. William thought the house was far enough away from the Joss House. But after the Joss House fight and the newspaper article, William felt his father was still living in his backyard.

The second family drama came hot on the heels of the first. It involved one of William's brothers, and it was also a fight, though it happened in Cairns. This time it was over a woman. Not a girlfriend, not a wife. William's brother wasn't even involved with her. He was covering for a Chinese friend whom the woman had taken up with though she had promised herself to someone else. William's brother was assaulted in the street for his involvement. The story of the altercation made it to the local paper, which everybody in Innisfail read. Three Chinese men, it was reported, had been fighting in Cairns. The paper gave colourful accounts of the prosecutor's cross-examination.

Who started the altercation?

The complainant. He called the accused a cock-eyed philanderer!

Is there bad blood between the men?

Not directly, Your Honour.

On and on the report went, describing the unseemly events, yet William couldn't get past his brother's part in them. Why get involved in the first place? On the night the report landed, William was unable to eat his dinner. He read it and seethed over his corned beef and potatoes. He didn't talk to Christina about it. She could do without the worry. Instead, he raged in his belly to the point of indigestion. Already dragged down by his father, now he felt dragged down by his brother too, caught up in their Chinese dysfunction.

Four weeks later, after his brother's trial had concluded, William himself was brought before a court on a different matter. He'd been called as a witness at an official inquiry into the circumstances surrounding the death of a pedestrian. The dead man had been hit by a taxi driven by a colleague of William's. It happened on Goondi Hill Road at about 9.15 pm in a thick fog. William was following his friend's car and witnessed the whole thing. Though he wasn't at fault, by association his driving came under question. He attempted to distance himself from the accident, telling Senior Sergeant Shersby at the inquiry that he did not have a clear view through his windscreen at the time, on account of the heavy mists. He also said he didn't think his electric windscreen wipers were even working. That prompted Sergeant Shersby to ask if William thought that driving in that weather was safe for his passengers, considering the issue with his wipers. William's name and involvement was printed there in full. The implication about his driving was clear.

The three reports made William nervous. He felt everything for him was now at risk: his income, his standing in the community – and with a child due any minute. William tightened the family finances and grew more anxious and more controlling with Christina, criticising her purchasing of vegetables and herbs when they could easily have grown their own. As her pregnancy drew to its inevitable conclusion, William made mental notes about how he would handle the child. He resolved to be like concrete, immovable and certain. He'd keep his brothers and especially his father well away.

The baby, a son, was born in the Innisfail hospital to a cooing Christina and an apprehensive William. Christina calmed her husband as best she could. She pointed to the child asleep in her arms, his brow more like Christina's, not creased like William's.

'Don't infect this boy with your worries. What do you think he knows about the last few months?' she asked her husband.

'Nothing, I suppose,' replied William.

Christina smiled and nodded. 'Then don't tell him.'

She was right, thought William. The past was a weight, but it needn't be carried forward, it needn't burden his child.

'I know we thought of naming him William,' he said, 'but now I'm having second thoughts. Why should he have my name?'

'Then call him Willie,' said Christina. 'Willie Bolin. He sounds like a whole new person.'

Jiāngshī

Through the next week of nights, Stephen found ways to avoid people. He passed successfully unseen between towns, between mining camps and railway sidings and minor points of interest on the Queensland tourist trail. Outside these patches of artificial light, the bush flooded in to reclaim him. Night birds and bats mobbed him. Weeds and creepers tried to tangle with him. As he lay face down during the days, opportunistic creatures climbed aboard. He woke to their movement and their weight. Parts of him were particularly attractive to them: the places where the broken skin exposed his flesh to the air. Inside his clothes, skin was rubbing off too, on the insides of his legs, in the crotch of his pants, on the sharp bones of his shoulders, around the neck of his shirt. At all these friction points he felt no pain, just a sense of things taking their course.

Carried by the breeze, microbes arrived, as well as mites in his clothes; small flies landed to lay their eggs in the folds of his skin. He expected he would be a rotted mess before too long and that the ants would have him eventually during the day, if not the worms and beetles and larger bugs who worked more quickly. But his motion during the night – the walking, jogging, jerking – controlled their numbers by knocking them off him in clumps. It was the idea of them that bothered him the most, a phobia from his former life. Eventually, he felt the urge to wash.

On the shoulder of a road just north of Rockhampton, Stephen saw a billboard advertising a resort. It promised weddings and functions, free wi-fi and cable. There were flames that licked the underside of the word *steakhouse*. Beneath that was a qualifier: *coming soon*. A yellow panel announced *GOLD* but not the metal kind, the liquid kind – Fourex. Stephen wondered if the advertising ever worked. Then, at the bottom, he saw a word that seemed to work on him: *POOL*.

It was a small, low-set resort, arranged in a horseshoe. The driveway curved around its outer circumference. Cars were parked nose-in to the kerb. As he entered the property, his feet made popcorn sounds on the gravel driveway. He stepped off into the soft mulch of a garden bed so he could phantom past the first of the motel rooms.

At the rear of the horseshoe complex, which sat facing the bush, he found the pool, surrounded by a fence. It was the shape of a fried egg with pale shallows and a deep-water yolk of indigo blue. Three timber gazebos occupied its far shore. To the right of them, a blue spiral fibreglass slide made two sharp turns. There was a ladder that rose to the top of the slide and Stephen would have climbed it if he had been alive. But he was incapable of play. Across from the slide, six masonry columns spat elegant arcs that broke the surface of the water, radiating ripples.

It was late. Stephen had no idea of the exact time but he hoped the people in the resort were asleep. The brick paving was still wet: swimmers had used it recently. Though the pool was surrounded by the rooms, Stephen chanced it.

He ran his insensate hand over the lip of the fence until it located a latch. He found a set of steps at the shallow end. As he entered the water, he lay down. He didn't care if he sank. He had no fear of drowning. Could he be any more dead than he already was? Face down, he felt no reflex to breathe. His clothes soaked though quickly, and he sensed the microbes and bugs begin to migrate to the shrinking dry land of his back and his buttocks and the rear of his head. They were marooned for a moment until he bent at the waist and submerged his head, drowning himself and them.

His body drifted to the bottom. Bubbles were released from inside his clothes, and from inside his body too. A dirty slick of dust and dead bugs and worn-off skin rose to the surface.

Stephen lay there for some time. It was cool and profoundly quiet. The tinnitus of crickets and cicadas was muffled. Relief. For a moment he fooled himself into thinking he could stay there, that he'd lost the internal compass that compelled him to walk north. He was still suspended in limbo, but at rest, the most at rest he'd felt since he died.

The pause was short. A thundering shockwave pulsed through the water around him. Then he felt arms reaching around his chest, slipping under his pits, lifting him, pulling him to the surface. He was dragged backwards through the water, up onto the shallow ledge and then, with much grunting and swearing, his sodden corpse was dumped over the lip of the pool onto the paving. He felt skin from his back scrape off on the hard concrete, but he didn't cry out. There was no pain, just a feeling of separation. More of him gone.

As the water trickled from his face and drained from his ears, he heard the desperate mumbling of a woman. She was panicked. She placed her fingers against his neck, searching for a pulse. He could have told her not to bother. Then, the same fingers were wedged between his lips, pushing his jaw open. They explored the cavity of his mouth, finding nothing but tongue and teeth. Deserting his face the woman began thumping on his chest.

One, two, three, four, five. The woman counted out thirty compressions, bouncing with urgency, making small, frustrated whimpers as she executed her rhythm. At the count of thirty, she stopped, and seemed to be preparing herself for something. She swallowed audibly, then she pinched her thumb and forefinger over Stephen's nose, and he felt the wet warmth of her mouth closing over his.

It was the embarrassment that caused Stephen to sit up. Rigid, he bent on the hinge of his waist. He wanted to apologise to her as she fell back onto the pavers. She was staring at him as if he was a miracle, or perhaps a monster. She assessed his form, the fact that he wasn't breathing heavily or crying out or vomiting up water, and then she was shouting.

'What the fuck?' she screamed. 'I thought you were drowning.'

She was middle-aged, strong-boned and freckled. She was soaking wet, her hair limp over her ears. Her oversized pale pink t-shirt was translucent across her breasts, which Stephen could see quite clearly in the light from the pool. She must have felt him staring because she covered herself with her arms. But Stephen wasn't leering, he was keening.

In what looked like her nightgown, in her movements, she was his mother. She was Aileen. When she pushed him away, it was his mother, scolding him for being selfish. The woman's outrage was his mother's fear that Stephen had caused their family to fight. Because of his *lifestyle.*

'You fucking creep,' the woman said. 'You fucking deviant.'

Stephen thought of how she had carried him from the pool. He wanted to crawl back into her arms. But the woman's invective smashed at his chest. His mother had never been this brutal. Perhaps this was everything she had never said out loud.

He must have looked quite strange to the woman, crumbling the way that he did, turning in on himself. Perhaps she was still in shock or maybe she thought his stumbling away was all part of the cowardice of a rapist, faced down by a victim with pluck. In any case, she didn't follow him.

Stephen was mortified by the vision of his mother that had just played out at the pool. He cut back through the rear gate and rushed around to the ring road.

Now he was out of sight, the woman resumed her shouting.

'You're lucky I didn't fucking nut you! I will tear you apart like a fucking cooked chook if I see you again.'

Her voice followed him into the night.

'Fucking backpacker sleazebag! Fucking foreign rapist! Go back to where you came from. Stay out of my fucking pool!'

1938

Hetty Milne covered her good scarf with the oiled canvas square she kept for rainy days. She pulled both over her ears, securing them beneath her chin. With her hair protected from the frizzing damp, she mounted her bicycle and pedalled carefully along Bridge Street, past South Church Hall. Esk Mill took twenty minutes by bicycle. The cobblestones along the old streets slowed her down when they were wet. Once she got to the mill, she clocked in and made her way to the corner shed. Eleven other women waited for her so they could walk together across the yard.

The men called to them and whistled as they passed the bleaching and beater buildings. Hetty let the other girls blush and tighten their coats while she observed the men with practical curiosity, as if she was watching them under glass. The whistles weren't for her, she thought. When she arrived at the salles building, she got to work.

Hetty's job was looking for hairs, impurities, any imperfections in the rag paper. She had done many hours in the lesser position of collecting the rejects and outsides from other graders, ferrying them back for re-pulping or to be repurposed as wrapping paper.

But since one of her friends had fallen pregnant and left, Hetty had been promoted and was now a grader herself.

Knowing she couldn't ever make a mistake, she took her time. If she allowed one imperfect sheet through, she could ruin an entire order and, with it, the mill's reputation. On every sheet was a watermark, created by the raised wire and thread that had been sewn into the paper moulds. The pulp settled more thinly over those proud letters and when it dried, the light shone through the marks to reveal the sheet's origin: Esk Mill, Penicuik.

Hetty's foreman told her to imagine the watermark was her own name. It was a threat. Imagine your own name written on an imperfect sheet. She understood, having already been branded as the bastard child of a mother who later took her own life.

Lunchtime at the mill was signalled by a bell. With their food and cigarettes and their cups of tea in flasks, Hetty and her co-workers went to the railway siding inside the grounds. They stood around and ate their sandwiches and drank and smoked and plotted the course of their love lives. The salles girls all thought they had their only opportunity with the men from the mill.

Since the days of rag paper production, there had always been a rumour that the rags collected for pulping carried pox and cholera and that anyone who worked in the paper mills was likely to get it. Hetty herself had been warned about it by her grandparents, who said there'd been outbreaks in Ivybridge at the E and J Allen Paper Mill.

She applied for the job at Esk Mill anyway. The pox stigma was nothing compared to the stigma she already possessed. And now, at the mill, she and the other girls had plenty of stigmatised men to choose from, as the men outnumbered the women by at least three to one. The girls gossiped endlessly about their suitability for marriage. Hetty watched her friends pair up but she kept her own hopes down.

'You just have to try to keep going,' she told herself. 'Even if you have to go it alone.'

A man named Ewan Morris was having his lunch at the railway siding when a line of girls strolled past him. He stopped eating as Hetty appeared. It was as if his future had just stumbled into his eyeline. Daphne, the English girl who had taught all the girls how to apply lipstick without a mirror, pushed Hetty a little closer to him. Only then did she glance up from his sandwich to his face.

It was a thin face, though broad at the forehead. Hetty thought Ewan looked like a thinker, though he clearly hadn't been smart enough to get a job somewhere without a stigma. He had a seriousness about him, a permanent crease in the space between his eyebrows. But when he smiled, goofiness descended, due in part to the arrangement of his two front teeth, which stood out further than the others. His eyes were blue, like hers, but his hair was fair, or it would have been if he hadn't been a boiler worker who was covered in grime. He stayed far enough back from Hetty to avoid overpowering her with his sweat. She felt awkward that she'd been pushed forward. But then he was speaking to her. And then she was speaking back.

As weeks passed, the salles girls made themselves scarce whenever Ewan Morris came calling on Hetty Milne. They didn't want to stand in the way of her luck. They wanted her to have as good a chance as any other salles girl of being married before getting knocked up. They encouraged her when they approved of what she wore. They looked out for her if a hair fell out of place. And they always asked her how lunch had gone, what she and Ewan had talked about and whether he'd asked her out yet.

It wasn't long before he did. There was a movie playing that he wanted to see one Saturday. Bold as anything, he already had their tickets when he asked, and when she told him she'd have to check with her grandparents first, he smiled and said that was fine. He told her a story about his own family, about how he shared the burden of a war-broken father with his older brother and how his sisters ran the house around them.

Ewan had both a father and a mother? Two sisters and an older brother? Hetty couldn't imagine such a house. His father was at home, but his mother was away, taking a 'vacation' in Bangour. She knew what he meant by that: his mother must be a bit funny in the head. Bangour was a hospital for the mentally infirm. She didn't ask him to elaborate. She just liked that he was prepared to mention it. Now she could be open about her family too. It didn't seem much worse than his.

When Ewan asked Hetty's grandfather for her hand, the old man approved straight away. He had been worried about her limited prospects and he was happy to see that a young Scottish man with a sense of commitment still existed. He thought Hetty was lucky to have found Ewan.

Theirs was a simple wedding. The Presbyterian service was performed in the Penicuik South Kirk by Reverend Robert, who had done the funeral service for Hetty's mother, Elspeth. The Reverend Robert was also glad to see Hetty had encountered better luck. Her grandparents and her Uncle Henry were the only family members to attend the wedding from her side. Ewan's sisters, Mary and Peggy, and his brother, Terry, attended from the Morris side. Ewan's father was also there, but he remained outside the church. His faith was just one of the things he lost in the war. As they said their vows, he headed home so he could put on the heat for them.

When the honeymooners arrived at the Morris house, Ewan bypassed his father and took Hetty straight to his room – or at least his half of the room, which had a curtained divider. He invited her to sit on his single bed while he took off his jacket and his waistcoat. Seeing the setup, Hetty couldn't shake the feeling that nothing about it said *honeymoon* to her. It was a Spartan's room, dressed for a man. But she wouldn't complain.

Ewan brought a fresh washbowl of warm water from the kitchen. He placed a clean towel on the bed for his bride to use. Terry would be arriving home soon from the reception, he told her. His brother slept on the other side of the divider.

'Don't rush,' Ewan said. And then he left her to it.

Hetty unbuttoned her wedding dress, which was on loan from a woman at the mill. She washed her face and her arms quickly, thinking at any time that Ewan or Terry would walk back in and catch her at it. Then she heard movement as Mary and Peggy arrived home. Their father boomed at them all to be quiet. Then he boomed at Ewan.

'Why are you keeping your new wife waiting?'

Ewan crept back into their half room with a flush to his face. His sisters giggled uncontrollably in the front room. His father told them to hush. A sheepish Ewan smiled at Hetty, who by then had changed into her nightgown.

'Sorry 'bout that,' he whispered, and then he undressed to his underwear and turned out the light. Hetty folded back the bedding and climbed into the bed beside him, and they were quiet, hesitant, nervous. Ewan's teeth got in the way at first when they kissed, but Hetty was happy with the sensation, despite the awkwardness. Terry left it as late as he could. When he knocked on the bedroom door and heard silence, he turned on the light in his half of the room. Hetty lay frozen, afraid to speak. It wasn't unpleasant to be lying skin to skin with her husband. If she could just detach herself from her embarrassment, she'd be fine. In the dark, she imagined a bubble, or a bell jar descending over their bed, with her and Ewan inside. A small, perfect world just for them. And then she fell asleep.

At six in the morning on 3 September 1939, Hetty woke with her face in Ewan's hair, inhaling the scent of his Brylcreem. She rose before him as she always did, moving quietly so as not to wake his brother, who snored and coughed in rotation beyond the divider. At 11.15 am, while Hetty helped prepare the family's Sunday lunch, Neville Chamberlain came onto the radio to tell the world that the German government had not agreed to withdraw from Poland as the British had demanded and, as a result, he had been forced to declare war.

It had begun as such a small day, Hetty thought. Now war was declared and, like his father before him, Ewan would be compelled to enlist.

When the rest of the family awoke to the news, they mobilised to the straight-backed chairs around the kitchen table. There was a morbidity that could infect even the rose-patterned wallpaper. The gas heater was on war rations already, and Hetty crossed her legs to warm her knees. Her father-in-law's presence flickered like a newsreel. His sense of duty, his need to take control, was being restored by every report. Though he came back from the Great War broken and moribund, Hetty could see he was now invigorated.

'They are unavoidable,' he said, 'days like these. We'll sacrifice what we can.'

Both Ewan and Terry could feel the weight of their father's words. After dinner, they huddled with him, stiff and insular. It was as if Hetty had already lost her husband to a military unit. He hardly spoke to her all evening. All she wanted to do was talk about other things, happy things, while they still could.

Over the next few days Ewan made his war preparations, finalising bills that needed to be paid and advising his supervisor at the mill that he'd be enlisting. Hetty watched him from a distance, reaching out for him whenever he passed. At the table, doing his paperwork, he ducked from her touch when she ran her fingers through his hair. He was irritated that she was softening him at a time when he needed to be hard.

Terry noticed that his little brother was ignoring his wife. He emptied his wardrobe and packed his clothes away in paper to be stored in a chest under the stairs. After making the couch up as his bed, Terry and Ewan drew back the curtain divider and pushed their beds together for Ewan and Hetty to use for their final night together before he had to go away. The gesture wasn't lost on Hetty. It made her feel seen, but she also wondered how she would feel with all that space to herself.

In a letter she sent to the front, Hetty announced that she was late, then in another that she was pregnant. When the baby arrived, slippery and blue, Ewan was still stationed with the 14th in Burma and couldn't be contacted. There had been no letters from him for two months. Mary and Peggy took one look at the mess on Hetty's bed and announced to the midwife that they were never getting married. The midwife winked at Hetty while working on the baby to rub life into her lungs. Hetty allowed herself a moment of weakness. Tears rolled down from the corners of her eyes while she waited for the baby to respond.

'Try to keep going,' she said to the midwife.

'We have signs of life,' the midwife reassured her, rubbing the child from a squawk to a full-blown scream.

In the upstairs room, Ewan's mother was pacing. She'd only been home a few days, since the Bangour hospital had been commandeered for the war effort. Ewan's father comforted his wife as best he could. But at the sound of the baby's cry, and having run short of her medication, she was suddenly shouting, 'When will Ewan and Terry be home?'

For five months, Hetty put off naming her baby. She was hoping for a letter from Ewan to answer the question for her. But there was no contact, no news from the front. Eventually, she named the child after her grandmother: Aileen. When she said it, the double-e made her smile. A rare thing when the mood was so grim.

On VE Day, the street became festive with women. Music blared from a gramophone perched on a side table. Little Aileen, two by then, was running between the dancers' legs. For her it was just a day to play, not a national outpouring. She hadn't been missing her father, didn't know what a father was like.

Hetty didn't share her fears with her daughter or let Ewan's MIA status affect their play. There'd been no news of his life or his death, so it was easy to exist in that way. But when VJ Day came and went, Hetty finally relented to grief. Ewan's father looked after Aileen with military discipline on the days Hetty couldn't get out of bed. Meanwhile, Mary and Peggy both found boyfriends to keep them entertained, men back from the war.

When Ewan finally did return, the shock was so profound that Hetty couldn't react naturally. She should have been happy to see him, but she fell into a deep shame for having believed that he was dead. Ashamed of her faithlessness, she slumped in her chair, unable to find the energy to fuss around her husband. For his part, Ewan didn't mind that she wasn't rushing at him. He was very unwell. His arms and legs were pitted with ulcerated tropical sores and his weight had fallen to the mass of his bones.

Aileen cowered behind the sofa at the sight of this strange, thin soldier who had entered her life without warning. She watched as he shook hands with her grandad and looked to her mother for explanation when the old man broke down, sobbing in the thin soldier's arms. Then Aileen watched as the soldier took his bag and his hat to the bedroom that she thought was hers. Her mother gave her a weak smile and then joined him in there, closing the door behind her. Aileen's grandfather motioned for her to step away. Then he turned up the volume of the wireless.

Three hours later, Hetty emerged. Aileen by then was asleep on the couch. Hetty gathered her up and took her to a rearranged bedroom. The curtain had been pulled back across and one half of the bed had been returned to that side of their room. Aileen had never seen the space in this configuration before. In her half-asleep state, Aileen expected her mother to join her on her side of the divider, but instead Hetty went to the other and Aileen was left to sleep on her own, separated from her mother for the first time in her short life.

The Morris house took on a post-war facsimile of happiness. A sort of dutiful getting on with it, where they counted their blessings. Then, in a repeat of Ewan's miracle, Terry returned from North Africa, creating a sense that there'd been no war, just a theft of time. With the bedrooms full, Terry volunteered to sleep on the couch, thinking his sisters would marry soon enough and move out, and brooding all the while over the noise that Aileen made as a toddler. But within a year, Hetty and Ewan had a second child. A son. They called him Little Jimmy. If the living room was a pressure cooker before, Little Jimmy's newborn cries threatened to blow it up. Ewan resented Terry's dark silence. He knew what it represented: an unspoken truth about his marriage, about Ewan's failure to provide properly for his wife and children.

In a fit of self-reliance, Ewan bought four subsidised tickets, ten pounds each, for the RMS *Cameronia*, a 552-foot tourist class steamer cruiser to Australia. On the voyage, he was separated from his wife and children, sharing a cabin below the waterline with five other men. Hetty, Aileen and Little Jimmy shared with the women, topside. The ship sailed from Glasgow to Sydney via the Suez Canal with its ten-pound Poms, as they were known. They were off to satisfy Australia's appetite for a white and grateful workforce on a journey through now-peaceful waters to a promise of economic revival.

In Penicuik they had been forced to barter for basics. But onboard the *Cameronia* there was butter on all the bread. In the ports, brown people brought their exotic goods in little baskets, raising them up to the ship with ropes. Ewan bragged they could afford these things now. There was good work where they were going.

Yet the joys of the ports were short-lived. As coastlines gave way to oceans, life on the ship mouldered through long, boring patches of nothingness. There was just the routine of queuing for toilets and washrooms and militarily organised shifts for lunch and dinner. The men played cards and drank, like they were bivouacked on a campaign. The women were stuck with the children in their cabins like war widows again, missing their men.

Hetty was often seasick. She kept a bucket beside her bunk. During these episodes Aileen, seven years old by then, took on the big-girl job of minding her little brother. She took him up on deck while her mother tried to keep her lunch down.

One day Hetty was suffering in her cabin, lying on her bunk, swinging her legs off the end, when Aileen rushed in with Little Jimmy, all excited. There'd been some incredible news. Men were dressed in funny outfits up on deck. Some were wearing coconut bras and grass skirts. One man got drunk and forced another one to kiss a fish. They were crossing the Equator.

Perhaps that was why Hetty had felt poorly that day. She felt stretched tight inside as if something was about to snap away from its coupling. They had crossed into a new hemisphere.

'Was your father with you?' Hetty asked.

'No, Mummy,' Aileen replied, offended by the suggestion that her supervision wasn't enough.

'Just keep away from the silly men then,' Hetty said.

'Why?' Aileen asked.

'Because drunk men are no good.'

On their arrival in Australia, the Morris family were stationed at a migrant hostel in the town of Castlemaine, where they shared an asbestos-lined Nissen hut with another Scottish migrant family. Soon Ewan had a labouring job. Within a year, Hetty was pregnant again. Ewan seemed to accept the news without a stumble or a pause. As if he didn't feel the weight of it because he was being carried along by a whole country's momentum.

Jiāngshī

Waking face down beside the highway between Rockhampton and Mackay, Stephen's left cheek was still warm from the setting sun. His feet pointed to the south, his head to the north. Above him, a mist of galaxies drifted in the ink-black sky. Under his nose, broken windscreen glass cast a fragmented reflection. Stephen stood up, giving in again to the invisible thread that had been pulling him on.

Two nights prior, he lost his footing on the verge of the highway, falling into an unnamed creek. His fall was broken by a log washed there in a flood. He landed awkwardly on his back and felt a rib dislocate at the point of impact, one of the floating ribs. As he walked, he could feel it swimming inside him, circling his organs. It took Stephen all night to get out of the creek. Yet he slackened in the struggle, hoping the creek banks would defy whatever it was that had a hold over him. He slipped and fell, slipped and fell again. Eventually, the creek grew bored of him and let him climb back to the road.

Stephen hid whenever a car approached. He was terrified they'd stop to ask if he needed help. A man walking the Marlborough stretch was an oddity worth investigating. He wanted to remain invisible. Ahead he could see a small exit, or was it a driveway? On such a desolate stretch, it stood out. Curious, he watched a car turn in. Perhaps it was a backroad, less busy than the highway.

Following the car at a safe distance, he discovered that the road ended at a clearing with a house, colonial in style with wide verandas. Corrugated-iron tank. Pressed-metal balustrades. Nearby, a relative anomaly: a mobile phone tower called in frequencies from the stars. Just beyond that was a small shed and a run-down tennis court, surfaced in ant bed. Its dull white lines were drawn straight over whatever weeds had invaded it. Lamb's tongue and dandelion. But there was no tennis being played.

Stephen's senses were amplified by the emptiness. Around the tennis court, he could see thousands of tiny eyes shining out from tall grass. The occupants of the car and the people from the homestead ignored these things or didn't see them. Their focus was on carrying supplies to a patch of watered green in front of the court. They laid out a large poly tarp on the grass and ran a power cord from the house to a floodlight that drooped from a wire.

A bucket of sand was pin-cushioned with smouldering sticks that sent a mosquito-repelling veil of blue smoke across the entire setup. Incense. Stephen could smell it. Two men brought in packing pallets to build a makeshift bed while the women and children carried in cushions and pillows and a ragged doona. Then a gas barbecue on wheels was dragged from the house, along with a collection of plastic chairs.

The activity was orchestrated the way family friends do things. A well-practised routine, beautifully casual. The homestead, the dirt court and the water tank could have been the setting of a Steele Rudd story. A family on their selection, Dad and the Donovans – except the family jarred with that cliché. There were no red-bearded settlers, no fair farmer's wives. Four black-haired children were lounging about on the bed of pallets, feet facing the sky, chins on their elbows, watching four black-haired adults setting up a folding table, clicking the gas burner onto high. Then a wok, blackened by seasoning, was drizzled with sesame oil. Out in the scrub, where Stephen stood, chilli and shrimp paste made itself known. A cloud of umami, an alchemy he'd only discovered as an adult, as an inner-city gay. On the table, cold noodles sat ready, piled into a light green plastic basin. He tried to remember the family meals he'd had and wondered why they hadn't smelled as good as this.

Stephen was intrigued. He inspected the homestead, the plants that were growing around the base of the water tank. The metallic green leaves of betel spread outwards from the slab. Coriander and ong choy grew in the runoff from the downpipes and the leaking water tap. Bitter melon draped over the old wire arbour monstering a neglected climbing rose.

Stephen crept closer to hide in a stand of trees outside the floodlight's reach. How strange to see an Asian family in that remote locale. But why wouldn't they be there? Stephen thought about his own family, his father's side, how they must have started somewhere like this. Where they would have been regarded as odd, jarring with the landscape. Stephen shifted on his feet. There were worms in the ground, making tunnels where he stood. Ready to consume him if he stayed there too long.

A man from the group stood up from his seat. He made his way over in Stephen's direction and stopped suddenly. Had Stephen been seen? No, the man had located a pack of Lucky Strikes in his pocket and shook a cigarette free with practised efficiency, lighting it and then dialling a number on his phone.

A mushroom of smoke blew from his lips, enveloping Stephen's face. There was a fruitiness, but also an earthiness, to the breath behind the notes of the tobacco. Stephen felt that urgent feeling again in his solar plexus, as if a balloon was inflating in his chest. It was a reaction he couldn't control. It was all gut. All nerve. And Stephen was lightning fast as he lunged at the man from the darkness.

He knocked the man backwards onto a bed of leaves. The mobile phone was shaken from his hand, disconnecting the call. The man struggled but Stephen was stronger. He held him down with his two arms and his two legs in a circle of iron. Each limb operated like the claw of a mantis, curving around the struggling man's body, holding him still and quiet. Stephen's neck curved so his mouth lined up with the stricken man's lips. Then he inhaled with all his organs. His gut sucked up into a convex shape, like the cup of a rubber plunger, pulling something vital from the man. Nothing with mass or matter, but something important, something life-giving. And then the man was still. He was no longer struggling or even breathing.

Stephen pushed himself away. He felt vigorous. Restored. His joints felt more flexible. His limbs felt lighter. The parasites that had climbed onto him were fleeing. Ants were running from inside his clothes and flies were escaping from his hair. The worms in the dirt pulled back. As if he was on railway tracks, Stephen slid away from the man, back into the darkness of the trees that he had sprung from, back along the dirt road too, back onto the sealed section of highway.

There, he spun. Steered on his paranormal axis so he was once more walking north. Faster now. More freely. More like a living man.

1938

On the wide dirt road known as Ernest Street, Innisfail, William and Christina Bolin's house sat like an umpire's stand, watching over a game of rounders. It was after 3 pm. School was out. When the Bolins and their cousins the Los and a couple of ring-ins got together, it was intense. Eighteen kids under the age of eight, with at least six cousins per team. Barefoot and without hats. The summer had been hot. Everyone was burnt brown except for the fair-haired ring-ins, who were pink and peeling.

Swinging the one bat they had at the one ball they owned, they smashed it into the allotment over the road. Whoever had the bat raced around the bases. Meanwhile, the chasers went for the ball and got scratches on legs and arms from the Guinea grass. Every so often a tick found its way into their hair to attach itself to their scalp.

Willie Bolin had just found one on his head. He ran to his mother, Christina, who kept tweezers in her pocket just for that. With a dab of kerosene, she dislodged it. The tick freed its jaws, maddened by the kerosene. Christina nipped it between her tweezers and held it to the light to identify its species.

'I hope it's not a paralysis tick,' she said. 'Or you'll be stuck this way forever.'

Willie wriggled free to get back outside. Back to the game – but also out of reach of his father, who was never happy with Willie being a sook with his mum. Willie thought that must be why he had so many younger siblings: his father was always trying for a better son.

There were eight Bolins living in their two-bedroom house. Willie and his two brothers had bunks set up in the sleep-out, a closed-in veranda with no fan, just a wall of wooden louvres that kept out the rain and let in the breeze. Their three sisters occupied the children's bedroom, a room that was once Willie's. His parents had their own room.

Only the rain that made Innisfail a record town for floods could keep a Bolin kid inside. But rain was the family's worst enemy because it kept them in each other's faces. It was a compression test living that way. But out on the street, life was good.

They were making as much noise as a flock of cockatoos when a few of them noticed an old man marching down the lane that cut through all the way from Owen Street. The man was ancient, bent over and hobbling. Willie knew who he was, and when he finally clocked him heading their way, he got the others to quieten down.

Something about the old guy frightened Willie. The way he frowned and didn't look at any of them. It wasn't normal for someone not to say hello in Innisfail. Willie was the first to speak.

'Hello, Grandad.'

There was no answer. The old man shuffled on. The skin on his face crinkled into multiple expressions but none of them could be called a smile.

'Hello, Grandad,' one of Willie's cousins repeated.

'Grandad, Grandad, Grandad,' the children all started shouting in relay. 'Grandad! Grandad!'

Nothing. The old man kept walking until he was outside the Bolin house, and that's where he stopped. With no difficulty at all, he bent his knees and squatted, surprising Willie with his flexibility. There he stayed, like a stone statue that had been put at the gate for decoration. Willie looked to his siblings and cousins. It was a look that seemed to be a signal, and they teemed towards the footpath outside the Bolin house to watch.

The children's chatter brought Christina out onto the stoop. Just one glance at the old man and she was back inside, calling to William to come and sort it out.

William was angry. Always angry. Seeing the kids there, he shouted at them through a window. 'Go back to your game or get inside the house.'

The Los, who were afraid of their Uncle William, took off. They melted away, the rest of the Bolin kids with them. Willie stayed outside though. He wanted to prove to his father that he could be useful.

Shaking his head, William marched down the stairs and out to where the old man was squatting. He tried to drag his father to his feet, pulling at the old man's thin arms. He shouted into his face.

'We don't want you here. Go back to the Joss House!'

The old man snarled. But he wasn't moving. He was solidly planted. His wrinkled arms, thin as twigs, shook free of William and wrapped around his knees. His flat, narrow feet stuck like Araldite to the footpath.

'Suit yourself,' William said, then stormed back into the house, shouting to Willie over his shoulder: 'Don't talk to him!'

When the Bolin kids came home for dinner, their grandad was still sitting out front. Each of them passed him with a suspicious expression, except for Willie, who felt sorry for him, having witnessed how he'd been treated. After dinner, Willie watched his grandad through the louvres of the sleep-out. In the streetlight he could see mosquitoes buzzing around the old man's ears. After dinner, when the whole family had retired to their beds, Willie tried to stay awake as long as he could. He kept looking through the louvres and the old man looked back as if he was watching him too. Eventually Willie's lids felt impossibly heavy, and sleep took him off duty. When he woke, his grandfather had gone.

It was Sunday. There was no mention of him over breakfast. It was as if he'd never been there.

Two years later, William Bolin was reading his morning paper when he noticed policemen walking up the front path. Wanting to head them off before anyone saw, he opened the door.

'Mr Bolin, is it?' said one of the officers.

'What's happened?'

The police were stewing in their woollen uniforms. They were brass-buttoned up to the neck. The sun was belting heat onto their backs and roasting their scalps. Their hats were off, and William feared the reason for this.

He took his own hat off the rack, slid into his shoes, no socks. He didn't give the police a chance to speak as he left the house, motioning to them that he would be happy to walk them to their car.

Christina was pegging out sheets on the clothesline. She heard the sound of an engine and assumed it was William's taxi heading off to work. In fact, he was sitting in the back of a squad car, waiting for the bad news to be revealed.

The police car with William pulled up outside the Innisfail ambulance centre, a twin-gabled building with an adjacent shed. One ambulance was reverse parked in the driveway. They were met by an officer who had done every jacket button one hole too high. After a quiet hello, William was led to the rear doors of the ambulance. Carefully laid out inside on a stretcher, and covered respectfully with a sheet, was a small and painfully thin body.

'That's my father?'

'You tell us,' replied the first policeman, who lifted the sheet to reveal Pan Bo Lin's face. William frowned at his father's sunken cheeks and greyish pallor. It wasn't pity he was feeling, but embarrassment.

William asked, 'Where did he die?'

'In the Joss House.'

William nodded as if he'd expected that answer. He inched away from the ambulance, wishing he had brought his cigarettes with him.

'We'll need you to sign some papers,' said the older of the two policemen.

William had a sudden thought. 'How did he die?'

The wrong-buttoned ambulance officer stepped forward. 'Senility,' he said, 'and various complications.'

William was relieved. At least he hadn't been murdered in a fight.

'I need some details from you,' the first policeman said, taking out a notebook. 'We have him listed as Pan Bolin, but we need a birthdate, other details.'

'Our family's not sure. Maybe 1840s. In Chikan, China, apparently. Put down gardener as his profession. He was married to my mother, Bridget Wilkie. She died in Townsville. They married in Maryborough.'

William was surprised that he could recall any of that.

'Who needs to be notified?'

William held up his right hand, as if each finger represented a sibling.

'Just Alvin, Clarence, Charles, Joseph, Mabel. I'll call them.' William didn't mention the family in China.

'Okay, that's all we need for now. We'll take him to the morgue, and you can make your funeral arrangements. Oh, and, uh … our condolences.'

On the drive back, William and the police officers spoke about the weather and the football from the weekend. Christina was still working in the laundry when William arrived home. Rather than disturb her, he started up his taxi in the street and Christina wondered why she was hearing it for a second time. He would tell her all about it when he got home, when the children had gone to bed.

At the age of twenty-seven, Willie applied for a railway worker's position in Port Augusta, South Australia. There, he'd have nobody to disappoint, no siblings to compare himself to and nothing to live up to. He was a young man trying to be as far from his family as he could get. In Port Augusta, he located a boarding house.

His dormitory was on the top floor of a repurposed bank building, built of sandstone quarried from Mount Gambier. It was owned by a couple who lived on the lowest floor. He and the other boarders, six of them, had an easy time getting on. They asked little more of each other than good humour. Everybody was given a nickname, whether they wanted one or not.

Willie's was obvious.

How ya goin', China?

He started a journal there in his careful hand on the first day of his stay. It was mostly an account of his working life. But he also described the men who came to the boarding house, stayed and went again. There were twenty who passed through, twenty young men from all over the place.

Bicycle Bruce came from Melbourne. His favourite sport was cycling. Willie wrote that Bruce kept his bicycle cleaner than he kept his bed. Russell the Muscle was a *physical culture type*. He was always on the floor, doing exercises in a puddle of sweat. Then there was Jack Smith, the mystery man. Nobody knew where he was from, where he was going or whether Jack Smith was even his name.

There were older chaps too, living across the road in a secondary hostel. It was a cheaper, more rundown place for the unemployed. One of the men Willie described as *Vic, the wino.* He walked into Willie's dorm one night while the other lads were out. Willie had heard of pansies before. Poofters too. But he never expected one to look like a railway worker. He always thought they'd be wearing a dress, fopping around with a limp wrist.

Willie turned his hands into fists when Vic tried to climb into his bed. He threw whatever he could at the guy through the tangle of his mosquito net, and Vic bolted. Willie felt disgusted, but mostly offended that it was him and nobody else who'd won Vic's attention. He debated whether to tell anyone about it at all. The next day, when he reported it to his landlady, he tried not to sound like a sook, tried not to imply that anything had happened either.

'That old pervert from across the road snuck into our dorm last night,' he told her.

'Which one?'

'Old Vic. He tried to get under my mosquito net. But I smashed him one.'

Soon after that, Vic was evicted. But somehow the story got out, and Vic became a nightly joke for the other boarders.

'Hey, China. Let me under your mosquito net,' they whispered. And at night, as the lights went out, they said, 'Good night, China. Good night, Vic.'

'Shut up or I'll smash you one.' Willie would laugh, but he hated that the joke was on him. He was Vic's mosquito-net sweetie. The one all the perverts tried it on with. He hated how it implied he was weak. Nobody said that about Russell the Muscle or Bicycle Bruce.

After a year of this, Willie fell into what he described as a groove of ignominy. He needed to shake off the Old Vic story by finding a girl. But the only girl to pay him attention was the young daughter of the landlady. She was frumpy and freckle-nosed and too young, but she was better than the mosquito-net bandit. Better for William's reputation. He began by complaining to the lads that she was keen on him. He said he might have to give her one for charity. But as much as he promoted the story, he couldn't convince them it was true. And he ended up feeling sorry for the girl for lying about her.

One night, while the men around him played cards and drank beer and made him the butt of their jokes, Willie opened a letter that had arrived from his father.

She doesn't have long, it read. *She is weak and not accepting visitors. We are just waiting around for the end. Don't come home. There won't be time. She won't even know you're here. Get on with your life.*

Christina was dying of arteriosclerosis. Her arteries were failing her. Willie read the letter while the belly laughs of his dorm mates rattled the light bulb above his head. He'd been so keen to go to Port Augusta, fooling himself with his ambition. Now he had robbed his mother of his support. Now she was close to death, and his father … why would his father encourage him not to come home? How could he think he could deal with his grief alone?

He didn't say goodbye to his friends in the boarding house. He sat upright through the long, uncomfortable nights on the train to Innisfail, rigid with anger at his father for even thinking he should stay away. He was not like his father. It took four days and nights to get back to Innisfail, and the whole time he worried that he would be too late.

She died the day after he arrived. He told her the things he hoped would make her feel loved, not deserted. He wouldn't waste time talking about himself and all the things he had done in Port Augusta on his own. Nor would he burden her with his failures. They were his things, not her things, not family things. Willie regretted going away, regretted thinking about his future, but even more he resented what had been stolen from him. Now he had no mother, and no father he could respect. Most of his siblings had moved out of the home. Just his youngest sister, Dorothy, remained.

Christina's funeral was a muted affair, held under the ominous clouds of a North Queensland monsoon. It rained on the hearse as it made its way to the service at the Mother of Good Counsel church on Rankin Street. Christina's coffin was brought in, wet with splash from the downpour.

William didn't speak at the funeral. Willie didn't either. He sat darkly behind his father in the pews, next to Dorothy. His other sisters and brothers attended, but they were supported by their partners. They all had new loves. They had dispersed into their own families. Willie felt envious. He had nobody to go to. He wondered how different things would have been if he'd turned up with a girl, even the landlady's daughter.

At the end of the service, Willie walked home with Dorothy. Their father dragged his feet behind them. He used to lead the family, but today he was incapable. That night, in the sleep-out, Willie listened to his father's silence, while a cacophony of frogs sang a requiem for his mother in the downpipes.

Christina had been declining for months. Willie could have been there earlier if only he'd been told. There was a sense now that he was out of sync with his siblings. He was still getting used to the idea of his mother's illness while they all seemed so resolved about her death. He thought he might never come close to them again. He was the eldest, but he felt the most naïve.

This was serious now. He needed to grow up. Get a good job in Innisfail with better money. On the strength of his Port Augusta experience, he landed one almost immediately. But still he was a man nearing thirty who lived at home with his father and baby sister. He'd been away for three years, but it was as if he'd never left school.

With his new job Willie could afford a car. His friends saw that as an opportunity. He could be their driver to get them to and from their parties. While they drank and hooked up with girls, Willie stayed sober. Girls considered him too nice to make a pass. He had an adolescent aura, stunted by his youngish looks.

Then a new family moved into the house above the shop on the corner of Ernest Street.

In describing this event in his journal, Willie was unusually specific, as if he needed to prove it had happened. It was a hot

Saturday afternoon. He was playing rounders again with a tennis ball and a wooden stick, being the fun uncle and humouring the kids. He'd been backstop at the intersection with Lily Street when he caught a glimpse of a girl in white shorts and blouse on the rear landing of the top flat, two allotments away. She walked down the stairs to the shop. Willie described the feeling that came over him.

It was an electric shock, he said, *caused by the sight of her trim, cool figure, and the way she moved like a kite.*

He gave her a wave as she crossed. To his surprise, she waved back. When she emerged from the store with an ice cream in her hand, she waved again, and he returned her wave. Willie knew he was in love.

It took a week for him to arrange a proper introduction. His sister Dorothy was the patsy of the plan, but she didn't realise it at the time. Over breakfast, she mentioned to Willie that she was starting a local girls' marching team and was looking for new girls in town to join. She asked her brother if he knew anybody.

'The new girl next door?' Willie suggested, hoping his upward inflection, his delivery of the statement as a question, wouldn't give away his excitement. He hoped he'd sounded helpful to his sister. Like he had her interests, only her interests, at heart.

Dorothy recruited the girl that afternoon. In another 'helpful' move, Willie volunteered to drive them both to and from marching practice, twice a week. He had to go to football training anyway. He hoped the girl would ride up front with him. He kept his football jersey immaculate just in case. He was the cleanest player on the field.

Jiāngshī

Each night Stephen awoke in his body, his legs were still pumping and his compulsion to move was still strong. It was painful, that constancy. The consciousness of it was too much to bear. Stephen closed his mind down, his awareness of the rambling, the staggering. His perception of waking and walking faded, but certain memories of what he'd done tortured him.

When he arrived on the outskirts of Mackay, the smokestacks of the Racecourse Mill were as iconic to him as the Twin Towers were to New Yorkers. But with the plumes of smoke came a recent memory, the memory of the man with the Lucky Strikes at the tennis court. And with the orange dot of the moon came the image of the lit end of the man's cigarette. Alongside the mill, mountains of filter press cooked itself to compost, covered in acres of tarpaulins held down by bricks. This brought back the tarpaulin that the family had laid out at the tennis court, the image of the children playing there, their heads propped on elbows, eating their noodles, waiting for their poor father to return from having his cigarette. But he was gone from their lives now. Stephen had seen to that. He wondered which of them found him. What trauma he'd inflicted on those children. Would they ever recover?

As Stephen entered West Mackay, he hoped he was invisible to the traffic, just another figure walking in the night. There were people across the road, strolling in the opposite direction, heading home for dinner. He had no interest in them, and they had no interest in him. Eventually he arrived at a corner where he saw a sign over a building. The streetlight was out but the sign was lit, its lettering legible in the gloom. *Laundromat*, it read. *Washers and Dryers 24/7.*

The place was empty. Yellow bulbs made the interior look submerged in urine. A series of dryers had their circular doors open at odd angles, as if there'd been an earthquake. Stephen felt around each dryer, hoping for lost property, clothes that had been left behind, anything that he could change into. But there was nothing. He checked inside a top loader. If there was even something wet stuck to the inside of the drum, it would do, but again there was nothing.

He tried the door to the storage room out the back. His fingers were fused and curved in rigid arcs, the thumbs bent inwards. They gripped the doorknob, but it was locked. Angry, he noticed a sign above. It said to call a number if he needed assistance. What a joke. How could he call and what would he say?

I think I've killed a man. I need a change of clothes. Also, I'm dead.

The light on the console over one of the front loaders was blinking green. It was in credit. Stephen peeled off his shirt and rolled his pants down his rigid legs. They came off like a wetsuit that had been powdered on the inside. There was dusty mould growing on his skin. The dark street outside the laundry made the windows reflective and, for the first time since he'd left Brisbane, he could see his own body as he stood there, holding his garments over the bowl of the washer, ready to drop them in.

So, this was who he was now. The skin had been worn off his torso where the garments had been the tightest: on the clavicles, on the tops of his shoulders, on the elbows and the nipples. The exposed flesh wasn't red, but black, polished and hard. His chest was like a cage, the skin over his ribs rubbed lustrous in stripes. Around his waist, where the pants had been cinched, his skin was shiny too. Below that, his cock, a button in cold weather, was almost non-existent, rubbed off so the pubic hair was all that could be seen. In between these black patches, dusty mould. His face was the most terrifying thing. It was dry like a relic. Stephen tried to lick his lips, but his tongue was bark.

It would have been a horror for anyone to see him. A naked corpse holding a bunch of clothes over a washer. Stephen couldn't recognise himself in his reflection. But his relationship with the mirror had always been like that. He had always thought he was looking at someone else. It never showed the person he was in his head.

Eventually Stephen dropped the clothes into the washer, and he activated the switch. A fast wash. The bowl filled and he stood there for as long as the cycle took, staring at his naked reflection in the glass. When he retrieved the clothes, their dampness wet down his powdery skin and they clung to him as if they'd shrunk. He left the laundromat and melted into the street.

In a ditch outside Proserpine, he woke again, having walked through the night and slept another day. Lost hours and days were a relief. He was grateful for those.

1960

Ewan Morris's family thought he'd crave Penicuik's ordinary streets after his years at war. But being part of a lost unit in the Borneo jungle had done something permanent to him. It had made his home life feel too small. His parents' house too small. His job too small. His feelings for Hetty and his children. Everything was diminished. Even vast distances seemed small. He relocated his family twice after sailing to Australia. When Aileen was twelve, he moved them from Castlemaine to Brisbane, a distance of 1776 kilometres. When she was sixteen, he moved them further north to Innisfail, another 1617 kilometres by road. There, Ewan took a job as a boilermaker. The most uncomfortable job he could think of in the North Queensland heat. He was punishing himself, of course, punishing himself for surviving. But he was also punishing his family.

Alongside his punishments, the jungle returned to him at night in that murky phase between wakefulness and sleep. It was always the same image, Gurkha fighters, allies to the British with sugar bags of Japanese heads they'd lopped off on their night-time raids. The expressionless Japanese faces would come to Ewan in the dark as he counted them. He'd swing his fists in frustration at his pillow until Hetty woke him up. Then he'd move himself to the kitchen, where he'd drink until he was too drunk to count, too drunk to be awake.

Hetty made all the reasonable excuses a wife could make for her husband. They were the things that war wives often said to their neighbours, to the bosses of their husbands and to their children. *He's just having a bad day. He's just a prickly personality. He just needs you to be quiet.*

She had the make-do instincts of an orphan. If she could avoid a confrontation, she would. She missed Scotland and felt every move was a new emigration. But she didn't complain. She didn't believe there were any choices for a mother of young children to make. She would take what she was given, in case it was given to somebody else. That was just how she saw life.

Not her daughter, though. Aileen remembered a time when she had her mother to herself. A time before her father came home. She'd had a taste of how life could be better back at her grandparents' house, where she and her mother had their own room, without the curtained divider. She complained loudly about moving to Innisfail, the stinking hot town so far north. The humidity clamped her hair to her head and made mushrooms grow in her shoes. But when the girl from next door came over to introduce herself and asked her to join her marching band, Aileen felt a feminine kinship might be all she needed.

The marching girl's name was Dorothy. She was confident and cool in fashionable clothes. Her hair was pin curled and black as a car tyre, styled like a model from *Vogue*. Aileen touched her own wispy hair when she accepted Dorothy's invitation. Then she was dragged across to Dorothy's house, where the flashy uniforms were already laid out on a bed. White and red, with contrast piping and tailored shoulders. The skirt was relatively short, and Aileen thought deliciously that it was likely her father would object to that. The girl was Chinese, though she spoke like a North Queenslander in blunt vowels with a nasal tone.

Two weeks later Aileen felt confident enough to tell her father that she had joined a marching club with a friend. In the kitchen, her mother was apprehensive. She rattled pots on the little stove while she listened. Little Jimmy played with a small wooden car on the floor, unaware that his sister was crossing a rubicon. Ewan was in his special chair, his singlet and shorts damp with sweat. He packed his pipe with the tip of a blunt finger. Didn't look at Aileen while he spoke.

'Waste of time, marching,' he said.

Aileen was surprised that was all he said. He didn't order her not to go. She didn't wait for another cue. At sixteen she was loath to hug her father, but in her instant elation she almost did.

On practice days, Dorothy's brother Willie hovered around the girls, disguised as an older brother supporting his sister but sending smiles in Aileen's direction. He watched her in the rear-view mirror of his car as he drove them to practice. If he bought them a frozen Bijingo, he'd hand Aileen hers first. For her part, Aileen was amused by the attention. Gradually she allowed him into view until in a few months' time she couldn't look away.

Willie was a completely grown-up man. But to Aileen, that was a bonus. He was old enough to drive. He owned a Holden FJ in two-tone – canary yellow and white. He had a nice haircut and wore smart jackets and long pants. He had a job, and he played football with the men of Innisfail.

Crucially, he was nothing like her father, Ewan, who sat shirtless and hairy at the table whenever the family ate. Willie was polite and he was kind, and he was well dressed and he was

Chinese. The same version of Chinese as his sister, with that broad Australian accent.

One afternoon after marching practice, Aileen decided to sit in the front seat with him. It annoyed Dorothy, who was forced to sit in the back with the gramophone. A box for a friend: not a fair trade. Willie had changed out of football gear into a pair of nice trousers, but there was a weeping gravel rash on one of his knees and the blood spotted through the fabric. Aileen wanted to touch it to see if it caused him pain. She kept glancing over to see if the seepage had spread. When she looked at his face, she caught sight of a drop of sweat travelling from his temple to his chin. She wanted to catch it in her handkerchief, to keep it as her own. The perfume of his kindness. Salty but also sweet.

It took less than a year for Willie to propose. He picked her up from her work at the Innisfail department store. In the twilight, near the canecutters statue, he asked the question that she'd suspected was coming. She gave him a tentative yes. But she kept the proposal buttoned up. First, her father and Willie must meet.

Aileen knew her father liked to dance. She thought that if she invited her father dancing, he'd appreciate how grown up she was. Then if she danced with Willie, dressed as nicely as he always was, Ewan would see that his daughter had chosen someone decent, and he would be more open to Willie asking him for her hand in marriage.

On the evening of the dance, as the band played 'Mack the Knife', Aileen picked her moment. She handed her brothers over to her mother, stood up and made her way out onto the floor, bold as anything. She was wearing a hooped skirt and her bodice was tight. Her father had criticised her dress earlier. But what was she doing with it now on the dance floor? Aileen was spinning and making a show of her legs, a confident young lady in a fashionable skirt. Ewan scowled. Hetty looked uncertain. But it was all part of Aileen's plan. She curtseyed in her father's direction, an over-the-top invitation to him, and then she was pulling him up on the floor. Soon he was gripping her too close. It was something he had done with her before. She felt she was being forced or compelled around the floor. After the third number, Aileen wanted Willie to make his move, to rescue her from her father.

'Dad, there's someone here I'd like you to meet.'

Though he'd heard what she'd said, Ewan held his daughter tight and continued to move her around. They circled the venue one more time. Willie stood at the perimeter watching them. Aileen remained a silent hostage as they passed Willie again. When the song finally ended, Aileen motioned Willie over, hoping he'd think of something charming to say. Hoping he'd get on famously with her father the way he got on with the other men at the football.

Willie approached with quiet confidence, but he could feel the tension in the air before he even spoke.

'Sir …' he began to say.

Ewan looked Willie up and down. Who was this? He glanced at his daughter, whose eyes were communicating secrets to the young man. In that moment, Ewan was thrown somewhere else. He was not in the dance hall anymore. A bullet broke the sound barrier as it cracked past his ear. Ahead, voices, boots on the jungle floor. Cold mud seeped into his socks. Ants were crawling and biting at his legs but there was no crying out, just an order to stifle his breathing. Overhead, monkeys howled at the birds that flew up, panicked by the sound of shots. It was the snare drum, the intro to 'Sing, Sing, Sing', the Benny Goodman song.

Standing on the dance floor, Willie boldly held his future father-in-law's stare. Ewan grimaced at the shape of the young man's eyes.

'Go to the car, Aileen,' Ewan hissed, shaking her off his arm.

Six weeks later, Aileen wrote to Willie from Brisbane. It was a letter he'd been dreading, though the details were patchy. The brevity of her sentences made Aileen's words inanimate and mechanical. Her father had put his foot down. No wedding. Their family's move to Brisbane would be permanent.

Between the lines, Willie searched for Aileen's tears. At his desk at his prized job, he pored over the letter. With its finality, Aileen's message felt like it had been delivered in a different language. Except for the way she signed her name. The stems of the A in Aileen had flourishes that she'd drawn at their terminals. They were curled with such care like little snails. Was there something in that? A coded flirtation? A clue that she hadn't given up on herself and their love?

It would take him a while to recover from the shock of her leaving. He was glad he was working late that night. He could keep the raw emotion of his first big break-up hidden from his father, concealing his weakness.

A month and a half later, Willie was relieved to hear from Aileen again. This time, she wrote the message he hadn't dared to hope for. She had booked a ticket back to Innisfail, and she needed somewhere to stay. She didn't offer an immediate explanation. But she still wanted to get married. Willie was elated. He wrote back to tell her he would pick her up from the station in Townsville.

Aileen sat upright for the thirty-hour journey, on a rattling heap of a train filled with sugar town workers. Her mother had found the money for the fare by selling her sewing machine to a neighbour. The men who sat opposite Aileen took pity on her, a young girl travelling alone. They scratched their ears and attempted to cough up mistimed bawdy jokes. Their good-natured efforts were hampered by their maleness. Hairy, smelling of beer and with arms like tree trunks, they were as subtle as cheap music boxes, all tin gears and grinding teeth, unable to charm the seventeen-year-old girl in their midst. Eventually they left her alone.

Willie was waiting as planned, freshly shaven, smelling of Brut 33, a clean, soapy fragrance that made Aileen wail the moment she saw him. Willie reached for her bag. He shepherded her under his arm for the walk to the car. Once they were seated in private, he kissed her timorously and asked her what had happened, how she'd been able to defy her father. While the engine idled, Aileen tried to explain how her mother had paid for her fare. How she worried about her mother now, left to deal with her father alone, along with the news of Aileen's return to Innisfail.

Willie listened quietly to the disjointed story that Aileen told him. She was holding something back. It was a lot for a girl like Aileen to make such a decisive journey. Her previous letter hadn't even sounded like she was considering it. Now she sounded depressed, resigned. Hardly happy.

'What made you decide to do all this?'

'I missed you,' she said.

'I'm glad you did,' Willie replied. He thought of his own father and how he had still not completely broken away from him. He felt weaker than Aileen. He pictured her at the dance, the last time he had seen her happy, and remembered then how she'd been dragged so cruelly around the floor. Her father's hand too tight around her waist. He realised she'd looked afraid.

'Did he do something to you?' Willie let the words out rather than choosing them wisely. But something about the memory made him feel justified.

Aileen put her hands in her hair, almost as if she might pull it out in hanks. She appeared to be thinking hard, considering what she could tell him. A decision passed like a cloud across her face, and her jaw muscles hardened. She stared at the rubber car mats on the floor as she replied.

'I just have to try to keep going.'

Willie had a glimpse of something unsaid, and he had the sense he should help her lance the boil. If there was one to lance. 'From what? Tell me.' But he was following his own momentum now, certain he knew what Aileen's father had done, and he erupted. 'That mongrel!'

Aileen touched his arm. 'No. Don't.'

'Why not?' Willie was ready to drive to Brisbane to confront Aileen's father about it. To punch him in the face.

'I just ...!' Aileen shouted the words, a sound Willie was shocked to hear. 'Have to ...' And then with sudden calm, rubbing Willie's forearm, she repeated, 'I just have to try to keep going.'

'It won't spoil anything between us for me to know,' Willie pleaded.

'It will. Let's just keep going.' Aileen pointed towards the road.

Something about the way she wouldn't look at him, then, made Willie settle. If she couldn't look at him, it would be the end for them. No marriage like that would work out. Wasn't it enough, he told himself, that she was there with him? She had trusted him with the next phase of her life. He needed to stay in her trust. He owed her this agreement. To respect the silence that she wanted. He just wished what had happened was clearer to him.

Willie had organised for Aileen to board at a neighbour's place in Innisfail, but he worried now it would be a bit too much dealing with strangers again after such a traumatic trip. He suggested that they stay overnight with one of his Townsville brothers. 'Just to give ourselves a break,' he said. Aileen agreed so long as she didn't have to explain herself any further.

She hadn't met Vernon or his wife, Margie, but she was excited to learn that Margie was from England. It would be good to have someone in the family who was born in the same hemisphere. They chatted over afternoon tea while the brothers caught up and drank beer.

There was a barbecue dinner that night, followed by an uneasy silence when Vernon and Margie announced it was their bedtime. Aileen felt instantly awkward. She didn't know if Willie expected her to sleep with him. But he had already decided. He opened the linen closet and gathered his own bedding for the living room couch, leaving the spare room free for Aileen.

A clock ticked loudly somewhere in the kitchen through the night, and Willie was woken on two separate occasions – once by the sound of a flushing toilet, and the other by a bush curlew. But in the morning, he was rested and optimistic.

Margie cooked them eggs and bacon for breakfast, then she took Aileen for a tour of her garden. There was an arbour in the backyard, draped with a deep green loofah vine. Its large five-fingered leaves and pendulous pods looked untamed to Aileen.

Margie showed her a pod that had dried. She peeled the brittle skin off its surface, then shook out a handful of seeds from its gauzy husk.

'It's a good scrubber for bathing,' Margie told her. 'People pay for them in the shops.'

Aileen marvelled at the structure of the thing, its veins and tendons and open vessels with no flesh left in between.

On the drive north to Innisfail, grasshoppers leapt at the windscreen, killing themselves in the process. Willie kept his eyes firmly on the road. He listened as Aileen grew chatty, letting her do most of the talking. He knew she'd done something monumental for him. He understood what it was like to be far away from your mother, to strike out into the world alone, to make a life-altering choice like that. He couldn't shake the idea that something bad had been done to her down there, but he wouldn't bring it up again. She seemed to be talking herself into a better mood.

They arrived at midday. Aileen was introduced to her new landlady, his neighbour, an Italian widow. Willie left her there for a few hours to settle in and said he'd come back to bring her round for dinner. At the Bolin house, Aileen got the reception she expected from Dorothy, who had grown distant from her when Aileen had taken up with her brother. While she waited for Willie to make dinner, Aileen began to obsess again about the trouble she'd caused her own mother. William arrived home to find his son cooking and his fiancée weeping on the step. His stupid son, he thought. Why hadn't he noticed?

Out on the landing, stacked against the weatherboards were small colourful food tins recycled into ornate planter boxes. William told Aileen he had made them himself, curled the tin with pliers. Every step on the stair had a plant, some chives, some tomatoes, marigolds and a pungent variety of geranium that he explained was good for repelling mosquitoes.

Aileen stared at them through her tears. The refracted light gave the planter boxes a coloured aura. She complimented her fiancé's father on his handiwork and wondered why he and Willie didn't seem to get on.

William hoped his son's fiancée would stick around. His boy was lucky to have her in his life. When she turned eighteen, he would be happy to walk Aileen down the aisle to his son and see them off on a branch of their own.

Aileen sent her wedding invitations out the month before her eighteenth birthday. She sent one directly to her mother, pointedly addressing the envelope to Mrs Hetty Morris, not Mrs Ewan Morris. Inside it said, *Bring the boys.* Aileen knew she wouldn't come. It tore at Aileen's heart not to have them there. But at least they had been invited.

On a call made from a pay phone in Murarrie, Hetty wished her daughter a happy day. They spoke for nearly an hour, coin after coin dropped in the slot. Aileen did most of the talking, describing what was planned for the wedding. Her dress was short sleeved for the weather, with a fitted bodice and a skirt that fell midway to Aileen's ankle. Underneath was a hooped petticoat that made Aileen want to stand like a dancer in a jewellery box. Aileen said in their practice run for the ceremony, Willie had been nervous. He had stood stiff like a soldier on parade. Hetty had a flashback when she heard that.

The ceremony was held in the Presbyterian church, then everyone was ferried in a fleet of William's workmates' taxis back to the family house. William had spent the whole previous day killing, plucking, dressing and then roasting a dozen ducks that he'd fattened up for the occasion. Duck feathers still floated around the backyard, blowing in the breeze and catching in the spiderwebs threaded through the pomelo trees.

When the reception got to its boisterous end, the twenty-five guests formed an arch of honour. With rice falling through Aileen's hair and down Willie's collar, the couple raced to their car for their honeymoon drive to Mission Beach. They had hired a small cabin for the weekend as a modest gift to themselves. A proper honeymoon was booked for the following year. Aileen wondered if she could talk her husband into a trip to Brisbane.

With cans rattling from the chrome bumper of their FJ and Aileen plucking rice from Willie's lapel, they talked nervously about little things, keeping the subject matter light, as if their future depended on this one happy moment – as if the wrong conversation might ruin their chances and then they'd be unable to find their way back. Despite those nerves, there was a feeling of accomplishment in the car. Like they'd climbed a mountain and were rolling down the other side.

With the help of a football friend, Willie cleared a hilltop plot in the new Innisfail suburb of Hudson to make way for the foundations of their house. Guinea grass grew deep-rooted there. Out of the adjacent rainforest, the territorial call of a male cassowary echoed like wood blocks. The prehistoric bird emerged to join them for lunch one day, swallowing a Valencia orange whole. They watched it travel down its neck.

Snakes stayed away from the sound of Willie's hacking. Willie dislodged tussock by tussock with his heavy mattock. He'd hoped more friends would have come to help, but a happy husband can do a lot by himself. Aileen did what she could with a rake.

She dragged the cleared weeds to a mound in the rear corner, where they rotted in the rain and became compost overnight.

The skeleton of the house rose on short stumps of concrete, while the house was built out of hardwood milled out of trees from the Ravenswood rainforest. The walls were lined with Masonite, the joins concealed by pine moulding and the floor was laid with linoleum.

What Aileen disliked most about Innisfail were the ants and spiders. In old houses they entered through gaps in the floorboards. But she was in love with her new house, which was modern and clean and sealed. The small kitchen had overhead cupboards that they painted lemon yellow, and a stainless-steel sink. There was an electric hot water system that piped directly to the kitchen and the bath. Aileen sat at a borrowed sewing machine for four weekends, making lace curtains to cover the hopper windows. They painted and tiled and concreted and built garden beds and weeded and weeded and weeded. It was as if the forest would overcome their marriage if they didn't beat it back ferociously.

The stages of their love soon changed. Curiosity gave way to familiarity. Spontaneity gave way to routine. Lust gave way to pregnancy.

In her first trimester, Aileen was carrying home a string bag weighed down with groceries. In the crook of her left elbow was a parcel of brisket, wrapped in butcher's paper. She was stepping over a pothole in the road when she was distracted by a bird that might have swooped her and in her fright, she slipped and fell.

There were men in the pub nearby, and they heard Aileen cry out. The parcel of brisket had tumbled onto the footpath just outside the pub door. When they got to her side, Aileen was haemorrhaging on the kerb, her face pale; it was obvious she was in trouble. The men were in a bigger flap than she was, until a barmaid had a quiet word in her ear.

'Where's your husband?'

When Willie pulled up outside the Innisfail hospital with Aileen in the back seat of his car, a flock of rainbow lorikeets was doing squadron passes through the umbrella trees. The birds squabbled and shrieked overhead as Willie carefully helped Aileen to the footpath. There was a nurse smoking a cigarette on the hospital steps, an experienced midwife who knew immediately what she was looking at. Stubbing out her cigarette, she took Aileen's arm and thanked Willie for helping, which he thought was strange. But he remained at Aileen's side for the walk to the emergency rooms; all the while, a trailing pattern of red drops landed on the polished floor. When the midwife had found Aileen a bed, she thanked Willie once again for his help and asked him where Aileen's husband was.

'I'm her husband,' he said.

The midwife was unable to suppress her surprise.

'I'm her husband,' Willie reiterated, more emphatically.

Aileen reassured the nurse, 'Yes, he's my husband,' and nodded firmly to confirm it.

The midwife attempted to cover for her embarrassment by asking them questions about the pregnancy. 'How far along are you? Have you been experiencing any unusual pain?'

Later, after surgery, after the loss of the baby, while the hospital lights brought moths to the ward, Aileen tried to direct her anger towards the midwife's question.

'*Where is your husband?* How dare she.'

She scowled across the room at the woman in the opposite bed, who was pretending to read a book propped up in front of her. Aileen turned back to Willie, sitting glumly in the chair beside her bed. She stroked his arm and he reached for her hand, which he lifted to his olive brown lips to kiss. The woman in the bed opposite turned to her other side to give the couple privacy. Was there a tone of judgement about her?

A few days later, at home, Aileen brought it up again. The bedroom was practically melting in the afternoon light that streamed through the lace curtains. Willie tried to do what he could for Aileen, bringing her iced water in a jug from the kitchen. Frogs were singing in the grass. The neighbour across the road was shouting at his kids to come inside.

'It's a growing town,' Willie said. 'She can't be expected to know everyone.'

Aileen shook her head as if she was getting rid of something caught in her hair. 'But she shouldn't assume we're not together.'

'It's probably because you're a Protestant and I'm a Catholic,' Willie joked, and it worked.

'That's why Dad never liked you,' Aileen said, trying to follow him into a better mood. She admired her husband's face, his lips and especially his smile. He was the most positive person she knew. Taking a deep breath, she made a pact with herself to try to be the same.

After a few months, when the painful edge of the miscarriage had blunted, Aileen allowed herself to be loved once more and they hoped that the next child they conceived would make it all the way.

Nine months later, she was rewarded for that faith, giving birth to a girl they called Carmel. Fifteen months after that, Aileen gave birth to a second child, a son they called Stephen. And then their little family was on a roll.

*

'Things happen quickly when they happen quickly.' Willie was telling Aileen how he'd been denied a pay rise and how that had inspired him to apply for a new job out of town. With apprehension, he was testing the waters, describing it as a management job, and then watching her face for any negativity. Encouraged, he added further detail.

'It's …' He observed her face again. 'It's in Proserpine.'

Aileen grimaced, making it plain she hadn't heard of the town.

Willie tried to reassure her. 'I'm sure you'll like it. The boss, Mr Lessing, has offered us his holiday house not far from the town at Cannonvale Beach, to live in for free, as a temporary stay while we sell the house up here.'

At the mention of selling their house, Aileen felt somewhat manipulated. Willie had saved the worst part till last, and the thought of leaving their new house for an old beach shack frightened her.

'It's the best job in Proserpine,' he added, quickly. 'The pay is very good, a manager's salary. Twenty-five per cent more than what I've been earning here.'

Twenty-five per cent more than what they'd been struggling to get by on, was the truth. 'The timing couldn't be better,' Willie said, glancing across to a bassinet in the corner. There, a third child, Leanne, who hadn't exactly been planned, let alone accounted for, was gurgling away, as if her cuteness could offset her expense.

Lessings was Proserpine's only department store. Along with the mill, it was the pride of the town, and sat on the corner of Lessing Street and Mill Street. That's how important it was, as if the town had been built around it.

When Willie's application turned up on his desk, Mr Lessing hired him on spec. The other applicants had written from a bigger city, like Townsville or Cairns, like Rockhampton or Brisbane, and Mr Lessing thought that sounded like a problem for sure. Why would they want to move to a small town like Proserpine? What were they running away from? Would they become bored again and leave?

Willie Bolin, on the other hand, came from Innisfail. Mr Lessing had passed through it a few times on his way to Cairns, and he remembered thinking how similar it was to Proserpine: both were quaint sugarcane towns that flooded when it rained. One wet season, he'd been stuck overnight in Innisfail and talked to a couple of the locals. People knew everybody else's private business there, just like they did in Proserpine. He could imagine the town when the cutting season was on and the mill was in full swing, how the cinders from the burn-offs would settle over everyone's washing, and how the wives had to learn to cope.

In his application, Willie mentioned his wife. Mr Lessing pictured her: stoic North Queensland stock, untroubled by a ruined wash. Immune to small-town gossip. Resistant to boredom, with a talent for making do. The Bolins were a good choice on paper. A family with little to lose and twenty-five per cent more to gain.

The drive from Innisfail to Proserpine took them seven or eight hours. They passed through lowland stretches of sugarcane fields and plantations of bananas to get there. The floodplains were carpeted by summer grass, punctuated by stands of cyclone-warped eucalypts and dotted with hump-backed cattle. In the distance, the violet ramparts of the Leichhardt Range held back a hotter, drier interior. The main road was a single lane. The Bolins overtook trucks, tractors and slow motorists, tucking back in wildly to avoid oncoming cars. In the moments they were caught behind, they closed the vents of their dash to keep out the fumes.

By around Home Hill, the tension was rising in the rear seats. Baby Leanne was in her bassinet, squeezed between an irritable Carmel and their bored and exasperating brother. He was stretching the corners of his eyes wide with his index fingers, making a face.

'Stop it, Stephen!' Carmel whined.

They drove their car over a low bridge. Carmel turned to her window, hoping to see something better than her brother, but the view of the creek was obscured by trees. On Stephen's side there was at least a sugarcane train passing by. Carmel attempted to count the carriages but the car sped through too quickly. The train was like a frame of film flickering through a projector and of course Stephen was back in her view, making faces, pulling at his eyes and poking out his tongue, making la-la-la noises, hoping for a reaction. His voice took on a maddening rhythm, like a noisy miner.

Willie tried to ignore what was happening behind. He turned up the radio, but his son's voice droned on.

'Stephen!' he exploded.

Aileen flinched at the uncharacteristic aggression in her husband's voice. She reached across to touch his hand.

'It's alright,' she said carefully.

Willie ignored his wife. Fixing his stare on his son in the rear-view mirror, he snapped again, 'Stephen!'

Stephen went silent, frightened by his father's anger.

Aileen swung her hand over the back of the seat to slap Carmel's leg. 'You should know better,' she said.

An indignant Carmel bleated, 'It wasn't me! He was doing Chinese eyes.'

'Your father's driving,' Aileen replied in a fed-up tone, taking over as disciplinarian. She could tell her husband was tired. But also he was treating Stephen harshly, and when had that started to happen? The radio pulsed with a lush Bacharach melody and the lovesick trumpet of Herb Alpert teamed with an overinflated cumulonimbus cloud to take the heat off the car.

They stopped for petrol at a Shell on the outskirts of Bowen. Aileen stayed in the car with the baby while Willie took Carmel and Stephen to the toilet. Carmel went into the Ladies alone while Willie took Stephen with him to the Gents. Stephen stopped at the door, repelled by the smell, wanting to go with his sister.

'You're not a girl,' Willie said, grabbing him by the arm, making him stand at the urinal, which was dry and rusted and fetid. Waiting for his father to finish, Stephen stood and wept in the corner near the basin. As he washed his hands, Willie said to his son, 'Don't be a sissy.'

On the final leg of their journey, the sun dropped down to the hills. They bypassed the turnoff to Proserpine, following the advice they'd been given by Mr Lessing.

It was almost dark by the time they got to Cannonvale Beach. The esplanade had no street lighting and the house they'd been given sat low under a canopy of cottonwood trees. Heart-shaped leaves had fallen all around the building, staining the sandy earth with their tannins. They stuck to Aileen's shoes as she shuffled to the car's rear door to bring Leanne out in her bassinet. Meanwhile, Stephen and Carmel ran straight down to the water, which was lapping the shore, thin little waves tasting the sand.

Willie found the key under the mat as instructed. Getting inside the house was like breaking in. The door was misaligned on its hinges. Inside, the only source of light was a single unshaded bulb hanging from an extension cord. The room was open plan, just bunks against the wall and bookshelves filled with boxes of John Sands table games: Squatter, Test Match, Rummy Royal and Twister. There was a sink against one wall and a fridge that sounded like it had a miniature train set running around inside it. On the kitchen table, Mr Lessing had left them a note.

Welcome, Willie and Aileen. Make yourselves at home. There's an outhouse. The bog men come on Tuesday mornings. The shower is out the back. There's no hot water, sorry. See you in the shop on Monday.

Aileen had not expected makeshift digs. She was tired, hot and dejected, and unable to mask her feelings. Willie went out to buy fish and chips from a local shop for dinner. While he was away, Aileen washed Stephen out the back, standing him on a rock under a cold faucet shower. The rock was slippery with moss. It made Aileen feel yuck. With Stephen back inside and wrapped in a towel, it was Carmel's turn. She had been watching her mother's despondent expression and decided to cheer her up. Raising her hands to her face, she pulled at her eyes with her fingers, the way Stephen had done in the car, stretching them wide and poking out her tongue.

'Look, I'm Stephen, Mum.'

'Don't do that to your eyes,' Aileen said.

'Why?' Carmel replied, screwing her nose.

'It's stupid.' Aileen swiped Carmel's hands from her face and took her daughter's head in her palms. She looked into Carmel's eyes, as if she was assessing for an injury. 'You kids disappoint me sometimes,' she added.

Carmel felt suddenly cold under the dribbling faucet. 'He did it first.'

'Doesn't matter what he did.'

'Yes, it does.' Carmel was getting annoyed and ready to argue.

With a swift and stinging hand, Aileen collected her around the back of the legs. Carmel froze, gulping in air, humming it out through her nose, a suppressed wail. Her eyes streamed. Aileen pulled her daughter's arms into her pyjama shirt and yanked her pyjama shorts up over her skinny legs. She was frustrated with the child, but mostly annoyed with herself.

'This is what I mean. You make me cranky,' she said to Carmel. 'Stop crying.'

Carmel was finding it hard to stop. She felt her mother had been so unfair. Everything her brother did was blamed on her.

'No more silly eyes,' Aileen said, trying to soften her voice, running her hand over Carmel's hair. 'I was an older sister once too.'

Inside the house, Stephen was digging around in the books and games on the bookshelf, searching for something to annoy his sister with. Hoping for a spider or a frog.

Jiāngshī

Entering the outskirts of Proserpine, Stephen was experiencing something akin to yearning. Or the memory of yearning, because his heart was by now dried and black. The road snaked across a mostly featureless plain. Only the battens of cyclone-shredded paperbarks staked out the hidden creeks in the dark. He remembered their names: Lethebrook and Goorganga. The twin waterways flowed stealthily under the road. Their concrete causeways dropped off to nothingness. Drivers could steer off into that void. You could be swallowed up by the reeds and mud, but Stephen kept clear of the edge.

Guided by reflex, he walked barefoot, just as he had as a child, except for the tag on his toe that proclaimed him dead. He had never been back there as a man. Trucks rushed by him, their exhaust shoving at his back. Around the final turn to the town, he passed a motel lit by fluorescent tubes. A single-storey rectangular structure with coloured doors. It was tacky but Stephen recalled it as a fancy place, a child's idea of modernity.

He passed the house of a friend he'd played computer games with off cassette. Unpainted, it looked almost the same as it had back then. One afternoon they'd watched a porno together after school. The boy's parents both worked and weren't home. The movie consisted of garishly lit vignettes of straight-person sex in American scenarios. One involved a baseball dressing room – a handsome blonde player with an injury that needed tending by a nurse. Stephen had been unable to look at his friend while the movie played. When the tape rewound automatically at the end, Stephen couldn't stand up. He blushed in his seat, willing, willing, willing his erection to subside.

In the dark outside the house, he thought about that moment. He wondered about his friend. About his sexuality. Did he remember that video as well as Stephen did and what turned him on about it? What did he like? Stephen wondered what would have happened if they'd been able to talk openly. Whether Stephen himself would have admitted that he enjoyed the cocks most and if such an early admission might have changed the course of his life. How pointless it seemed now to have allowed shame to hold him back. The boy didn't figure in his life now. He should have risked being honest with him back then.

Stephen hurried on. He tried to avoid the lit-up Holden dealership and the Caltex petrol station and then the sensor light at the double-storey brick motel. He slipped past the Shell petrol station, and then the BP petrol station. On the facade of a newish two-level building, he saw a sign that read *Yoga Classes*. It disoriented him. It made him feel he had taken an offramp into a different town. The next sign was more familiar, more like Proserpine: *Pies and Pastries*.

The St Ewan Uniting Church was still where he remembered it. An oblong building with arched windows, its white stucco walls were reflecting the moonlight. Across the road the much darker red-brick structure of the St Catherine's Catholic Church lurked. Behind it, in the shadow of its authoritarian bulk, sat the Catholic school.

The concrete footpath gave way to a formal covered pavement and the detached buildings became a block of shops with masonry walls. Stephen felt cautious, though it was dark and deserted. He worried he might be recognised by someone from his childhood, though nobody was awake at that hour. The Grand Central Hotel gave off an odour he had always hated. Soured beer, it reminded Stephen of his father after work. But surely his father had been long forgotten by the town, and surely Stephen was unrecognisable in the state he was in.

The Ironside Building, once called the Eldorado Theatre, was next on his impromptu tour. Inside its curved front window, it had housed a kiosk selling lollies and sugary drinks, but now it was lined with racks of real estate photos.

There was an urgency developing behind Stephen's sternum. It compelled him to turn around, to back up and exit the town. But he defied it for a little longer, wandering further, past the Metropole Hotel, where he had his first alcoholic drink. A sickly sweet memory of cheap rum and Coke. To his left was the road that took you from the town centre all the way to the school. The blocks lined up in squares. Lawns were trimmed to the root ball. Twin concrete strips were poured only as wide as the wheels of a family car. Cane toads gathered under the streetlights, gobbling up disoriented lacewings. At the entrance, where the school gate stood open, Stephen recalled a memory of himself as a six-year-old on his first day.

He was running now, lighter on his dead, cold feet. The tag from his toe trailed behind him, past the bag racks, beyond the bubblers, through the awnings between the buildings. He was at the back of the school before he realised where he was going.

Then he was on the oval, revelling in the space, suddenly free of his melancholy. The grass out there had seeded. He stopped to tie a grass trap with two handfuls of strands. He knotted them and giggled with delinquent excitement.

That was when he heard them. Two voices near the fence, where the oval dropped into a ditch. He saw the tips of two school rulers, two ends pointed in his direction, the other two level with an eye. The voices shouted again, like a warning to their troops.

'Jap! Jap!'

Then the hammering of boyish ammunition, rat-a-tat-tat, in his direction.

He turned to face the sound. Nothing there but the empty oval and a path leading down to the school. Just his footprints in the morning dew, no others. His grass trap, his snare, was real but he had tied it by his own putrid hand. Then the voices returned.

'Jap!'

With their guns held in front they ran towards him, surrounding him, firing at will, shouting their warnings to their friends.

'Bang bang! You're shot. You're dead. Lie down.'

The nearest boy fired his weapon unnecessarily close. Point blank at the side of Stephen's head.

'You have to fall down now.'

And Stephen did.

'Stay there,' they said. 'You're enemy! You're dead.'

He couldn't shake the hallucination. He would have to wait for the dawn to knock it out of him. Wouldn't that give the school something to talk about if he fell down and just waited here. *Former student arrives back home for grisly visit.* It was a wicked thought. A horrible vengeful joke he should play on them. Was he that bitter about this place? Bitter enough to frighten the schoolchildren? Were those years really that bad to him? No time to consider. No rest for the driven. The ache in his gut had him standing again and the compulsion to walk north did its job on him. It made him move. It pushed him on.

1983

In a second-class carriage of the *Sunlander* train, Stephen shied to the window, ashamed of his tears. He should have been excited to shake off the yoke of regional Queensland, which would have typecast him for a mill job. He was enrolled to study media and marketing at the Institute of Technology in Brisbane's CBD. A sought-after degree. But he was already homesick.

He would be boarding at his grandparents' house in Murarrie, on Brisbane's southside. Short term, four weeks at the most. He'd only ever stayed there on holidays. His mother described those holidays as 'going to see Grandma'. But someone else lived there too, his grandfather Ewan. Those holidays with his sisters and his parents were exhausting. The Lone Pine Koala Sanctuary one day. The Currumbin Bird Sanctuary the next. The David Jones food hall on Queen Street, which was also a kind of sanctuary when the alternative was the tense atmosphere of that house in Murarrie.

His mother and father had once been banned from that house. They spent their holidays up north, never venturing below the Tropic of Capricorn, never driving beyond Rockhampton. But when their first child arrived, it was time to sort things out. To bring them to a head.

Willie Bolin had gone alone to Murarrie, leaving Aileen and Carmel stashed in a Brisbane motel. Hetty had let her son-in-law in. But at the sound of another man's voice, Ewan came barrelling out of the living room. Willie took a step back. Not to give way, but to plant his feet and to raise his fists.

'Do you want to see your grandchild or do you not?' he asked unflinchingly.

'I do not!' Ewan bellowed.

Neither expected what happened next. Hetty spoke up. 'If you do not allow me to know my grandchild, I will leave!'

Willie believed it was the raising of his fists that had earned his father-in-law's begrudging respect. Aileen said it was the way her mother had spoken up: she'd never done that.

Even on holidays Stephen could tell things were not right in that house, but it was still his idea to stay with his grandparents while he studied. He had reasons. For a month in Year 11 he'd been on a student exchange to a farm in New Zealand. A house full of sheep-farming brothers who were very boisterous with him. At the time he'd been confused over the thrill he'd felt being lit up in the beam of their unruly grins. Looking back, his thoughts about the experience were as yet unformed, and he feared the university boys' colleges would be a repeat and that he might have to face up to something he wasn't ready for. Carmel, who was already studying in Brisbane, boarded at the Queensland Country Women's Association lodge. But he couldn't stay there with her. His grandparents' small weatherboard house would have to do. At least it was a place he knew.

At night Stephen could see the lights of the city towers from his room, but no stars. Nearby were the holding pens of the Cannon Hill cattle yards. The herds mooed and brayed, soothing his country homesickness. But these were holding pens for an abattoir. After slaughter, bleeding pelts were sent to the boilers of the adjacent hide processing plant. When Stephen left the house to attend his lectures, he gagged at the smell of it, all the way to the train. That rank odour entered the carriage with him. Every night on his return home, he held his breath until he was back inside.

His grandfather spent his days downstairs, disengaged with the world, in a small room built between the concrete stumps. It was lined with translucent sheets of green corrugated fibreglass. The ceiling was bare, just the underside of the floor above. Attached by their lids to the joists were bottles of nails, bolts, screws, drill bits and old coins. In one of the jars, Ewan kept his medals from the war, tarnishing with lesser alloys. In another corner of the room, a gem tumbler rotated day and night. It rumbled like a storm, helping to drown the noises in his head. Lumps of agate, tiger eye, smoky quartz and petrified wood rolled around inside, knocking off their imperfections, smoothing themselves in a slurry of grit. Ewan supervised the work and smoked his pipe. He cracked macadamia nuts in the hand-vise on his bench.

Upstairs, Hetty kept the house as she liked it, with scenes of England on her curtains, and a clock with a Westminster chime that was wound and dusted weekly. She spent her days in the kitchen, making Ewan his meals. When it was time for him to eat, he emerged from below and she ferried his food into the living room, where he sat waiting in his easy chair with a collapsible table over his lap.

He only came upstairs to eat and to sleep. Without the noise of the gem tumbler to soothe him, he cranked the stereogram to the point of industrial deafness. Shostakovich or Mahler punched at the single skin walls. Then the television would go on at a rude volume for the news.

It was torture for Hetty, who flinched at all the crashing of cymbals and the rumble of the timpani. She made little ticking sounds with her tongue, trying to suppress the fear that some catastrophe was about to be announced, as it had been whenever the wireless in Penicuik had been turned up that loud.

Stephen walked a narrow path between his grandmother and his grandfather. He tried not to be obvious about taking her side on things. Every so often, Uncle Jimmy and his wife would turn up to conspire with them. They sat with Hetty in the kitchen, sheltering, keeping their voices low, joking in half whispers at Ewan's expense as he smoked and drank and fumigated the atmosphere with his orchestral rage in the living room. The kitchen camaraderie, the huddling, it made Stephen feel like part of a team.

His scores at school had been good enough for him to do vet science. But he'd chosen a business media and marketing degree instead. He was wooed by the spiel: the course promised a creative life, but not one where he'd starve in a garret. The other students in his course had their hair bleached or gelled and teased, like the English bands, like the new romantics. A barefoot boy from the regions, Stephen couldn't cut it with them. He tried wearing winklepickers, but they gave him blisters. He regressed to Dunlop Volleys, no socks. His hair was centre-parted, straight and black, shiny as a mangrove nut. It was virgin Chinese hair from his father, untouched by any process in a salon.

Hetty fed her grandson from the Penicuik cookbook. She boiled cabbage soup with mutton neck. Sliced pressed tongue for his sandwiches. Stephen tried to impress his grandmother with all he'd learned at his lectures – the sins of the military industrial complex, say, or how the patriarchy had control over the social, legal, political, religious and economic world. Hetty would say, 'I'm listening,' while she whisked dinner out to Ewan, tutting through the din of Mahler's Symphony No. 2, the *Resurrection*, blinking through the clouds of pipe smoke. Stephen would still be going when she returned. 'Women have been subjugated by home routines,' he'd say. 'Unless you object actively, you're an enabler.'

Meanwhile, Hetty considered her kitchen to be quite the feminist manoeuvre. The newly painted wall, the updated appliances, the new plates and cutlery she'd bought in preparation for her grandson's arrival – she had found the money for those things by saving, by working cleaning jobs at night. She polished the floors of the CSIRO building down the road while Ewan languished at home in his decades-long military funk. Those savings just didn't just happen by themselves.

She'd frozen her husband out of her bed many years ago, into the guest room and almost out of the house. Since then, hers had been a heroic campaign of dogged stoicism. Yet she was proud of her house in Murarrie, proud that she could host a grandson in need. Meanwhile Stephen continued with his lecture. He didn't stop to pause or to reflect on his ego or naïveté. He was in love with the newfound power of his intellect and the co-opted vocabulary of his tutors and peers. He had no sense of the part he was playing in that house of passive-aggressive deeds.

Two tall beers in on a Shostakovich Saturday, Ewan called his grandson out of the kitchen and into the living room. It was summer and Ewan was shirtless. The hair on his shoulders stood out from his skin. Droplets of sweat precipitated on each strand.

Stephen stood to his side so he could avoid the flow of pipe smoke wafting past him down the hall. Ewan asked questions that his grandson answered quickly.

Yes, he was around on the weekend to help mow the lawn. Yes, he'd do the edges and toss the clippings on the compost heap. Yes, he'd do a good job of it too.

Satisfied with his grandson's answers, Ewan felt the transaction was over. But Stephen lingered. He had just begun an assignment on tribalism and body adornment, and he had remembered Ewan's forearms were heavily tattooed. A dagger, drawn crudely in indigo dye. A snake winding its way up the blade, its diamond pattern smudged by years of Australian sun.

'Did you get that ink during the war?' Stephen asked, readying himself to be ignored or told to mind his own business.

Ewan scowled at his grandson's use of the word *ink*. He looked down at his arm and then back out into space, sucking three short draws from his pipe. On the stereo was another Shostakovich symphony. As it transitioned into the introspective second movement, he flipped his arm over so Stephen could see its underside.

'Ay, but I'll show ye something even more interesting.' He dared his grandson to look closer at his forearm. Stephen cautiously obliged. There was a scar from wrist to elbow. The join in the skin looked like pink linoleum, or as if it had been vulcanised. Ewan sat forward in his chair. His naked back made a Sellotape sound as it peeled free.

'Ye know what that is?' he asked, jabbing at the wound. His accent was broadened by the beer.

Stephen shook his head, knowing he was about to be told.

'That's the very definition of lest ye forget,' he spat.

Stephen could smell the ferment of beer on his breath. Staring into Stephen's face, his grandfather continued. 'Want to know more about it? I can tell ye all the gory details.'

Out of an instinct for self-preservation, Stephen broke eye contact.

Hetty must have sensed what was unfolding. 'Can you come out here to give me a hand?' she called from the kitchen.

When Stephen was back in the kitchen, she dropped her voice to a percussive whisper. 'Don't listen to his silly rot.'

Stephen understood that he'd stumbled close to an edge. He knew his grandfather had been a war veteran, but the idea of him at war had always seemed abstract. He'd seen the medals in his grandfather's bottles, hanging from the rafters. He'd watched *Hogan's Heroes* on television while his grandfather had been watching too. But now that his grandfather was pointing out his wounds and challenging Stephen to look, the war was alive between them. His grandfather was a difficult person. Did he have his reasons? There was something else though, in the way his grandfather had attempted to frighten him. Something bothered Stephen about it. How it carried an undefined weight and how it had been swung to land on him. There was a memory of a day at school of boys with their rulers lined up like guns, lying in ambush in the grass. Boys calling him Jap.

Ewan ate his dinner, then prowled down the hallway to his room. Hetty waited for him to close his bedroom door, then she rose, changed the channel from the news and turned the volume down to just a murmur. As she settled back into her chair, there was a line of demarcation redrawn across the carpet. As if the room had turned over its shifts, and this was Stephen and his grandmother's allocated time and space.

*

After graduation, Stephen felt his education pressing on him from behind, like a load he couldn't uncouple. He had spent fifteen years conscientiously applying himself to his schooling, rarely acting up, doing whatever parents and teachers and lecturers told him to do. For fifteen years he'd been a dependable son, applying for a course and then qualifying with a degree. But his parents didn't really understand his field of study or what it led to. They saw the word *degree* and they pictured that certificate with a wax seal framed on the wall of an office – the office of an accountant or a lawyer or a doctor or an engineer at a top city firm. They didn't picture him turning up for work in a black t-shirt and jeans at an office that was more of a nursery for fragile creative egos. They hadn't pictured him churning out junk mail and discount catalogues either.

But this was the career path he'd chosen. Stephen successfully applied for an internship at an ad agency. After a probationary period, he was hired. He grew a ponytail to celebrate. His father called him on the phone one night to ask how it was all going. Hetty was listening as Stephen tried to tell his father about his day.

'I wrote some good copy today.'

'Copy?'

'Dad, it's called advertising copy. The words. I write the words for ads. Someone else designs the pictures though.'

'What did you write?'

'Well, today I wrote, *Buy one, get one freezed.*' Stephen waited for a reaction. 'Do you get it?'

'No.'

'The brief was, "two ice creams for the price of one". So I wrote, *Buy one, get one free-zed.'* Stephen spelled the 'zed' out a bit more obviously.

'Say it again.'

Stephen groaned. Hetty chipped in. 'Buy one, get one free-zzzed,' she said from the kitchen, as if Willie might hear her from there.

There was a sound like the telephone handpiece was being struggled over. Then Willie said, 'Your mother wants to say hello.'

Two pay cheques later, Stephen told his grandmother he was moving to a share house with two of his study mates, Paula and Mandy. Hetty watched from his bedroom doorway as he packed his things. She felt helpless, like the night Aileen eloped to Innisfail. That was a lifetime ago, her grandson's lifetime. Back then her daughter had been running towards love. Now her grandson was running towards some dream. But what were they running from? The same thing: the choking atmosphere of her and Ewan's house. Not just the pipe smoke or the smell from the tanning factory. It was the unspoken, the stifled, the suppressed feelings that were never allowed out. Young people can't live with that kind of suffocation. Young people need to breathe.

In Stephen's share house, there were no taboo subjects. No demarcation zones. People were called out. There were no sibling jealousies either. The expenses were split. The cleaning tasks were democratically assigned. Decisions were made as a group operation. They weren't like family; they'd chosen each other. Stephen didn't have to bring anyone up to speed with what he did. They were all travelling at the same velocity, leaving everyone else behind.

The share house was a Queenslander on a sloping block at Bardon. Abandoned to the rental market by a widow, it was elegantly in decline, rained on by jacaranda flowers in spring and burnt gum leaves in summer. The fallen foliage collected in mounds, turned over and rearranged into other mounds by bush turkeys who lived with gusto in the gully. Under the house, redback spiders trapped skinks in their silk. Concrete laundry tubs became surrogate beer fridges, topped up on the weekends with ice. Cheap bottles of plastic-corked plonk swam with their detached labels in the slush. Stephen kept a bonsai in a box under the runoff. It was five years old and growing aerial roots into the dirt. It had been a housewarming gift from someone who thought Stephen might know what to do with it.

From his first day in the house, Stephen found himself stealing sideways glances at Mandy's boyfriend, Darren, who stayed over often. He was a rock climber with a compact body that he always found a way to show off. His shirt was eternally open. His shorts often teased a bit of crack. Darren was made to share the boys' bathroom and he treated it like a locker room, uninhibited with his nakedness. It was an unexpected perk, Stephen thought.

The other perk was the party life. Stephen's housemates knew all the protocols of piss-ups. Who to invite, who not to. At uni, Stephen had always left parties early to catch the last train to Murarrie. He'd never had a party of his own. Now he was part of a posse who did.

The people who attended looked as if they had been ordered from a catalogue. It astounded Stephen that these people could be his friends now. Taxis pulled up out front, disgorging their gorgeous groups. Others were ferried in the luxury cars of their parents, some in the rusting beach cars of siblings. Doors slammed and the drivers accelerated away as the volume of the party rose in metered degrees.

Out in the backyard, people talked over each other. Nobody seemed to be listening. Every so often someone would turn up who could silence the chatter. Dwayne was one of those. His hair, a dark architectural wedge, cut through all the beauty like it was butter. Black Wayfarers hid his eyes. Nobody could tell where he was looking, so nobody ever felt acknowledged by him. Stephen wanted hair like Dwayne's. How much hairspray would it take to make his stand up that proud? He touched his ponytail self-consciously as Dwayne passed, but it was black and slippery and obedient only to gravity.

Free-mouthed, often obnoxious, the party swept along on a river of alcohol. At one point, someone complained about rednecks from the country.

'South-East Queensland should secede. Draw a line at Rockhampton.'

'Draw a line at Noosa,' someone else urged.

Stephen shrank into his foldup chair. Did they not know where he was from?

From behind his sunglasses, Dwayne made his statement to the upper atmosphere: 'Then we'd have Sallyanne Atkinson as premier!'

There were guffaws and groans at the thought of Brisbane's lord mayor leading the entire state.

'Better than Joh,' Mandy said, and Stephen found himself agreeing with that. Joh Bjelke-Petersen, the incumbent premier, was a gerrymandering tyrant.

'The fact is she couldn't do the job,' Dwayne replied, replying to Mandy by addressing the birds.

'And why is that?' Mandy asked with a half-drunk hardening of her stare.

'Because she's a woman.' There was a coordinated flexing of elbows, of drinks to lips and eyes twitching sideways.

'Wait, there's a reason I say that,' Dwayne almost had to shout over the rising temperature. 'It's because she's a woman,' he continued, having quelled any outcry, 'that she'll be ignored in the party room. She'll be stymied at the table. Women don't get a fair go in politics. They never have.'

'And yet Sallyanne is mayor,' said Mandy.

Dwayne cracked a can under the heel of his Johnny Reb boot. He was too cool to be caught in an argument, and his Wayfarers could hide any annoyance. There was a quick conspiratorial look between him and Darren and then a signal that it was time for a joint. They both left for under the house.

The speaker system from the living room was wired out to the garden. The Violent Femmes were blaring, telling their tales of the young and awkward. Wonky out-of-tune instruments and loose drumming shook the ripened common mangoes out of their tree. The singer was complaining he was unable to get just one fuck. Dwayne told Darren between puffs that he didn't relate to the song in the slightest.

Shelley, Dwayne's girlfriend, was a firecracker by reputation, with short red hair and big rubbery expressions. They'd been together since uni, but she was defiantly her own girl. She didn't always hang with Dwayne at parties. She had her own aura.

The first time Stephen met her, she swept up to him on his way to the kitchen and announced: 'I'm following you.'

Initially, Stephen had wondered what people saw in her. Dwayne was gorgeous and she was less so. But Stephen was soon in her thrall.

'Do you know who you've got on your arm?' she asked.

'Who have I got on my arm?'

'I'm Dwayne's girlfriend.'

When she said Dwayne, she tilted her head and pursed her mouth as if she was suppressing a laugh.

'Who's Dwayne?' Stephen replied, surprising himself with his sharp reflexes.

Shelley threw her head back and slapped her thigh like a vaudeville comedian. 'I love you.'

She had laughed at his joke with such gut. She was unvarnished and boisterous with her affection. Not tomboyish, as someone had once described her. Just down-to-earth and honest about what amused her. Unselfconscious. But also, she seemed sincerely interested in Stephen, and that was seductive to him. He kept looking at her face, waiting for the mask to slip, but all he got from her was pure enjoyment. She meant what she said. She was loving Stephen. He wondered if he might love her back. Could that be a thing – platonic love at first sight? He felt relieved to have met her and be gifted her attention.

The morning after the party, Stephen woke up to discover several guests had stayed over. They were sleeping in clumps throughout the house, collapsed on couches and rolled up in rugs. The kitchen was swilling with paper plates, leftovers and empties. Stephen took a garbage bag, filling it as quietly as he could. Nobody stirred. Shelley was sitting on the back stairs, smoking a cigarette.

Stephen asked her if she'd even slept. Feigning outrage, she told him she had slept – with him!

'Were you too drunk to notice?' she asked. Then she shouted to the room, 'The mystery is solved. Stephen has a huge penis!'

'It's genetic,' Stephen replied, as coolly as he could. 'My mother is surprisingly well hung too.'

Nobody else laughed, but Shelley choked on her cigarette and made noises like she was turned on by the idea.

She and Stephen had almost cleaned up by the time Paula emerged from her room, and then Mandy and Darren from theirs. Mandy went straight to the stereo, which was magically back on its shelf. She slipped a record from its sleeve: *Zenyatta Mondatta* by The Police. There was a groan from Darren. Comatose guests stirred and raised like the dead. Where was Dwayne? People rolled off their couches and wrapped cushions around their pounding, hungover heads. Mandy and Darren had a running feud about her choice in music. He listened to The Smiths.

'Turn it down! If he didn't have his looks, you wouldn't be playing him,' Darren said, as Sting sang the chorus to 'Don't Stand So Close to Me'.

'What can I say? He has beautiful blonde hair and high cheekbones. And the man is tall,' Mandy replied, pointedly sizing Darren up. Stephen hadn't noticed Darren was short before.

'Sting is just perfection,' Mandy added. 'Paula agrees. Even Stephen is into him.'

Stephen felt welded to the carpet.

'Not in the way you are,' Darren said.

'Why wouldn't he be?' Mandy countered.

Stephen remained silent while the conversation revolved around him. It was better than being defensive.

'Sting would turn any man gay,' Dwayne said, rising like Icarus from under a pile of cushions and sheepskin rugs in the corner. 'I'd fuck him.'

There didn't seem to be anything more to say after that. There was no need to rewind to the statement about Stephen's sexuality. Stephen especially didn't want to seem uncool with being gay. His masturbation fantasies for years had made it pretty clear that he was oriented that way, even if it was still an untested theory for now. Mainly, though, Stephen worried about being irreversibly categorised as the sad housemate, someone to be tiptoed around. Time was running out for him to react. Then Shelley stepped in, with a loud and sarcastic laugh that seemed to be for Stephen's benefit and to Dwayne's detriment:

'It's confirmed, gay men have the biggest dicks.'

*

The next Friday, Darren's mustard-coloured VW Beetle farted loudly under the house. It spun its wheels trying to make a sharp left out of the driveway, avoiding the cement stump at the axis of its turning circle. Mandy was in the passenger seat with her head out the window, making sure the wheel arches cleared the fence. Paula was nursing a migraine in the back seat, surrounded by bags and an esky. The rest of their supplies were jammed in the small storage space under the front bonnet. Stephen ran from his room to wave them off, but he arrived at the window too late, just as they were accelerating up the street.

They were going to Stradbroke Island for a week. Stephen had told them that he couldn't get the Friday off, so he'd catch the barge over on Saturday. It was a lie he'd engineered to give himself a night to execute a plan of his own. The sound of Darren's Beetle driving off gave him a small thrill, close to sexual excitement.

The advertising agency Stephen worked at occupied a refurbished warehouse on the river. Its front foyer had black and white chequerboard tiles watched over by a receptionist with corkscrew hair, an English accent and a hard attitude. She drove the male clients and some of the female ones wild with it. Stephen kept his head down, working through a pile of corrections to his radio scripts. He moved words around, gave the clients what they wanted. It was not very challenging – grunt work, really. When 5.30 pm came around, there was the usual staff stampede to the ex-wharfie's pub on the corner. But Stephen packed up his work bag and left for the bus.

He made it home so early he had time to wander around the house. With Mandy and Darren gone, he took the opportunity to peek inside their room. There was a large box of tissues on one side of their bed, which Stephen assumed was Mandy's because she suffered from hay fever. There was also a lamp and a stoneware vase with dried flowers. The other bedside table had nothing on it.

Stephen sat on that side and took in the sight of Mandy's clothes hanging from every surface, including the curtain rails and the back of the door. Where was Darren's contribution to the space? He wasn't an official tenant, but he was over a lot. Stephen grew worried. Was Darren on the out?

Back in the kitchen, Stephen reheated some moussaka that Paula had made the night before. It had grown in volume as she prepared the ingredients until it filled two whole baking trays. Paula had suggested Stephen should eat the leftovers, rather than let the food go off while they were away.

The moussaka was full of garlic and Stephen rinsed his mouth with water after every mouthful. Then he watched some television with one eye on the clock. At 9 pm, he showered.

With a towel around his waist, he re-entered Mandy and Darren's room. He was looking for something in the wardrobe in the corner. He couldn't give up. Again, the garments hanging there were mostly Mandy's – all jeans and shirts and loose pullovers, as she hardly ever wore dresses. But Stephen was looking for something of Darren's.

There was one shirt in particular he wanted to find, and he did. It was hanging in the back. A teal-green, long-sleeved and loose-fitting cheesecloth shirt. Stephen tried it on. It was always hot on Darren, but when Stephen wore it, it hung awkwardly off his sloped shoulders and his arms failed to fill out the sleeves. Still, it was Darren's shirt, so Stephen couldn't give up hope that he too looked good in it.

At 10 pm, Stephen arrived in Fortitude Valley, parking his blue Corolla out of sight behind a row of buildings in a narrow lane. He walked quickly: the street was frequented by cops, and he didn't want to be noticed by them. There were rumours about harassments. It took him only a few minutes to find his way down a set of hidden stairs to an underground bar.

The drag queen at the door looked Stephen up and down, at his loose-fitting shirt and his country-style jeans. She noticed he was avoiding her eyes. Having seen that furtiveness many times before, she impatiently grabbed his arm, stamped it with ink that could only be seen under a UV light and let him go.

Inside, the music was loud. It took Stephen some time to adjust to the darkness. Through a wall of cologne and bare shoulders, he excused himself so he could stand at the bar. He was desperate for something to fortify himself with. It took a while for the barman to notice him but eventually Stephen got his rum and Coke, and then he hurried into an even darker recess where he could stand and just observe.

At 2 am, Stephen exited the club, but he wasn't alone. He had noticed a guy staring at him through the strobe light on the dance floor. The guy closed in as if in stop-motion with every flash of the strobe. Then he was right up on Stephen's toes and then against his mouth. The stubble around his lips and his earthy breath were a revelation to Stephen, who'd only ever kissed a girl for a dare. Up on the street, though, they stayed apart as they hurried back to Stephen's car.

Once inside, they were briefly law-abiding with their seatbelts. Stephen was relieved to see that the guy was, in fact, good-looking – blonde hair, sharp features. He was most likely older than Stephen but not by very much. The guy gave Stephen directions, while Stephen tried to think of things to say along the way. He was too afraid to discuss sex, and small talk seemed naff.

Luckily, the guy did not live far. They pulled up outside a

brick apartment block in Spring Hill. Stephen sat with the engine idling for a moment. Nothing had been expressly offered to him. He couldn't be sure he'd even be invited in. But he'd got that far on an assumption, and so he turned off his engine.

They walked up a narrow brick staircase, the guy motioning to Stephen to be quiet. As they entered his apartment, he asked Stephen to wait in the dark of the kitchen while he crept through to check on something. He returned in a hurry, hustling Stephen back to the door.

'My sister's here. I didn't think she would be. Can we go to your place?'

Stephen had always thought sex for him would be difficult. But the guy was determined and willing to go out of his way for it. For him. On the drive to Bardon, at the Normanby Fiveways, a cop car came up beside them. Stephen tried to position himself in a way that suggested a vast distance between him and his passenger. He was sure they were about to be arrested. As the cop car accelerated away, Stephen drove slower so it could outpace them.

At Bardon, Stephen led the way to his bedroom, feeling slightly guilty that he'd allowed a stranger into his housemates' sanctuary. Unsure of what he was expected to do, he undressed completely the moment the bedroom door was closed. He came just as quickly in the guy's hand, thinking that was what the guy wanted from him, that Stephen needed to prove he was enjoying himself. But the guy told him off for being selfish. He said Stephen should have held back and waited. Stephen reached for the guy's cock, wanting to make up for his mistake. He gave it a few unhappy pulls, but the guy tucked it away and stood back from the bed, wiping his hands on Stephen's doona. Then he asked Stephen to drive him home.

At his block of flats, the guy got out of the car without saying goodbye.

It was a guilty trip back to Bardon. Stephen worried that every motorist was somehow joining the dots. That they knew where he'd been, who he'd been with and what he'd done. As he fell asleep though, he eventually managed a smile. He could smell two types of cologne on the doona.

The next morning, while he was getting ready to go to Stradbroke Island, Stephen debated whether he could confirm to his housemates that he was gay now. Mandy and Paula once complained about a lesbian in their inner circle who was militant about telling every person she met that she was queer. Stephen decided to take a different tack. After all, he now had an anecdote about entering someone's flat for a hook-up and discovering his sister was home. *His* sister. That should do the job, he thought. That would make it clear.

He told them over dinner. Mandy looked triumphant. But for the rest of the weekend, Darren took every opportunity to slap him playfully and publicly on the arse. Stephen knew it was some sort of straight-man over-compensation and took it as horseplay. But he let Mandy and Paula be outraged for him.

Jiāngshī

As he ventured further north, the landmarks of his life opened more and more wounds. His memories projected onto the walls of sugarcane. The dry leaves close to the ground were in washed-out sepia tones like pictures of dusty ancestors. Up higher, Stephen's childhood came to mind in Kodachrome chlorophyll green. At the top, cane flowers hosted lurid memories of the sexual fantasies he'd suppressed as a teenager but taken up in real life as an adult.

Somewhere north of Bowen, where the land was flat and low, Stephen grew desperate to escape these visions. He thought he should go to the sea. It wouldn't be suicide for someone already dead. And it might kill off the pictures of those who weren't.

At a road sign – *Yellow Gin Creek, Youngoorah Bridge* – he followed the arrow on the asphalt signalling a right-hand turn off the highway. The road was narrower, with no centre line. It ran straight for a kilometre and then it veered away. Tension gnawed at his hips, then loosened as his direction corrected to the north. But it was a temporary reprieve.

The road veered again to the right until it reached the coast, and with it came an increasingly punishing ache. The air was humid and buzzing with insects. Two houses, dark and small, solidly built, were silhouetted against a deserted beachfront. Their windows were fortified against the weather. One house had its cinder blocks stacked on poured concrete that had been set over an exposed rock. Stephen could hear the gentle waves at its base, but it was pitch dark. The sea, an ink lagoon, protected by a flank of offshore islets, was there only as an idea.

Though he thought he'd evaded his memories for a while, one came back in a spasm. He saw a similar beach and a house and a rock with a shower, his mother pouring cold water down his shivering back, the stain of green slime on his feet.

In the house on the rock, a small dog detected Stephen's presence. Stephen heard its whimpers coming from under an awning. The sounds were pitiful. He hadn't seen a dog since he'd died. His family had kept dogs, and he liked their company, but he wondered how one would react to him now, in the horrible state he was in. What if he could give the dog a little kindness?

It scraped and pawed at the ground. Stephen awkwardly bent to his knees, reaching out, his elbows straightening painfully, his fingers elongating from his wrists. As he touched the dog's nose, it licked at his fingers, a brief hello, and then ... two of his fingertips were gone. Stephen pulled his hand back, inspecting it in wonder. There was no pain. No blood. Just the pale ends of his intermediate phalanges, separated from their distal brothers at the cartilage.

A sound came from inside the house. The door cracked open. A torch startled Stephen, scalding his face, then he heard a man's voice.

'There's nothing here for you, knobhead.'

Stephen drew back into the darkness, hoping to disappear. The torch's searching beam found him while flashing across his chest. It was a weak little lamp, a marine torch with a flat battery. It could barely cut through the humidity, let alone identify him.

'I'm out of booze if you're wondering,' the man said. 'So until we get the generator fixed, you're gonna have to wait it out in the dark over at yours.'

Stephen remained silent and still, as if the weak light was holding him there.

'Hear me?' The beam swung up rudely into Stephen's face. 'Ay, you're not Arthur. Who the fuck are you? And what the fuck are you doin' 'ere?'

Stephen scrambled backwards but stumbled and sat down on the rock. The torch found him again.

'Arthur! Arthur!' the guy shouted, calling over his shoulder, swinging his torch across to the other house and then back to Stephen, each time landing with decreasing brightness. 'There's someone out here, Arthur!'

'Fuck off, yer mad!' came a voice from the other house.

'I could be gettin' killed out here, Arthur!' said the one with the torch, a theatrical quaver in his voice. Then he seemed to realise that Stephen wasn't moving away or towards him either.

'Eh, you remind me of someone,' he said as he crept in closer. 'Yeah, you do. Hey, you remind me of … this guy in Prossy I knew. Arthur, you know Willie Bolin, who used to run the supermarket? Fuck me, you're his dead ringer, sunshine.'

Stephen was shocked. Curious too. Who was this guy? He couldn't remember any of the people his dad knew. *Also, did he say, 'dead ringer'? That's funny. I suppose Dad and I are both dead*, he thought.

'He was a funny little cunt. Went red in the face when he got pissed. Town Chinaman always propping up the bar at the

Prince of Wales on his smoko. Bit of an alco, I reckon. Arthur!' he shouted again. 'Check this cunt out! Do you remember Willie Bolin?'

Stephen stood up, growing angry now.

'Mate, you just stay there till I get Arthur to confirm this for me,' he muttered, as if it was some sort of game they were playing. Some sort of boozed-up argument he was trying to solve. He pushed Stephen to his knees.

'Maybe you're part Chinaman,' the guy said, ranging the dwindling light over Stephen's face. 'Awww, hey, hang on!' the guy said, breathing in a gutful of discovery. 'Are you actually related? You might be Willie Bolin's son. That little poofta Stephen. Are you that poofta, Stephen Bolin? I went to school with that cunt. Jesus, you don't look so good. Say something. Speak up!' Then, 'Arthurrr!' he shouted again. This time a light flicked on in the house next door. Not a strong light, just the flicker of a torch.

Stephen had no memory of being at school with this guy. There had been six hundred kids at his school. He tried to stand back up but was pushed to the ground again.

'This is fucking private property, mate. Are ya fucking trying to rob me? We're out in the middle of fucking nowhere, you realise. We ain't got nothing to flog. Wrong place, wrong arsehole to burgle, poofta. Come here.' He was winding himself up, bouncing from one foot to other. 'You wanna go me? Come here. Come 'ere!'

Suddenly Stephen was flat on the ground, his head pushed into the concrete slab by the man. He smelled of spilled bong. His weight was so heavy Stephen could feel the ribs in his chest bow and creak, about to crack. The man leant in over Stephen so he could see the intent on his face. The look was a warning. *Stay down.* He shoved Stephen hard, the heel of his hand on Stephen's cheek. But the pressure was too much for Stephen's disintegrating skin to bear. A section tore off and slid from his face, and with it, the man's centre of gravity slipped. His elbow struck the concrete, and Stephen heard a sound like a spoon scraping out a pumpkin. It was followed by a volley of curses.

'Ow, fuckin' ow! Arthur, he's fuckin' ruined me. Look what he's done. Come out ya fuckin' house, ya chicken cunt, and help me out!'

The man had rolled off Stephen and was clutching at his shoulder. Stephen flipped himself back onto his feet, hinging from the waist in that grotesque way, and he wondered if the man would rise and run to his friend's house now. But no, he shouted at Stephen, pleading, holding his shoulder as if it were broken. 'You've dislocated my fuckin' shoulder, Stevie Bolin.'

Stephen noticed the torchlight was shining out through broken venetian blinds in the house next door. He felt the presence of someone uncertain behind it. The man at his feet was balled in agony. Eventually, his breathing steadied, and he opened up his posture, enough to reach out his hand – for help.

'Pull my fuckin' arm, will ya. Fix what you fuckin' wrecked.'

The man was moaning. Despite the abuse, Stephen felt pity for him. He'd been responsible for the guy hurting himself. He reached for his hand and pulled. There was a wrenching sound and the man cried out, but the shoulder was restored to its rightful configuration. The man rolled over and groaned. The dog joined him. It leapt on, but it wasn't biting, it was licking. Stephen touched his own face. A pikelet-sized piece of skin was hanging loose, just under his left eye. He tried to push it back into position.

Just then the neighbour's door opened. Stephen had to go. He was a danger to people even though he was outnumbered. Even though he hadn't done a thing. He was right to keep away from people, he thought as he swivelled and lined up again with the road. Could Arthur see how strange his motion was? Were there others here, in this settlement of short, squat buildings, watching him perform his terrible walk?

Obeying the ache, he moved swiftly back along the lonely road, back to the highway, driven by a growing sense of guilt and horror. He was a rogue organism. He had cheated death, stolen actuality, held on to something that was not rightfully his anymore – his life. And he'd been identified. He disliked that part the most. Always had. Always hated being linked to his father, the town's Chinaman. Stephen's childhood embarrassment. What a fucked-up son he was.

1989

It was Christmas. Joh Bjelke-Petersen had been smashed at the last election, and Wayne Goss was about to decriminalise homosexuality. Tony was the first gay man Stephen took beyond the bedroom and into his friendship. Tony lived with a bunch of other young gays on Brunswick Street in a run-down mansion divided into single-bedroom flats. His other name was Roxy Rottenbox, which he used when he was in drag, which wasn't very often, just every now and again, just for a laugh.

Tony called Stephen 'Asian Jesus'. When Stephen looked offended, Tony said he didn't mean to be rude, he just meant that Stephen had long hair and was a bit of a prude. That was all. But Tony had categorised him so definitively as Asian, Stephen thought. Why not Scottish Jesus? And it wasn't that he was purposely a prude. Stephen had got clear messages, many times, that he just wasn't some guys' type. Too short, perhaps. Or too slender. Or too Asian? He didn't need reminding.

He learned a lot from Tony about where to go on the scene, which clubs, which bars. He also found out which parks, shopping centres and toilets were beats, though he had no desire at all to have sex in public. It was illegal anyway, and Stephen was afraid of being jailed. Not to mention the embarrassment of being charged. How excruciating it would be for his parents to find out about him that way.

From the gays, Stephen learned who Nina Simone was, and that it was Liza with a z, not an s. He learned the canon of Kylie, though he was not into pop. He learned that Friday night was new trade night at The Beat Megaclub, when the undergraduate-gays would be out on the prowl. They were young men who were still closeted, and more likely to be into guys like Stephen – Asian or part-Asian guys with fewer masculine features, guys who took them back to their adolescent experimentations.

Trixie Lamont ran the door at The Beat. Her job was to screen the fakes, the undercover cops and the poofter bashers, and she'd beat up those liars if it was called for. Stephen and Tony and their friends would delay their arrival until midnight. They'd be charged up by then on pineapple juice cocktails that they whipped up at Tony's flat. Pineapple juice made your cum taste better, Tony said. Or so he believed, because he didn't like to suck.

Stephen was inevitably carded at the door. The guileless group mascot, the perennial newbie. He watched his friends work the room, amazed at their confidence. He was petrified but desperate for attention. Against the rear wall of the dance floor, gyrating in his own space, he stole sideways glances at himself in the mirror. Observed how he appeared to other men. But he would angle his head so the shadow of his jawline was deeper, and he'd move to where the light made the smudge on his upper lip look more like stubble. He tried not to see his father's features in the mirror, but instead the features of his mother's brothers, his Uncle Jimmy and Uncle Allen. Could he see them? Were they there in the strobing light? Could he fool himself into believing that they were all he saw? Stephen drank some more until the dance floor swirled and he stumbled and staggered. Men shoved him and he was groped. They felt around his chest and his crotch and his arse for free, until somebody finally pulled him in closer and held him there long enough to make him think that he might actually be their type. Not the person he saw in the mirror at home, but the person he saw in the mirror at The Beat, under the strobe lights. Someone better and hotter, who was only visible through the haze from the smoke machine.

Stephen's sister Carmel went into labour and was rushed to the Mater hospital on the day of the 1996 federal election. It was her second child with Matthew, who did what men often did in that situation: he called for backup. Excited that she was soon to be a two-time grandmother, Aileen came to the waiting room with Willie and Leanne. Aileen had invited Stephen also. She told him everybody would be there. But Stephen was on family strike. He was hosting an election party at home.

Aileen and Willie had retired to Brisbane. When they moved, they made what they thought was the only sensible decision: to buy a house in the outer suburbs near Carmel and Matthew, so they could help out with any child-minding duties. Meanwhile, Leanne lived bayside, a forty-five-minute drive away, because she wanted to smell the sea. Stephen took a different approach. He moved to the inner city, which he considered to be a gay haven.

Seven months into her pregnancy, Carmel had begun complaining to Stephen about how Aileen and Willie had been all over her and she needed a break from their interfering. Whenever she called, Stephen tried to find an excuse to cut the call short. He was on his way out, or busy with people. The phone in his flat wasn't that private. Shelley and Dwayne, who were now his housemates, were often tangled on the couch and listening in, and he was conscious of their judgement.

'It'd help if you were more in the picture,' Carmel said at the end of one rant.

'I don't do the suburbs,' Stephen replied, thinking Shelley and Dwayne would approve of the burn.

'What a wanker.'

'What can I say? Babies, happy families.'

'You're the one that's sounding like a baby.'

'Um … am I? How's Matthew, by the way? I hear he's got a shed set up. He and Dad been trading whipper-snipper tips? Do they have to fight to decide who fixes your taps?'

'Oh, poor you. Just get involved.'

'I'm not complaining.' Stephen gave a long-suffering grimace for the benefit of Shelley and Dwayne. 'I'm just … trying to work out what you need from me that you don't already have out there.'

Stephen waited for Carmel to reply. There was a pause, as if she was working out what to say, but instead she hung up. Stephen always expected that kind of volatility from his sister. He kept the handpiece to his ear, wondering if he should say something to pretend he was ending the call. All he could think of was, 'Anyway, I gotta go.'

When he put the phone down, Shelley asked, 'Was that your sister?' They had discussed her many times before. Stephen had complained how she'd been a bitch to him throughout their childhood. That was how he'd described her to his friends.

'Correct,' Stephen said.

'When are you going to come out to them?'

'I think never.'

'Fair enough,' she said, rolling back in under Dwayne's exposed armpit. 'Fuck 'em.'

Stephen flopped onto the couch under Dwayne's other armpit and tried to get the conversation out of his mind. He was sure he had been in the right. There was nothing about his life that interested Aileen and Willie in the slightest – nothing that competed with grandchildren, at least. Their eyes glazed over whenever he spoke about his work. They didn't understand half of the stuff he went on about, as they put it. Things about his career. Things he was proud of. They were always asking him when he was going to settle down and marry. He told them he was too busy with work to meet people, the only answer he thought they would accept from him. When he talked about his personal life, he used *people* and *friends* and *they*, choosing his pronouns carefully. Too much of *he* this and *he* that and they might start asking questions. Or would they? He wasn't sure and tried to convince himself that he didn't care. If Carmel wanted her own life, she shouldn't have had children. Why was she trying to involve him?

Stephen was never going to go to the hospital to wait for Carmel to push out a second child. The big election-night party that he was having with his housemates was a convenient excuse. But at least his housemates knew who he was. And they were all interested in the outcome of the election. He doubted his family were. They were so insular, allergic to the wider world. He wouldn't, couldn't join them in their little hetero cheer club at the hospital.

Early on in the evening, the election result was becoming dismally clear. The announcer on the broadcast was ready to call it: a landslide to the Liberal and National Coalition. The prime minister, Paul Keating, and his Labor government had been resoundingly defeated. At that, Dwayne disappeared outside to smoke and Shelley stood up to use the loo. The imprints of their bodies stayed behind with Stephen on his second-hand Art Deco three-piece setting. On the television, the announcer was giving a breakdown of seats won and lost. Finally, he came to the electorate of Oxley.

'Pauline Hanson seems to have won that seat.'

The controversial young candidate, a woman who had been disendorsed by the Liberal Party just prior to the ballot, had won her seat as an independent. As Shelley rushed back into the room, Stephen realised she had almost the same hairstyle as the victorious Hanson. It wasn't something he could joke about at that moment. Shelley screamed at the television, breaking Dwayne out of his stupor on the deck.

'That fucking racist?! Unbelievable! Fuuuck this stupid country!'

Then Stephen's phone rang. It was Leanne. Carmel had had a boy. Mother and child were doing well. Stephen thanked his sister for the call and hung up. In the intervening minutes, Shelley and Dwayne had descended into an argument.

'Why are you saying I should calm down? Who even are you?' Shelley was in full Hollywood flight, her fingers splayed in anguished stars on either side of her face, her eyebrows in extreme arch.

Dwayne shrugged. 'I'm not worried.'

'People voted for an outright racist!'

'So what.'

'Why are you not completely fucked off?'

'Because this is just democracy. That is how it works.'

Shelley stormed off towards Stephen, then she reversed direction.

'It's a fuckedocracy!' she yelled, centimetres from Dwayne's face. Stephen was shocked at her aggression. He'd never seen them argue like that but it gave him a sense of where their relationship had got to. They were complete opposites. Dwayne was ice-cool, Shelley was red-hot. Stephen cringed a little at their pantomime.

'She's entitled to her opinion just like you are,' Dwayne argued flatly.

Out came Shelley's finger, right in his face. 'Arsehole. That's not what you think.'

'Don't tell me what I think.'

'Someone has to. Or you'd think nothing. You're fucking empty.'

'Empty?' Dwayne took off his Wayfarers. Some days Stephen half expected there'd be no eyes behind them. But there were. Tonight, they were red, extremely stoned eyes. They swivelled around in their lazy wrinkled pockets begging for love. Looking to Shelley for an apology. Perhaps even just some attention. It was shocking to see Dwayne like this. *Poor Shelley*, Stephen thought. *Everybody thinks he's a rock star and only she knows he's not.*

Dwayne eventually slunk off to bed, leaving only Stephen and Shelley. She cried on his shoulder for a bit.

'I just feel so let down,' she said.

'Australians are stupid,' Stephen said.

'Dwayne's such a disappointment.'

'He's just stoned,' Stephen insisted, but he knew he was trying to forestall a potential problem. The breakup of his inner-city bubble was not something he could handle right now.

Shelley sat back from him and tilted her head to size him up. She didn't say anything. Then she stood, straightening her top. 'You've convinced me.'

In the morning, she announced she was dumping Dwayne and moving back in with her parents. She said she wanted to go overseas.

That afternoon, Stephen found himself driving Shelley to her parents' place. He hugged her at their gate, as if she was already in the departures lounge at the international airport. Then, instead of going home to a devastated Dwayne, he kept driving.

On the road, the burring sound of tyres on the asphalt and the vibrations through the steering wheel gave him a kind of paraesthesia that verged on formication, a crawling on his skin that helped him pinpoint his extremities so he could disassociate a bit, get outside of himself to look back in. Was he really that determined to maintain his stupid feud with Carmel? If his family ever found out about his sexuality, it would be his father or his grandfather who'd have the biggest problem with it. He might need his sisters and his mother to take his side. He should be a good uncle to his niece and nephew. And then there was Shelley. He should have tried harder to convince her to stay.

Aileen and Willie had a barbecue planned that Leanne only told Stephen about out of courtesy, not really expecting him to show up. Carmel, Matthew and their two children, Sian and Jaydn, would be there. Leanne was bringing her new fiancé, Timothy, along. Stephen's grandfather, Ewan, had been unwell and was recovering in hospital, so Hetty was free to attend too.

Carmel watched Stephen arrive with a sense of weariness. Did she have the energy to walk a tightrope with him? She hoped they'd find a civil equilibrium. Aileen had been cooking all day and while she and Leanne fussed over the lunch, Carmel was kept busy by her new baby boy, Jaydn. Hetty was entertaining Sian.

Stephen greeted them all with a practised breeziness and then he moved through to the living room, where the three men were gathered. Two generous recliners sat claustrophobically close to each other, upholstered in velour. In one sat Willie.

It was news time. Timothy was talking to Matthew, below the volume of the television. Matthew spoke above it. He had the confidence of someone who had already proven himself to his father-in-law. When Stephen entered the clique, the conversation paused for greetings.

'What's news?' Matthew asked, a manufactured airiness to his voice.

'Nothing much!'

Willie shifted his head in Stephen's direction but kept his eyes glued to the screen. 'Bloody Labor government's gone. I suppose that's one good thing.'

Stephen felt his hopes for a trouble-free family day begin to fall away. Politics were a powerful motivator for Stephen. It made him feel good about his intellect to engage in it and reminded him of how much time he'd spent outside the naïve circle of his family and Proserpine. Willie's provocation was hard to resist but Stephen wanted his father to feel there'd been a purpose to his visit, that he hadn't just come to argue. He knew his father was a National Party supporter, though. Could he deflect away to what he thought was neutral ground?

'Yes, and how about that woman from Oxley? The redhead? Pauline Hanson.' Stephen said her name as if he was having trouble enunciating it.

'Yeah, good on her. She makes a lot of sense,' Willie replied, quickly and definitively.

Stephen had been expecting his father would see her the way he himself did, as an electoral curiosity. Something to have a laugh about. But he felt his blood pressure spike. She was a terrible bigot! Stephen was sure he had to challenge his father on his opinion.

'Are you kidding me?'

'No,' said Willie. 'She makes some good points.'

'Like what specifically?' Stephen regretted the word *specifically* the moment he said it. It came off as patronising, supercilious. But it wasn't his fault he had conviction, or education. His father was clearly wrong.

Matthew and Timothy inched towards each other. It was their cue to leave but they mustn't have wanted to be obvious. Or perhaps they were curious about how it would end. Willie shifted in his recliner, adjusting himself so he was able to speak to Stephen over his shoulder.

'Well, she's not gonna give handouts to the Abos for a start.' It came out through the side of his mouth.

Aileen had been listening in from the kitchen. 'It's *Aborigines*,' she shouted, though Stephen wasn't sure if she was objecting or just correcting.

Willie rolled his eyes. 'Aborigines,' he said, turning back to the television.

Stephen didn't want his mother fighting his battles for him, so he spoke up.

'You know what else Pauline Hanson said?' Stephen felt calm, confident he had the perfect argument for his father. 'She said, we're in danger of being swamped by Asians.' He let the words hang in the air, watching his father for a reaction. But Stephen got nothing, so he pushed harder.

'You know when she says that she's talking about you, Dad. When she says Asians, she's actually talking about you.'

When Stephen had heard Pauline Hanson deliver her maiden speech, there was a visceral feeling about his objection to it.

His intellect was offended by her racial politics, but his body also gave its own reaction. The speech raised his blood pressure and caused him to cringe – not out of embarrassment, but as if he was ducking. Was she talking about him? About his father? His family on his father's side? She was wrong and she was stupid, and he was prepared to argue against her ideas intellectually. Stephen also wanted to punch her in the face for the insult, but still, he knew her words had currency with certain people; for that reason, he suppressed his anger and tried to use his intellect.

Now, faced with the idea that his own father was a Pauline Hanson supporter, he could feel his emotional maturity slipping away. Stephen had never called his father Asian before, not to his face, but he sincerely wanted to shock him. Actually, he wanted to save him. He wanted to punch through the argument and show his father how stupid he was. How deluded.

Willie kept his eyes on the news. Stephen stared at him, waiting for him to react, but his father was unmoved. He wasn't going to be schooled by his son, even if it was his adult son, even if he had been to university. When he was sure that Stephen had been made to wait long enough, Willie finally spoke, directing his words to the television.

'We are,' he said.

'We are what?' asked Stephen.

'We are in danger of being swamped by Asians.'

Stephen steered clear of Willie after that, not just making himself scarce at family events, but living in self-imposed exile from them.

The months passed easily. Stephen had an easy distraction – the gay scene. There was a new club open, an old pub that had been reclaimed by the gay community. A boring hotel once used by country people for their city stays. It was less about the dancing there, more about the mingling. It bridged a socialising gap between daylight hours and clubbing hours. Tony had to drag Stephen kicking and screaming there. Stephen couldn't believe an old-fashioned pub could ever be a safe space for gays. Yet here was one, right on the street, with a drag queen behind the bar.

Stephen used that pub to replace some of what he'd lost. He'd been burnt by his father and felt deserted by his sisters and his mother, who refused to acknowledge the differences that kept him away. And he missed Shelley, who had moved to the UK. He decided he needed more casual friends to replace the fixtures in his life and to give him a place where he belonged.

Eventually, though, Stephen felt compelled to give it one more go with his parents. He'd won a slew of awards and been given a pay rise, and he wanted to show his father and mother he was a success. In the back of his mind, he felt he might even owe it to them. He believed his parents saw only his failures – the lack of a spouse, the family conflicts he supposedly caused – but he had built a career for himself and he was good at it. His parents might not understand his job, but they understood awards, and maybe they would share in his pride. He called his mother and invited himself over.

When his mother met him at the door, she showed no sign of awkwardness. But it was different. For a change, she avoided asking him how he was. Instead, she asked how his work was going. That was his cue. He told her about the awards he'd won. Best in show for an ad he'd written for the trains. She nodded enthusiastically. So far so good. Stephen was sure she was making an effort to be impressed, but he was grateful she was trying. His father, who must have heard Stephen come in, hadn't joined them immediately, which was a relief. Stephen asked his mother how everybody else was. He was prepared to mask up for his mother's answer. She made comment after comment about Carmel's children. About how much Jaydn and Sian had grown. About how Carmel and Matthew had their hands full with them. Her enthusiasm for discussing her grandchildren was unlimited.

Stephen took it all in quietly, though little balls of anger were germinating and being extinguished just as quickly inside his skull. None of his honest reactions escaped his lips. It took a lot of energy to lock them down. If he could just make it through the lunch, he could tell himself that he'd achieved what he'd come here for.

It was delicious that Carmel and Leanne didn't know about the lunch. He hadn't told them and he was glad that his mother hadn't either. He wanted to be a fly on the wall when they found out. He hoped they'd be miffed and feel excluded, the way he often did. But of course, they were there in the conversation.

His mother conjured up a rotisserie chicken and a baked zucchini slice, and mashed potato on the side. His father was still not at the table. Surely he'd heard Stephen arrive. Was he down in his shed? Stephen wanted to ask, but settled for a safer topic.

'Did you make this slice?' he ventured.

'Yes.'

'Whose recipe is it?'

In his ruminating at home, while he was planning the visit, he had imagined broadening the subjects of conversation to dangerous things – even opening his heart completely to his parents. It had seemed a fantasy. Would that opportunity ever present itself? Would there ever be a right time? He knew they would never ask him directly about his love life. They would never make it easy for him because it wouldn't be easy for them.

It was so alien to their world to ask about sexuality. It just would never occur to them. Not ever.

Here at the lunch table, Stephen had his mother on her own. He began to think he might never have this opportunity again. He might never feel this reckless again either, like a door had opened, and he knew he would walk through it.

Aileen noticed him frowning. 'What's wrong?'

Stephen was about to reply, but he struggled to gain control over what he would say, how he would speak. He didn't want to sound irritated. He didn't want to stutter. He swallowed his words until he could think of something neutral. But before he could do so, his mother spoke again.

'You look constipated.'

Stephen couldn't help it then. A reply rushed out and he couldn't catch it.

'Mum, I have something to tell you.' The tone was wrong. Too angry. He wished he had been more casual.

Aileen's antenna was up. 'Do I want to know?'

Stephen gritted his teeth and held his blood pressure down as best he could, but it was surging.

'Probably not. But it's too late. It's gonna come out now or never.'

Aileen was caught in the moment, and she knew it. She watched her son struggling to form his thoughts, trying to articulate a thing of great importance to him. She knew something bad was coming for her too, but she couldn't think of what it might be or if there was a way to stop it from happening. Her son looked so pained. So out of control.

Stephen wished his mother could help him do this, but she was only staring back at him in fear. He had to stumble on. 'Are you sure you want to know?'

'I don't know. Do I?' Aileen asked, breaking eye contact, realising her hands had been cutting into the rest of the chicken, as if she was despatching the bird for a second time.

Now or never, Stephen told himself.

'Okay, okay, okay. I think you should know. I don't care what you think. But I'll tell you anyway. I'm gay.'

Aileen's face twitched. It was a minute movement of the space between her eyebrows. Then she quickly got herself under control and a neutral expression descended. She lifted her eyebrows and then her eyes.

'Are you sure?'

Stephen gave her a smile, all teeth. It was all performance now, nothing natural, nothing real. He was puppeteering his face.

'Mum, you don't know how hard that was to tell you.'

'Why?'

'What do you mean, why?'

'Why would you want to be gay?'

Stephen ran his hands through his hair. 'I don't *want* to be gay.'

He was immediately annoyed at himself for saying that. For falling into the trap laid by decades of negative impressions. His father calling people pansies. His mother laughing at homophobic jokes. Somehow, in this moment, she'd turned all his pride into shame. It was so easy for her.

'Then why would you?' Aileen asked.

'Look, Mum. I just am, alright?'

'You'll be ostracised.'

He wondered if this torture would end. 'By whom?'

'By people.'

Stephen knew that his mother couldn't help being who she was. He knew she wished this whole conversation wasn't happening. At the same time, she was drawing him a diagram. A big circle surrounding all the people in the world, her world, which included his father, his sisters and everyone else she knew. And then she put Stephen outside the circle. She was telling him to get back inside the circle, at least. But still, she was singling him out. He knew it, and he also knew that it was hopeless for him to tell her that. He'd dreamed she'd become an ally, a PFLAG mum, but that concept was way too foreign to her.

'You're acting as if I've got a choice,' he said. It was the best thing he could think of to say. In other environments, that would be the clincher. Unarguable. Reframing the debate away from nurture back to nature. Should he say that his sexuality was genetic, that he was born this way? Would it convince her? Fuck no. The phrase would mean nothing to his mother, who had given birth to a child she had designed in her head.

All Aileen could understand from his answer was that he was hurt and that she hadn't found the way to get through to him. She knew she was supposed to be happy that he'd told her, but she was certain he was making a mistake and would lead an unhappy life. She was just being honest with him. Why couldn't they rewind this conversation? Aileen felt lost and incapable of finding an exit.

'Don't tell your father,' she said finally.

'Why?'

'You know how he gets.'

Stephen was shocked that she was cutting him loose that way. But also, in a humiliatingly large part of his brain, he was relieved that she'd said it aloud. That she'd given him an out. He realised at that point how much of his family's structure was built on a foundation of fake happiness and the comfort of silence. Its success as a unit was dependent on getting along, fitting in, avoiding conflict, doing what was expected and everyone fooling themselves into thinking it was all okay that way, even if it wasn't. That was what his mother meant whenever she said, 'I just have to try to keep going.'

It had taken a lot out of him to tell her. He had no strength left to go through the whole thing again with his father. And anyway, his mother had already told him it would go the way it always did. His father would say something that would upset Stephen and then Stephen would storm out and there would be another major rupture. It was damaging to everyone. If Stephen pursued the subject with his father, he would be hurting them all. His mother was urging him not to rock the boat, not to cause a bigger family problem. She was telling him to suck it up. To jam himself back into the closet, for the sake of the family.

Stephen pushed his plate away. It had been an even bigger disaster than he'd imagined. If he'd felt let down by his mother before, and distanced from his father, he was even further away now. He no longer knew why it had occurred to him to tell her. He was angry with himself. It had all come out so defensively. He felt like a child in her presence. He felt like he had cheated himself, by losing control. He had never wanted to tell her. He knew it was more sensible to keep it from her forever. At least that would have left him with his fantasy coming-out experience that was coloured pastel like a happy dream. Not this monochrome reality. But now he knew the truth of it. There was no hope of them ever accepting him or understanding him. He'd lost the benefit of the doubt and received pity in return. He was officially the sad case of the family.

Aileen was gazing fearfully in the direction of the rear stairs. She could hear Willie coming up for lunch. She turned back to Stephen for some reassurance.

Why don't you have any thoughts of your own? he wanted to say. *Why don't you ever take a stance that isn't his?* But instead, he pushed his chair back and stood up. When his father entered the room, he went over to him and patted him on the shoulder.

'Good to see you, Dad. I've got some news.'

'What is it?' Willie asked.

Aileen looked as if she would faint.

'I'm saving up to go overseas.'

Jiāngshī

The night was in its dying quarter as Stephen passed through Ayr, a small town of sugarcane farmers and Italians. The Bruce Highway repurposed itself at the first intersection to become a street of shops. Stephen passed a mango vendor's cart, not yet open for business. The lights were off at the municipal pool. Stephen swam there once at an interschool carnival, but now the smell of chlorine reminded him of the resort outside Rockhampton. Stephen hurried past a police station. Beside it was a park built out of concrete. Bronze brolgas fished for breakfast in a form-set billabong.

It started to rain. Stephen relaxed, knowing wet weather kept people inside their homes. Quivering drops landed on his dusty skin, causing mildew spores to explode off its surface in little crown-shaped formations. At a roundabout, a weathervane swivelled on a sandstone obelisk, confirming that Stephen was still heading north. The awnings of thrift shops and fried food takeaways kept the rain off his head for a few blocks until he arrived at the Queens Hotel. It was a building with more gravitas than the town hall, but it smelled of beer and armpits and the deodorising blocks they used in urinals.

After that, there was no cover. Stephen walked through ankle-high grass that seeded the footpath alongside darkened hip-roofed homes. A curved brickwork fence funnelled rainwater through the gates of a school, a pretty missionary-style structure with a lifted skirt, its legs in the water. Just seven kilometres down the road, Ayr's conjoined twin, a town called Home Hill, was sleeping too. The sugarcane between the two towns was uniform and straight and featureless. It made the distance imperceptible. Stephen passed through Home Hill just as the sun was pushing the cold air of the night away. Then a wall of cloud that had already dumped heavily on the distant ranges dumped on him.

He was woken the following night by a tickling sensation. The flap of skin that had dislodged in the struggle at the beach had wriggling tadpoles feeding on it. He sat upright, hinging at the waist, disturbing them. They fled into the current rushing around his body and were sucked into a culvert under the road.

Stephen wished he'd been dragged in there with them. He flipped himself onto his feet to climb onto the road. There were a few cars in the distance. Stationary. Their rear lights were blinking through the downpour. Their front windscreen wipers were madly sluicing rainwater, losing a battle against the storm. Their occupants hardly noticed him as he passed by. Some were on their phones, making a call or sending an SMS. Others were just waiting, staring ahead. Stephen looked as bedraggled as anyone would be in that rain. He trudged unnoticed to the head of the queue to see what the holdup was.

The causeway ahead was flooded over. Its white roadside markers bent in the current as water poured from a banked-up creek to the left and down an embankment on the right. There were cars on the other side, their headlights reflecting on the water so it shone like metal, the causeway treacherously indistinct beneath the smooth and rapid sheet.

Headlights from behind framed Stephen. He imagined their drivers reading the words on his shirt, *YAY GIR MY STIR*. Would they think he'd been drinking? From the nearest vehicle, a man shouted, 'Don't be a dickhead.' But Stephen had no fear of drowning. If he was swept under a rock or trapped by a tree root or taken by a croc, that would be a good outcome. It would end his interminable trek and he'd be at rest. It would be merciful.

He entered the water, feeling with his feet for the concrete, watching for approaching debris to carry him away. He followed the white centre line until he was midway. The car lights across the causeway shone back in his eyes, blinding him. He was calm as he lost his footing, calm as he slipped from the road, calm as he was pulled under by a rip. He heard people in the cars opening their doors, calling out to him, running to the water's edge. He remained calm amid all of that and then there was nothing to remain calm about. Because he was gone.

1998

If you leave a scab alone and don't pick at it, they say it will heal. Yet Stephen didn't heal. His coming-out experience had wounded him and he kept going over and over it until his memory of the moment festered. For the next two years, while he saved to go overseas, he met for his family's birthdays, he turned up for their Christmases. But his intolerance had its own momentum, and he used every small irritation as justification for his resentment. Flights were expensive, in the thousands. Saving up took him longer than he expected.

When the money finally came together, he was weirdly unprepared. Overseas had been the goal. But he'd been so focused on the escape, he hadn't yet decided on the destination. To America? New York seemed scary. To Scandinavia or Germany? He was worried about the language barrier. Then in October, Stephen received a letter postmarked from London. It was from Shelley, who had heard through friends that he'd been saving for travel. She played it cool, describing how things had been for her and what she'd been doing all that time. She told him she had everything she wanted in life. A good job that paid stupid money, a nice place to live, a packed social life. She then mentioned in a casual way that a flatmate would be good, if only she could find one.

Stephen was on a plane to London by November, keen to grow his career internationally and to live with someone he already knew. He'd missed Shelley. He'd been living alone and hadn't enjoyed it.

The flight stopped over in Singapore, where it must have been convention season. Stephen felt like the only lone traveller in the airport. On the final leg, he was unable to sleep. He watched a movie, then attempted to get drunk on red wine. But it only blocked his sinuses.

As he flew into London, his ears screamed at his brain with the pressure change. He saw rows of council flats and tried to remember the theme to *Coronation Street* to distract himself. He forced a yawn and tried to swallow and then, mercifully, his plane landed.

Shelley had given him instructions on how to get from Heathrow to her flat in Queens Park via the Tube. The stations were a blur, appearing one after the other in rapid succession. At Cockfosters he awkwardly caught the eye of a woman sitting across from him. He'd noticed her looking at the Australian flag that Stephen had sewn onto his bag. He'd done it so he wouldn't be mistaken for an American. They were being targeted. But Australians were neutral.

'Cock and Fosters,' she said. 'Two of my favourite things.'

Was she coming onto him? Stephen was too tired to work it out. He arrived at Shelley's flat at 4 pm, after being awake for nearly forty-eight hours. Shelley welcomed him in with a hug, pushed his bags into a corner and then dragged him back out the door, wrapping a scarf around his neck.

It was only then that he felt the chill. Stephen hadn't noticed it when he arrived. He'd hurried from plane, to train, to the back of a black London cab and then into Shelley's central heating. Now the temperature reassured him that he was no longer in Brisbane. He couldn't stop marvelling at the vapour from his breath. While he walked, he listened and tried to answer Shelley's questions about the trip.

'Any hot guys on the flight?'

'Nope.'

'How was the food?'

'Hideous.'

'Was the alcohol free?'

'Thankfully.'

'Did you sleep?'

'Not a wink.'

They arrived at a fish and chip shop. Shelley told Stephen it was the most English thing she could think of to do to welcome him. Stephen couldn't help thinking of Pauline Hanson, who was known to run a fish and chip shop in Ipswich. He was annoyed to be reminded of her even after forty-eight hours' travel to a different hemisphere. There was a queue of people who were waiting for their order. A Caribbean woman with an incredible array of hair beads was conversing with friends and outdoing Shelley in the chat department.

When Stephen took just a scintilla too long to react to a point Shelley was making, she was onto him. 'Am I boring you?'

'I am just flogged,' he replied.

'Well, you can't go to sleep until bedtime, otherwise you'll have terrible jet lag.'

Stephen blinked to keep his eyes open. On the way back to Shelley's, he felt impossibly lost. Nothing about the streets looked familiar even though they had only just walked them. London seemed too tightly bricked. Back in the flat, he went to the toilet, where he hung his head in his hands as he sat on the bowl. He was jolted awake when his elbows fell off his knees. The chips were cold when he returned to the living room, but he ate them while Shelley chatted about her work.

Stephen's jet lag felt like porridge. He was subsumed by it. He was also starved of sunshine, and overwhelmed by the cold. He felt his arteries were clogged with fat. The northern latitude light refracted oddly off his skin. His face developed a cast, as if it had been anodised by two hundred years of industrialisation, coated by coal and arsenic and petrol residue.

Every day, Stephen hoped his head would clear, the way a hangover normally did, the day after, or the one after that. He went to bed hoping he'd feel energised when he woke up, but each night he failed to sleep, and he woke unrefreshed.

His bedroom at Shelley's had a low, cigarette-stained ceiling with a clear, tulip-shaped light shade that hovered just above his pillow. It made him feel like he was a bug caught under a jar. His throat grew sore from the heating. Every morning he woke up feeling as if he'd been intubated. Stephen's eyes grew itchy, his scalp grew tight, and his anxiety raged unchecked. It possessed him. His patience and focus abandoned him.

For breakfast, Stephen drank two cups of black coffee, one after the other. It worked temporarily, enough to get him showered and dressed and motivated to leave the house. But the moment he stepped from the threshold to the footpath, the jet lag would descend again, and he'd be dragging his feet through to the end of the day.

The nearby Bakerloo Line took him directly to the ad agency district. There he gave out copies of his CV to the receptionists at each of the flashy companies. After a fortnight, he had nothing to show for all the foyers he'd haunted. One day he visited a different precinct and wondered why the doors to the foyers were closed there. The coffee shops were filled with people still, and they looked at Stephen in his business jacket as if he'd stayed out all night and was doing the walk of shame. In a way he was, because it was Saturday. He hadn't noticed. At the Tube station, Stephen's frayed brain made him choose the wrong platform and he almost got off at the wrong stop. He tried to pay attention to the Tube map and not to fall asleep, but there were no easy wins. He felt as if his brain had been bubble-wrapped and put into storage along with his career.

After a month of rejections, he decided to play the one card he was most reluctant to play: a family connection. His father's sister, Auntie Dorothy, had a son named Tye who had moved to London years ago and had made it in agency land. Tye was the creative director of a company that did dry corporate work. But if Stephen could jag a job there, he'd at least have a bolthole in London. He'd never met this cousin, at least not that he could remember, but he had a phone number.

The call began awkwardly. Tye recognised Stephen's North Queensland accent enough to believe that he was indeed his Australian cousin. Tye's own accent, by comparison, was closer to Mayfair on the Monopoly board. Stephen tried not to sound cloying and needy.

On the day he'd arranged to meet Tye, the Bakerloo Line was overheated. Stephen stood with his portfolio jammed between his feet, holding on to a pole, guarding it as if it was turf that he'd conquered in a battle. He was sweating inside his puffer jacket but the carriage was too crowded for him to remove it. As the palm of his hand perspired on the pole, Stephen could see the grime of the city mixing with his sweat and running down his wrist in rivulets.

When he got to the foyer of Tye's workplace, Stephen asked the receptionist if he could use the bathroom first. Stephen washed his hands there and tidied his hair. He took his puffer jacket off and rolled it in on itself. Out in the foyer, seeing him emerge from the toilet, Tye stood back as if Stephen might be infected with something. Reluctantly, he shook his cousin's hand.

There was not much family resemblance in his cousin's face. Tye was half-Chinese like Stephen, but the reverse combination. His father was Scandinavian. Stephen assumed that was why Tye had the masculine features he did. The jawline, the full beard. And his hair was wavy. Tye got lucky, he thought.

Every page of Stephen's portfolio was met with a look of prepared enthusiasm. Stephen had seen it before: his cousin was humouring him. The leg up he thought he was getting now felt like a humiliation. The London porridge gobbed down again. Dejected, Stephen started to down-sell his experience, flicking through the pages and telling his cousin what he shouldn't waste his time on. When Tye made compliments, Stephen batted them away. It was Tye who closed Stephen's folio for him.

'It's tough over here,' Tye said. 'Let me buy you lunch.'

At a small pub on the corner of the block just down the road from the agency, Stephen nodded as Tye explained that Australian agencies weren't terribly well regarded in the UK. Stephen might have to start again at the bottom. In Asia, however, Australians were doing well. An untalented friend of Tye's had snagged a job as a creative director in a large multinational in Vietnam. Tye told Stephen, 'Just speak English there and you're hired.'

While they drank their pints, Tye asked after Willie and Aileen. Stephen rolled his eyes and said his dad was a Pauline Hanson supporter, but Tye didn't know who that was.

They parted ways outside the pub and Stephen used his copy of *London A–Z* to retrace his steps to the station. Back on the Bakerloo Line, he began to rearrange the pages of his portfolio. He pulled out the pieces that he had been most embarrassed about. He tucked them into the back, in a sleeve that couldn't be seen. In the end, only two pieces remained, and Stephen reviewed them with a mixture of disappointment and injustice, as if they had been cheated out of a fair hearing.

Accepting that he might not crack the London ad agency scene, Stephen took a temp job as an administrative assistant. It was a three-month foot-in-the-door at a famous PR firm called Id Communicado. He rationalised that the company would look good on his CV, and he'd finally have some work experience in the UK to speak of. But there was a catch. The position was in Edinburgh.

On a wet Saturday, he and Shelley caught a cab to Victoria Station so Shelley could wave him off from the platform like a lover (not a mother). She said she'd keep his room vacant. An incentive to come back. Stephen thanked her, promising it would be a short-term separation. Like lovers having a break. 'We get leave passes, right?'

Shelley laughed him off.

He arrived in Edinburgh in a mist. As he disembarked the train, damp rolled down the back of his jacket and in through his neckline. Soft daylight fell over Waverley Station through its skeletal glass roof. Unused bicycles in racks languished beyond a fenced barrier. Shivering, Stephen hurried with his suitcase towards the exit. Outside, he hailed a taxi, keen to get to his accommodation: a B&B on Barony Street that had been advertised as student rooms.

The B&B owner gave Stephen a surprised look when he turned up, as if she'd been expecting someone else. They'd only spoken on the phone, their two distinct accents messing with each other's ears. She introduced herself as Hayley and she ushered him inside the four-storey townhouse, a red sandstone residence. Four floors seemed a lot for one woman, but she explained that her kids had all grown up and moved away. There was no suggestion of a husband and Stephen was afraid to ask.

The top floor was divided into three small rooms with a shared bathroom for student lodgers. His room was neat and spartan: a single bed, a framed painting of a cat above a chair, and a desk that sat midway along the opposite wall to the window. There was an empty three-shelf bookcase by the door, and a set of drawers. The rug on the floor was shagpile and orange. Acrylic, Stephen guessed. He'd expected stains, being a rental, but the rug seemed clean and the room was otherwise spotless.

Stephen felt Hayley was genuinely excited to have him stay. She asked him if all his family was in Australia, and he said yes, though his mother, Aileen, was born in Penicuik. They chatted about the chances of that. Later, as Stephen was stacking his clothes in neat piles, Hayley returned with a district map. Penicuik was circled to show how close it was. She explained to him how the public transport system worked, then invited him to join her for dinner.

There were no other lodgers so the dinner was intimate, but the conversation was still easy. Eventually, Hayley navigated back to family.

'So, if your ma is from Penicuik, where is your da from?'

'Innisfail,' Stephen replied.

'*Inis* … *Fáil* … the stone at Meath … near Dublin?' Hayley looked confused.

'No. Innisfail is a small town in northern Australia.' Then, to put her out of her misery, he added, 'He's gold rush Chinese.'

'How fascinating,' she said.

Was it? Stephen supposed it was.

The next morning was cold, but he felt invigorated. He pulled on a set of New Zealand merino long johns that he had shelled out for in Australia. They were a luxury, but he was glad he had them. He added a shirt, long pants and a jumper. He left his work clothes hanging on the hook behind his door so the creases would straighten out during the day. He'd start the job tomorrow. Today would be a day of sightseeing.

He thought about heading up to Edinburgh Castle, but that felt too touristy. It was something anybody could do. Because he was there, because he might as well, he decided to try to find his mother's family home, the one she lived in as a child, though he had no idea of the exact address. He recalled her talking about the local landmarks, the paper mill, the church. He thought it would be easy enough to find.

Hayley had prepared him a hot bowl of oats and a cup of tea for breakfast. She had eaten her own already, so she left him to it. Then, Stephen departed for the bus station with Hayley's map in his pocket.

On the bus through Edinburgh's southern suburbs, Stephen wondered why it all seemed strangely familiar. Many of the houses were historic and made of sombre stone. There were modern conveniences, mobile phone towers, electricity pylons inserted here and there, but the past centuries still dominated.

Stephen had only ever lived in sunlit spaces and landscapes ruled by tropical greenery. Yet this world of cobblestones and narrow misty lanes soothed him. It was an odd feeling.

There were at least three streets that could have been his mother's. Stephen walked up and down them, trying to recall the photographs from her photo album. A couple of modern houses had gone up like gold crowns over crumbling teeth. Stephen wondered if the foundations of his mother's house might be under one of these.

He took perspective photographs, trying to match by memory one his mother had shown him, with a house on a curving road. In the original photo there was an old man wearing a flat cap and a tweed jacket. His mother was a toddler then, holding the old man's hand. Her hair was cut into a straight bob. Did she say the man was her grandfather? Why hadn't he paid more attention?

Maybe he could send her a photo as a politeness. To show her the interest he'd taken in her world, even if she hadn't shown a deep interest in his. If he could find the actual house, that would be a coup. There were several that could have been it. He laughed to himself at the thought of channelling his genetic memory, like his mother had a remote control that was guiding him up and down the streets.

As he headed back to Edinburgh, Stephen thought about his mother's soft power. When he was little, he'd watched the Edinburgh tattoo on television with her every year. On occasion, she would play her Kenneth McKellar record, *Roamin' in the Gloamin'*. He knew all the words to the songs. When Scottish pipers were playing on ANZAC Day, she'd draw them all in to watch it with her. His mother's ways had seemed so kitsch at the time, like scenes enamelled on a biscuit tin. But now he felt the solidity of her childhood. By comparison, Stephen felt his own was the equivalent of a season's growth, easily cleared away with a slasher and a machete, or a gale from a storm. His North Queensland footprints would be well overgrown. Nothing was permanent up there.

Stephen surprised his co-workers with his typing speed if not his talent. He was quickly seconded to the office of the Edinburgh Regional Head, a man with questionable grammar. Having never been a secretary, Stephen didn't know the protocol. He summarily fixed sentences, reworked weak phrasing, turned passive language into active, made the man look good. He didn't worry about offending him. He was on a short-term contract.

In a couple of weeks, Stephen was promoted to a better position, writing the company's media releases. He sat higher in his task chair from then on in. It was better work, closer to a proper job. It might even give him a decent shot at a position in the London branch.

Back in Brisbane, an envelope addressed from Edinburgh arrived for Aileen. She opened it to find Stephen's photographs in full colour.

Everything looks very different, she wrote in return. *Glad I didn't go all the way over there to see it for myself. Have you got a job yet? Or will you be coming home soon?*

Rules at Barony Street were loose. Stephen could come and go as he pleased. But he was considerate, if not secretive. If he arrived home late, he'd remove his shoes on the stoop so he could climb the stairs in his socks, two at a time up three floors. He supposed Hayley was so used to students that she'd given up on any curfews.

She never mentioned how late Stephen came in, or asked him where he'd been. And he wouldn't have told her. The men he met in the bars of the New Town often led him into shameful places.

They were mostly tourists, these men. They went out at night for the same reason as his: to pick up other men. They often had their own hotel room to return to; if not, they knew of a place where he could get off quickly with them in private. Sometimes it was a landing dock of a commercial building or an alcove under a footbridge. Never a public toilet. Stephen hated those. He kept a map in his pocket for finding his way home afterwards. With the buzz of the sex powering him, he'd retrace his steps back to a landmark he recognised, and from there he could find his way to Hayley's.

His accent had become his trump card during these encounters. It always came as a surprise to the men when they heard it. They told him he sounded like Jason Donovan, the implication being that someone with Stephen's dark eyes and olive features shouldn't sound like he did. As he pulled them closer in the dark, he sometimes talked with an even harder mouth, in the harsh tongue he'd used in North Queensland. It was his bogan tongue, something he would use when he wanted to be ironic. But in Edinburgh, it carved out a niche for him. He was a fantasy for the metropolitan ear. It might have been a confection, his cosplay for Friday and Saturday nights, but it helped him to feel he had some control over who the men thought he was. He could surprise them.

At work, he curbed the accent and adopted the tone of a reliable secretary. They called him 'sweet' at Id Communicado. Sweet little Stevie Bolin from Australia. And with Hayley he spoke like a respectful lodger.

One Saturday, Stephen came home at 3 am to find his landlady waiting for him in the hall, speaking on the phone. The streetlight through the door harshened the features of her face. He heard Hayley referring to him in third person.

'Hold on, he just turned up,' she said. 'I'll put him on, and you can tell him yourself, dear.'

Stephen hurried over to Hayley, using his eyes to ask for more information. She was emanating compassion. He tidied his hair as if the person on the other end might be able to see him.

It was his mother, sobbing. Stephen found it difficult to get anything out of her. He had to wait for her to breathe. Eventually she formed her words, but she still wasn't making much sense.

'He's at the bus stop,' she said. 'He's gone to get something to eat at McDonald's and then he's catching the bus home ... Terminal.'

None of it added up. 'Who is at the bus stop?' Stephen asked. 'What terminal?'

'The cancer,' Aileen replied.

The conversation was disorienting. His mother was in Australia. He was with Hayley in Edinburgh. But where was he being asked to be? Stephen ran his fingers along the coiled wire from the handset until he found the end where it entered the phone.

According to his mother, his father was at the hospital. He'd gone there to get some test results. He went alone because he didn't think it was anything serious, but now they'd found cancer, a lot of cancer, and it was untreatable. The doctors had told him he should make his arrangements.

Because of the strange details, the words didn't sink in. His father was at McDonald's, getting something to eat. Was he hungry? How could he be hungry? Why was he catching a bus home with such terrible news? Where were Stephen's sisters?

'I wish you weren't over there. I wish you were here,'

his mother said. 'If you were here, you could pick him up. Your poor father … on the bus.'

Saliva pooled in Stephen's cheeks. His mouth, which he'd used expertly only an hour ago on a Welshman's cock, was losing its composure. Stephen tried to keep it together, but his strength was failing. His mind was racing to the thought of his father's death. At a bus stop. With a pack of McDonald's fries in his hand. Stephen was eating his gums away, chewing his lips.

He felt useless. Hayley stayed by his side as he attempted to calm his mother. His words seemed inadequate. He was a hemisphere away. Too far away to get involved. He had left them all behind. He channelled his sensible office voice in an effort to sound controlled.

'I wish I was there too,' he told his mother.

'Will you come home?'

It was a question that begged an answer, forced an answer. He pushed his free hand into his pocket as if he was searching for spare change and then he pulled the pocket inside out, so the lining hung like a rabbit ear from his hip. Where was his money? He'd spent it all on booze while he was trying to impress the Welshman, trying to pick him up. Stephen didn't want to make any false promises to his mother, but the words came out anyway, as if they were already in his system, already in his lungs.

'I will *try* to get there.' Then weakly he added, 'Can't Carmel pick him up?'

His mother's reply grew sharp. 'She's working. Don't worry. We'll manage.'

After a lengthy silence and a stilted goodbye, Stephen hung up. Hayley stepped aside and allowed him to climb the stairs alone, which he did, two at a time, quietly in his socks.

⋆

Flying home felt like something he could do, but it also felt like the exact opposite of what he should do, because it would dishonour something important. He had expended so much effort in trying to disconnect his self-image from his parents' approval. He felt he'd only just started his big gay life in Edinburgh, untethered from the inner awkwardness he knew was created by his parents and his upbringing. Did his father's terminal diagnosis also mean that Stephen's life was now terminal? Had his freedom been just a temporary excursion?

The prospect of being curtailed left him seeking something wild and unyielding to hold on to. He stayed on longer in the clubs, desperate to hook up. On the side he made friends. They were locals from the New Town, big, loud lads who were unapologetically gay. But there was something else about them that Stephen was drawn to. Though they were coarse, they were accepting. Like his father, they were ornery, but what they said wasn't offensive. Their humour was brutal and base but they also poked fun at their xenophobia. They weren't coolly ironic either, like his friends back home. There was no posturing, no intellectualising. They were just cheap and friendly.

Marvin, an overweight party boy with bleached hair cut too high over his ears, was the first to adopt Stephen as a friend. Ham was the second. He got his nickname because his arse was huge. Then there was Neanderdoll, a hulking fem queen with a serious brow. And Robert-the-Second, a Glaswegian with an impossible-to-understand accent. Stephen told them his mother had come from Penicuik, and that was all it took for him to gain a seat at their table. Stephen got the nickname Hen.

'Hoo's it gaun, Hen?'

He didn't tell them about his father dying back home in Brisbane. He didn't tell them that he was delaying flying home to see him. He didn't tell them any of that and they never asked.

Stephen dragged out his uncertainty for a month, telling himself there would be time to decide while he waited to be told there wasn't. In the meantime, he learnt the one rule the Edinburgh New Town lads held sacred. Nobody went home until they all picked up.

There was a collective gasp of outrage one Saturday night when Stephen slid out early through the club's rear fire exit with a German guy who lived in a bedsit near Stockbridge Market. On the walk there, the German asked what Stephen's nationality was. Something about his forward-leaning posture made Stephen feel like the German wanted to dissect him, and so he needed to answer cryptically. He said he was Australian.

'You're something else though.'

'I'm half Scottish,' Stephen admitted. It was all he wanted to give away, so he reached for the guy's crotch, hoping to change the subject. He lingered there while the guy inspected Stephen's face.

'I love mixed-race guys,' he said.

The walk to the German's place was urgent. The fuck just as urgent. Stephen left awkwardly, making up some excuse about having to work early the next day, though it would be Sunday. The walk back to Barony Street was just one foot after the other. When Stephen climbed the stairs, he noticed for the first time that the treads made faint squeaking sounds with each step. His thick socks didn't muffle the sound at all. His clothes scraped the walls. His body was noisy. His blood pumped so loudly against his own eardrums he was sure Hayley could hear it too. He wished the world was already awake. What time was it in Australia?

The next morning, Stephen called his mother. It was already the evening, her time. Stephen asked how his father was.

'There is nothing to report,' she said. 'We're just waiting. There's some treatment underway. It's all palliative. We are just trying to keep going.'

When the phone rings in the night it's never good. Stephen was home at Barony Street for a change, dead-to-the-world in his bed. The ringing vibrated through the airlock of his sleep. It rattled his brain stem to shake him awake. At first, he thought it was a smoke alarm. From his bed he could see his door was ajar. The inhale and exhale of the house had pushed it open, and the light from the communal bathroom across the hall was a blade on the rug.

He was moving before his body had time to catch up. As he glided down the stairs, his hand felt for the patterned wallpaper, the embossed roses. He felt he was stepping into a void. Blue flickering light from Hayley's television licked the gap under her door. He found the switch for the stair light on the second floor, then he continued on. The phone stopped ringing for a moment, but then it started up again with renewed gravity until he snatched it off its cradle.

Stephen had somehow known it was for him. Carmel responded to his hello with a grunt of surprise.

'Finally.'

'What's news?' Stephen asked.

'Why aren't you coming home?'

Despite her abruptness, her words gave him an unexpected feeling of relief. Was he not going home? Had they assumed he wasn't?

Carmel's voice was just an electronic signal coming through the phone wire. It couldn't hurt him from a hemisphere away, surely. He opened his eyes fully to the darkness of the room while he considered his reply. He had never wanted to see his father die or gasp for breath or spasm in pain. The thought of watching that seemed unnecessary and he wondered why his family would want to be there. He could be fooled by the distance into believing his father wasn't dying at all, that he wasn't taking his last breaths. Except his sister was trying to remind him. She was right inside the bubble of their father's death and paying it forward.

'He says he misses you.'

'Give him my love.'

It was the better way, not speaking directly, just through a messenger, an interpreter. The translation could be polished by whoever delivered it. His mother would erase his gay life, make up some other excuse. She'd have a plan to manage the message. But if it was Carmel, would she editorialise? He wasn't sure.

'Is there much point in me trying to get there?' Stephen asked. He knew it was the wrong thing to say, but then he always said the wrong thing to his sister. They were always opposites.

Carmel surprised him by avoiding the combat zone. 'Oh, darling,' she said. 'I really don't think I can answer that. I'm sorry you're alone over there. It must be hard being so far away.'

Stephen didn't know how to react. His mind wandered to Hayley telling him why she had installed the wall phone near the door, a strange place, but she had put it there so that lodgers could have private conversations without the rest of the house listening in. The phone sat above a console table that housed a figurine, a pastiche of an African woman with a gold skirt, a gold turban and an unlit tea light in the pot she carried on her head. She was turned to the side, the look on her face impassive, as if she, too, was trying not to listen in.

'Honey?' Carmel asked. 'Are you okay?'

His sister's softer approach chipped away at his hardness. He blinked, trying to stop tears forming. He could only remember her being this gentle with him once, asking that sort of question. Was he okay? It was during one of their holidays to Murarrie. They'd been fighting about kid stuff – something one of them had said to rile the other. He had snatched at a book she'd been reading so he could throw it away from her, to injure her without touching her. But she was always prepared to go a bit further. To get physical. She scrambled over him, not caring if she kneed him in the process. He pushed her off. A tit-for-tat shoving contest ensued until he had pushed her so hard the little bookcase behind her toppled over. Just as that happened, their father entered the room. A tower of frustration, he lost it momentarily, delivering a volley of sharp kicks while Stephen tried to roll away.

'Pushing a girl,' their father said, coming and coming, 'try me now, you bully. You little bully.' Stephen was being challenged by a mountain, while also being told that he was the danger.

'Stop it!' Carmel shrieked. 'Stop kicking him!' Then to Stephen, 'Are you okay?'

He had been shocked to hear her talking to their father that way. That she was the one who stood up to him. Stephen felt weak. Powerless. He felt shown up, reduced by her bravery. When their mother appeared in the door, their father rumbled back down the hall.

'Honey?' His sister was still on the line.

Stephen gave Carmel a quick reassurance that he'd try, and then he hung up the phone. He couldn't bring himself to accept the moment for what it was. The gravity of his father's illness, the sympathy exhibited by his sister when she should have been berating him. He decided he shouldn't think too hard until the morning when his head was clear. He climbed to the second floor and switched off the stair light. The light in the communal bathroom was still on when he reached the landing to his floor. He switched that off too.

By the next morning, his sense of entitlement was restored. He rationalised that he hadn't done any proper living in London yet. He called Shelley to tell her his Edinburgh contract was nearing the end but he didn't mention his father. Shelley sounded excited to hear he was coming back to London and that his promise about returning after three months had been true.

On the day after his return, Stephen took a trip into Soho, where he purchased two red t-shirts that shouted the slogan, *Some People Are Gay. Get Over It!* London Pride was on the next Saturday. Stephen had coaxed Shelley to do the march with him. He purchased a red lipstick from a Russian woman who was selling cosmetics on a blanket on the footpath. He purchased four red bandanas and a set of red leather studded gloves from a sex shop. The cashier, a man with an exhausted expression, tossed two London Pride badges into the plastic bag with Stephen's items. Stephen thanked him and caught the Tube back to Queens Park.

In his room, he removed his pants so he was standing in front of his mirror in his underwear. He tied two bandanas together at one corner, wrapping them around his hips, knotting them at the other corner so they covered his crotch but revealed the tops of his thighs. He tucked his underwear up higher so it couldn't be seen, and then he tested his walk. The look was a tonic for his energy. He felt electricity in his scalp. He loved how the dry London air kept his hair crackling and textured and high on his head as if it were loaded with hairspray.

On the day of the parade, he and Shelley rose early and ate

conscientiously, lining their stomachs with eggs and bacon. Then they took turns to shower. Shelley joined Stephen in his bedroom afterwards, where he already had their outfits laid out on the bed. She did his makeup for him. She told him to look up to the ceiling while she drew in his eyes. When they watered, Shelley sang 'No More Tears (Enough Is Enough)', but he didn't tell her his tears were real. She drew a beauty spot on his shaved upper lip. She overdrew his lips with a lip pencil and filled them in with Stephen's lipstick, telling him he should take it with him for touch-ups throughout the day. Shelley had a fit when he threw the lipstick down the front of his underwear. She said it looked like he had two dicks, one bigger than the other. Stephen said, 'One for the pink, the other for the stink,' and they guffawed, filthy as a couple of old drags.

Wearing matching t-shirts and their bandana skirts, they each slipped on one of the studded gloves and chose shoes that could get them comfortably through the march. Then they admired each other in the mirror before Shelley raced off to her room, returning with two fanny packs, studded just like the gloves, but in black. She told Stephen they were for house keys and wallets, but when he looked inside his, he discovered she'd filled it with condoms and lube.

Stephen told Shelley her gesture meant a lot. Before he could launch into a cringeworthy speech, she told him not to let the condoms get past their use-by-date.

'Like mine always do,' she said.

He reached over to hug her, but she pushed him away while she went to call for a mini cab. Stephen watched her arse walking away. She really was a cracker. But she was his cracker now, not disappointing Dwayne's cracker.

⋆

Two weeks after Pride, Shelley came home from work unwell and paced around her bedroom in pain. Stephen had been out at a club and returned, half cut, to find Shelley with her head in her hands, sitting on a kitchen chair, jiggling her knees.

'I'm sure it's just a UTI,' she said.

'You might have gonorrhoea,' he said.

'Great. An immaculate infection,' Shelley joked back.

Stephen didn't try to say anything funnier. He asked if he could get her something from the pharmacy. She dug out an old prescription that she had for antibiotics. On the way down to the twenty-four-hour chemist in Kilburn, Stephen felt a powerful sense of protectiveness over his friend and over his life in London.

On his way back, with the pharmacy packet sweating under his armpit, Stephen felt this appreciation for Shelley morph into a criticism of himself. Of his need for Shelley and what she represented, a sort of failure on his part to be able to exist without someone like her to lean on. Someone safely female. What kind of a man was he?

Depression is a creeping predator. It camouflages its attack. You don't always know it's there. Other people can't see it either. Those attuned to it can sometimes smell it, but depression stays downwind. While you're concentrating on whatever you're doing, depression is approaching you from behind, softly from the shadows. Then when you finally notice it, you become too afraid to face it down.

To help him to sleep, Stephen began taking herbals. He tried them all. Valerian, chamomile, then supplements like vitamin B. But the alcohol he drank in the clubs was keeping him awake. He tried polaramine from the pharmacy and then he got a prescription for temazepam when that didn't work.

On the strength of his Edinburgh connections, he landed a temp job in copywriting at Id Communicado's London branch. He was writing media releases to begin with but he was keen to get back into writing ads. But each night he found he needed more of the sleeping meds to settle himself down. And when he woke with the inevitable hangover from taking too many of them, he struggled to even want to work. Struggled to come up with anything good.

He tried every stimulant he could during the day. Coffee, sugar and alcohol. He drank more and more. Then he tried Valium. He felt exhausted from the drugs, but also from the masking, from faking energy and attitude whenever anyone looked his way. He told himself he was still a young gun when really he was worn out and on a backwards slide – back to Brisbane probably, back into the lowlands of his family.

Shelley noticed it well before he did. She found him unexpectedly at a bar she'd been frequenting in Shepherds Bush. She had gone there because she wanted a break from all the Englishmen she'd been meeting in Soho. She found she could relax more amongst Aussies, and a lot of them lived in Shepherds Bush. The bar was the unofficial Australian embassy, a steak house branded in outback kitsch. Shelley thought Stephen would hate a place like that but there he was. She had to ask.

'What the fuck are you doing here, sunshine?'

'Same thing you're doing,' was his answer. 'Picking up.'

Shelley got the feeling he was being evasive. 'Shazam,' she said. 'Wonder twin powers activate!' They kissed fists, one of their jokey rituals.

'But dressed like that?' he asked, pointing to her outfit.

Shelley looked down. Her shirtdress was a bit casual for London, but this was Shepherds Bush, not Soho. Stephen, on the other hand, had taken to wearing slutty club gear anywhere. Mesh singlets and torn jeans, a bit of eyeliner. He looked fried, and it wasn't just the outfit. Shelley wondered if he was on something. He was glancing around the bar a lot.

'What's the real reason?' she asked.

Stephen didn't like the question. 'Won't these blokes be put off if they see you talking to another guy?' he said, pissy.

'Not one dressed like you,' she replied, laughing loudly at her own joke so it was clear to him that it was meant as one. Normally he'd come back with something catty. Instead, Stephen kept his eye on the door.

'Ah, it's pingers,' Shelley said. She was trying hard not to judge him, to keep him close, to play it cool, but she was worried about his escalating drug use.

Stephen reached across to the hem of her shirtdress, hoisting it up into his fist. He was trying to tie a knot in the corner of it. 'Here, let me fix this for you.'

He'd pulled it so tight he was revealing her knickers. Shelley tried to hold her dress down, but he kept on, knotting it with his fist until she could hear the thread in the hem pop. All the time, Stephen kept talking, rapid fire. 'This doesn't suit you. It needs to be hotter. I'm tired of you coming home lonely and sad. Whoever it is you try to pick up needs to know you're up for it.'

Shelley tore her shirtdress from his hand. He'd overstretched it. The dress hung limp along the left side of her knee.

'Well, that's … hot,' he said, stepping back, blanching at the result. He walked away before she had the satisfaction of a reply.

The next morning, Shelley came to his bedroom door. It was nearly eleven, so she thought she was safe to wake him. His blind was pulled down, and the room was dark. As she approached his bed, he shouted at her. 'Relax, I'm not dead!'

'Glad to hear it,' she replied.

'Did you get a root?'

'None of your business.'

'Well, it is, actually,' he said, flicking the bed clothes to the side as he sat up. 'It's exhausting being the only slut in the house. Bring yourself down to my level.'

'So, you've been a slut then,' she said. 'Again.'

'I have, Mummy,' he said, pitifully.

Shelley should have been annoyed by him, but instead she felt sorry for him.

A week or so later, Stephen was out again when Shelley received a phone call from his younger sister, Leanne. She was getting married and was hoping that Stephen might make it home – 'for that at least,' she said. When Shelley asked what she meant, Leanne told her the whole story. 'Our dad's been moved to a hospice,' she said. 'Can you just let him know the situation?'

Shelley knew he'd been lying to her about something. And he hadn't been his usual self. She asked Leanne when they'd found out their father's cancer was terminal, and was dumbfounded to hear it was that long ago. 'No, he didn't mention it,' Shelley told Leanne. 'I had no idea. I'm so sorry.'

Shelley saw Stephen's behaviour now for what it was, and she was distraught at the thought of him bearing this burden alone for all this time. She promised Leanne she'd try to convince Stephen to return home to Brisbane, to attend the wedding and to get there before his father passed. Though she was colluding with her best friend's sister, Shelley was really colluding with herself too. She was sure that if Stephen didn't go, if he didn't deal with his issues, she'd lose a friend. He was being self-destructive, and she was worried he'd make a life mistake. Or if he maintained his troubling trajectory, he might say something cruel to her that would turn her away. She'd always enjoyed being around him. She didn't want to fear him or fear for him.

The following Tuesday, Shelley told Stephen she was bringing home a bottle of red wine and a butter chicken curry for the two of them. She'd chosen an early night in the week, when it was unlikely that he'd be clubbing.

'Your sister Leanne called me,' she said after both of them were on their second glass.

He stared at his curry, then picked up his wine, swirling it flamboyantly. 'Oh, lovely Leanne. What did she say?'

'That I should try to talk you into going home.'

'Trying to get rid of me, are you?' he said, a sour look on his face. But then he hardened his chin, and the question turned into a challenge.

'Leanne's getting married,' Shelley continued.

'Good on her,' Stephen said.

'You should go. It'll be good to sort things out with your father.'

'Like what?'

'Come out to him?' Shelley wasn't sure how he'd react. She'd been out of harmony with him for weeks. She couldn't read his moods anymore.

'He's already dying. Do you want me to kill him twice?' Stephen watched Shelley's reaction. 'Don't bother looking surprised. I know Leanne would have told you.'

Shelley began to get upset for him. She could hear in Stephen's voice an indelible bitterness. She felt partly responsible for it, by being his gay cheer squad, by taking his side against his family, by urging him to get away. But that was before everything he was now dealing with. That was before he was running out of time. Back then, when her default was to side with him, they were only young. The serious years were gaining on them both.

'Oh my god. Your family is so odd,' she said. 'Your commitment to estrangement.'

'You're the one who said, *fuck 'em*,' Stephen complained.

'Listen,' Shelley insisted. 'I want you to go. Actually, I need you to go. It'll be better for us.'

Stephen could see she was serious.

'Well, a straight wedding will be something fabulous to look forward to,' he replied. Then he poured them both the dregs of the bottle.

On the flight back to Australia, Stephen developed a migraine. It was sudden but not unusual. He'd been getting them lately, but he'd been managing them. Without his home cabinet of pharmaceuticals, though, he couldn't treat it. The pain burrowed parasitically behind his right eye to feed on his brain and interfere with his sight. When he raised his eye mask to look at the screen in the back of the headrest, his vision doubled.

He was on the aisle. The window seat was occupied by a young woman with an asymmetrical blonde bob. She was listening intently to something through her earphones. Stephen tapped her on the shoulder to ask if she could lower her shade, because the daylight was adding to his torture. Her face was like two photographs taken one on top of the other. The first had the warmth of the woman's natural skin, the second was brighter and more electric. Stephen couldn't work out which was real, which to speak to, so he addressed them both.

'Could you two pull down the shade, please?' he asked, wincing at the volume of his own voice.

The woman didn't speak or remove her headphones, but she complied. The dual exposure aligned momentarily but then it separated again. His optic nerve attempted to force the picture back into alignment, but the pain of the effort was worse than the light. Stephen felt he should apologise to the woman.

'I'm sorry. I have a migraine,' he said, squinting.

Now his voice sounded as if it was detached from him, as if it was coming through a small speaker on a transistor radio somewhere a few seats back. The woman removed her headphones finally. But she replied to the question she thought Stephen had asked.

'Just a week,' she said, 'thank God.'

Stephen realised she must have thought he'd asked how long she was going away for.

'Sorry. That sounds a bit negative about poor old Brissy,' the woman added.

'Not really,' Stephen replied.

A bell rang within the cabin. It was muffled, as if it came from behind a wall somewhere, as if it had been meant for a whole other group of people in another room. The seatbelt sign flashed red, and the cabin groaned a little as passengers sat up in their chairs and corrected their posture. Stephen turned to look down the aisle, then back at the woman, but suddenly she wasn't just a random woman: she was Carmel. Carmel was saying that a week was more than enough time to spend in Brisbane.

'Just not looking forward to it,' she said with some distaste.

Stephen thought if Carmel wasn't looking forward to it, she should try being in his shoes. 'Me neither,' he said.

'What are you going for, then?' she asked.

'You should know. You're the one who's been pushing for it,' he replied.

Carmel gave him an odd look, as if she thought he was stupid.

Stephen wanted to give her a stupid look in return. He pulled his eyes wide the way he used to when they were kids, when he'd tease her about her eyes, when he joked that she looked more Chinese than he did.

Carmel now seemed weirded out.

Stephen threw his head back to laugh. *Oh my god, she's still so humourless*, he thought.

For a moment, the cabin rattled with the arrival of the promised turbulence. They sat in silence together, feeling the vibrations through their seats, their necks pressed into their headrests. Then the seatbelt sign went off again and the cabin relaxed.

A flight attendant made his way down the aisle. He smiled at Stephen, who suddenly lost all interest in his sister. His eyes followed the attendant's trim body. Once he'd gone, Stephen turned back to Carmel. She looked offended.

'What's wrong with you?' Stephen laughed to himself. *Get used to it*, he thought.

Carmel huffed and turned away. But of course, it wasn't Carmel at all. It was just the pain behind Stephen's eyes making him a bit crazy.

The flight attendant came by again. Stephen casually grazed his hand, lingering too long on his sleeve. He asked for a red wine. When it arrived, Stephen opened out his tray table and tried to operate his movie screen, but his migraine pulsed again. So he drank his wine, hoping he'd be anaesthetised by it if he just had enough.

The day after his return, Stephen went to see his father at the hospice. He was jet-lagged and hungover. He was convinced it wouldn't make any difference going there, not even for his mother's sake, not even just to make a show of support. Leanne, who picked him up from the airport, had already told him that their dad was completely out of it on painkillers. The rest of the family avoided similar straight talk, especially about Stephen's delay. Dealing with that could be deferred, but that didn't mean the issue went away. It had arisen from a permanent rupture. People don't let go of things just to get on well in a hospital room. Just so they can deal with a loved one's death with dignity.

Stephen tried to accept that he would always be a stranger to his father. That he was supposed to let his father die, let him drift off believing Stephen was one thing when really he was something completely different. But what if his mother had been wrong about her husband? What if his father had proven her wrong? What if he could have handled the knowledge that his son was gay? Could Stephen have helped his father redeem himself? Helped him cast off his intolerance and small-mindedness? What about his father's dick-brained support for Pauline Hanson? Stephen shook his head at that one. How did his father lie to himself that way? How did he only hear what he wanted to hear? That was some deep-seated delusion. That was a victim punching down on his co-victims, hoping to climb on top of them and maybe get out of the hole they were all in.

Stephen couldn't imagine resolving anything with his father. And there was something faulty in having hope. Something weird about using the threat of death to bring his ideas and those of his father together. Why couldn't it happen when everyone was well and happy? And why was it not his father's default position to accept his children? Was that even something a son should have to dream about getting from his father? Shouldn't a father accept his child no matter what? Death was just a convenient way to tidy up inconvenient disagreements. It was all just deathwashing.

Stephen watched over his father, shrunken on the bed, sleeping loudly, snoring with an open mouth. An intermittent beep sounded on an intravenous device that was attached via a clear plastic tube to a cannula sticking into the back of Willie's hand. The skin where the needle went in was so thin it was ruched by the adhesive tape that bound it.

There was a smell that was unmentionable, a mix of shit and disinfectant that people were meant to put up with, given the circumstances. Stephen felt he should shallow his breathing in the room, that all the oxygen inside should be reserved for his father, who seemed to be barely existing in his final sliver of life.

Aileen had hugged Stephen briefly when he arrived. She spoke but barely made a sound, as if she was afraid to wake her husband. Nothing would make him stir, yet still she whispered.

'Would you like to hug him?'

'I don't think so,' Stephen told her.

Aileen rose and pulled him closer to his father's bedside. He was forced to comply. She lifted Willie's hand, gesturing at Stephen until he took it in his. Aileen stepped away then. Happy to have achieved this reunion, nodding as if things were right again.

Stephen felt under scrutiny. He suffered his father's hand, counting down the seconds though he had no idea how long he should be holding it. Was it a ritual he didn't know about? What was his mother expecting from him? The hand felt chilled by the air-conditioning, already disconnected from his father's heart. It wasn't moving. It was just a weight.

Stephen considered whether he should feel for a pulse. Instead, inexplicably, he leaned in and kissed his father on the forehead.

Then he bent over his father's ear and surprised himself again by indulging an urge to tell his father his truth.

Was he really going to do this? Now? With his mother watching? It was so quiet she would surely hear. How would she react? Would it disturb her to know that her son had chosen this moment to defy her wishes? Was he really going to tell his father he was gay, right now? Would the truth make the old man unhappy for the rest of eternity? It would be the poison of a final failure, knowing his only son was still broken, not a proper man, not able to carry on the family name. And he couldn't do anything about it. He couldn't respond. He was lying stricken with cancer, his body failing, while his one male heir was healthy and young, and despite that, he was not able or not prepared to perform his assigned biological function. Was Stephen really that selfish, to want to do that to his father? To tell him who he was?

The moment passed. Stephen sniffed back a tear instead of speaking. A mistake. The earthy smell of his father's earwax gave him a primal reminder of the interconnectedness of their bodies. Their earwax smelled the same. They were the same man. Stephen was part of his father, and his father was just like him. He was a legacy of his father's biology. Their family line was wrapped up in that smell. And if all the breeding had gone right, and if Stephen hadn't turned out queer, the family line wouldn't have ended there in that room.

Willie would've believed that Stephen should be reproducing a version of himself, providing children and grandchildren. Carmel's children weren't enough because she wasn't carrying on the name. As for Leanne, soon to marry, soon to have children too, she couldn't carry on the family name either. She was a girl.

It didn't make sense for Stephen to think of himself as the end of a line, but somehow he knew that his father had thought that, and perhaps was even thinking it now, lying there in front of him. His father hadn't been that interested in Stephen's mind, or his soul, just his genes, just his male body. But Stephen couldn't give his father what he wanted. He had failed his father. He had failed the line. The thought and the smell of the earwax drew bile up into Stephen's throat and he turned away from the bed.

Aileen had been watching her son, and she misinterpreted his turning away as an expression of grief. She thought her son was already missing his father, bringing to an end their family's rift. Her son's distance had bothered her greatly, but now, in Stephen's reaction, there was evidence of a reconnection. And for her it had come just in time.

Jiāngshī

Stephen came to under a small jetty, wedged behind its concrete footings. He was above the tide line. A shredded washed-up tarp shrouded his corpse. He tore it back to free himself. Above him, he heard voices, laughter, young people. Around him, dried prawn heads, pieces of fishing line, driftwood and fish scales decorated the rocks. It was dark and the sea was calm. Through the boards of the pier, slivers of streetlight fingered down onto him, shadows passing through.

It was despairing to wake up again. Why could he not end it, this violation of his nature? He recalled being pulled by an undercurrent into a submerged culvert back on the flooded highway outside Home Hill. That experience should have been enough. Why was he not still trapped in a muddy eddy in a forgotten tributary of the Burdekin floodplain? Why wasn't he washed out to sea? Had he somehow been dragged back in on the tide? Had his body been retrieved by a stupid crocodile, stashed beneath the jetty to be eaten later?

There were new wounds on his arms and legs. How did he not lose a limb, or something else major? New parts of him were blackened by the processes of decay. But miraculously everything still functioned, and he was able to move. Once again the feeling in his hips returned, the ache that made itself known, like waking to a tumour after sleeping through your meds. And once again he obeyed the urge, working his way out from under the jetty to head north again. A small, stepped series of rocks led him up to a concrete walkway.

Though it was night, there were people up there, a lot of people milling about. Their exuberant interactions matched the excitement in their voices. Stephen hesitated and looked for ways to skirt around the revellers. But as he edged up onto the walkway, a figure approached and spoke directly to him. It was a thick-set man, his legs chunky and his body curving at the shoulders like a preppy ape. He was dishevelled, his checked shirt covered in dirt and his collar askew.

Up close, Stephen saw the man's face was wet with blood, and his eyes had dark rings around them. He had the look of death. Just like Stephen. Was he a dead man stuck in limbo too? The man slapped Stephen on the back and then his face broke open, a manic smile through bloody teeth.

'Nice one,' he said, looking Stephen up and down with admiration.

Was this how the dead dealt with each other? By slapping you on the back for your sins? Congratulating you for staying on your feet?

Other dead people began to congregate around him, each of them in as poor a state as the other, wounds on their faces, blood dripping down their chests or leaking from their mouths. They were smiling too, laughing, guffawing. They surrounded Stephen, leaned in close to examine the flap of skin that was hanging from under his eye. One produced a camera from his pocket to take a photo.

'That is really convincing,' he said. 'Outstanding work. You can walk with us if you like.'

Stephen merged with the group. They accepted him. But he realised he'd been mistaken about them. The camera. These people weren't dead; they were just pretending. Their injuries and decay were just makeup. They had blood capsules in their pockets and latex scars on their faces, and they were on a zombie walk. When he first read about it, he'd laughed at the idea. It was another imported American concept, more proof of their culture's insensitivity to death.

Why hadn't these fools noticed Stephen's odour? The larvae of beetles and flies? Perhaps they were too busy with each other, taking photos and admiring the deception of their own injuries. They were moaning and crying out, clawing at the sky, dragging one foot behind the other, tearing at their clothes. It was all so over the top. They walked in loose formation around the perimeter of a tidal pool, past a sign that said *KIOSK ON THE STRAND. HOT FOOD. DRINKS. ICE CREAM. COFFEE.*

Stephen understood where he was immediately. He knew this place. The Strand esplanade in Townsville, though he hadn't been there in decades. He was at its easternmost point where the Rockpool, a manmade fancy, sat fringed by windswept palms. It was a grotesque coincidence that he was there with this Hollywood-effects underworld army.

Wary of his potential for violence, Stephen lagged at the rear. He watched as the living zombies teemed onto the boardwalk ahead of him, their horde elongating as it thinned to three or four people across. They snaked along the beach, wove in and out of the trees like a gruesome river inundating the land. He hated that he needed to follow in their wake, but he had no strength left to defy what urged him on. His musculature was becoming insecure; his nerves were misfiring; his skin was almost black and shrunken to the flesh, hardened in places like leather. On the joints, where the skin needed to be flexible, a carapace had formed, the joints hinging noisily beneath. He had no will for defiance either.

Up ahead, a cloud of blue smoke worked its way through the branches of the trees. The filmmaker John Carpenter would have been proud of that lighting. Festoon bulbs had been draped between the taller palms, and music was playing. The bass line thumped at Stephen's chest.

Eventually the zombies merged with normal people, people without wounds or decay or cracked posture. Couples, retirees, families with small children. The younger ones cowered behind their parents as they arrived. The elderly shook their heads, but nobody objected. The zombies walked through with surprising ease.

Stephen felt hidden within the group, and as he walked through there was no recoiling. The living had finished with the spectacle. People went back to gathering around their small marquees, admiring the goods on display. The interruption had been brief. There was a vendor selling illuminated box-jellyfish mobiles that undulated in the night air while children ran their fingers through the benign tentacles. A fairy floss vendor in bright hot pink enticed them away with enormous halos of spun sugar on sticks.

Stephen was beginning to be outpaced by the zombie walkers. Their direction disagreed with his anyway, and with the throbbing ache in his hips. Between two marquees, he noticed a vinyl-walled alley that he could slip down, drawn to the darkness. He ran his hands along the sides of the tents. Where his fingertips were missing, the bones vibrated with sensitivity. He could feel something building. Could it be hunger? Impossible. His stomach was hard and had shrunk to the size of a walnut. But as he passed an open gap, a smell of burning sesame oil, chilli, ginger and five spice drew him to it. Stephen could see a makeshift kitchen inside. Flashes of heat hit his dehydrated retinas. On a stove, a wok was being rocked and scraped and banged with a metal spoon by a young woman. Her black hair was tied back, wet with perspiration. Around her waist, her apron was dirty with flour and grease and char. The skin on the back of her neck was the colour of milk tea.

Stephen realised too late what would happen. Synapses at the junction with his spine locked his focus on the woman. And then that lethal surge at his core, the fist in his solar plexus, it twisted and pulled so he was strung like a bow. The cavity in his chest curled in, driving his arms forward. He stepped out of the gap to wrap all of himself, all of his moving parts, around the poor woman. His arms and legs were hooked around her waist, pulling her down with him onto the floor. At first she was on top of him, and his head nearly dislocated from his neck in its effort to link with her mouth. Then the power vacuum inside him started up.

The woman screamed into Stephen's black tongue. He swallowed her sound, sucking in any hope of her rescue. He was in control. She spoke muffled Chinese words that quelled a hunger in him too, a hunger that he had felt only three times before. At the bus stop, at the roadworks, at the tennis court – and now here in Townsville, at the back of a food tent.

Stephen felt sickened by what he'd done but incredible at the same time. He felt energised, revived. Gently, he eased the woman onto her side in a coma position, hoping in vain that he hadn't killed her too. He pushed out through the gap, moving down the alley between the tents. What was done was behind him. But the truth followed. He had attacked again. He had answered an urge that was unholy, unfair and unprovoked. Why couldn't he just let people live their lives? Why couldn't he be satisfied that his own had ended? Why couldn't he accept his fate? Why did he have to do damage to these people?

His brain convulsed with disgust, but his legs moved with renewed vigour. As he broke through the cordon of tents, the crowd casually stepped out of his path. His appetite had been sated. They weren't his type anyway.

2001

The invitations to Leanne's wedding were printed on expensive linen-textured card with gold edges. The calligraphy was elaborate. It read:

The Seymours and the Bolins cordially invite you to the wedding of Mr Timothy Seymour and Miss Leanne Bolin.

Leanne had worded it carefully, referring to the Bolins in general. Not 'Mr and Mrs Bolin'. She knew her father would be gone by then, though she felt slightly guilty for not holding out hope.

Stephen was surprised his sister had chosen Miss as her honorific. He had always thought of Leanne as more of a *Ms*, and had expected she'd do the feminist thing and keep her name. Now here she was, in a white hooped skirt with frills and lace, as Timothy waited at the altar. She walked herself down the aisle, wearing a bowls club badge of Willie's pinned to her dress. Through that one gesture of Leanne's, Willie's presence was felt by everybody in the room.

Leanne had invited random people from work to fill out the numbers, as if a full house could lift them out of their mourning.

Stephen was asked if he wanted to bring a plus-one, but he declined. The Brisbane gays could look good in a suit, but why submit them to the indignity of all the questions they'd be asked? Instead, he decided to play the eternal bachelor and come alone.

The reception was joyous, but a physical torture for Stephen, who had a headache again. They'd become more frequent, but he'd been too busy applying for jobs to see a doctor. At least it gave him a valid excuse if a matron tried coaxing him onto the dance floor. Leanne and Timothy's hetero-flexing male friends could do that job tonight. Meanwhile, he scanned the venue for secret signs of the other team, his team. Were there other men like him batting away horny older women? The guests were all so well dressed that it was interfering with his gaydar. Also, the raging masculinity of the groomsmen was winding him up. He thought a couple of Timothy's cousins might be fun to flirt with. It took his mind off the pain in his head.

Bored with the dance floor antics, Stephen inspected the dessert bar. Leanne had planned a serve-yourself affair. There was a standing board of vivid donuts hooked on wooden pegs. They were iced and sprinkled with lurid candy sand. Beside them, two tall glass vases were filled with chocolates. The children at the wedding, who had never seen so much sugar at one table, had been circling those all night. There were broken tarts and slices, as well as pieces of wedding cake that had already been plundered. While he tried to decide what to ruin his teeth on, a waiter carrying a bottle of white wine closed in. Stephen felt a change in the atmosphere as the guy refilled his glass.

He was wearing the same uniform as the other waiters – white formal shirt, black halter apron – but his collar was open and spread two or three buttons wide. Above the apron, Stephen could see into the cleft of his chest. The hair on his head was blonde and curly and unfashionably cut. It was growing out of the style that it was in. Every other youngish man at the function was freshly groomed for the event, but the waiter seemed casually aloof from all of that. That was what grabbed Stephen's attention.

The waiter leaned in close to Stephen's ear.

'Your glass is as dry as a nun's ninny.'

He was dripping with camp.

'How very dare you,' Stephen replied, delighted to have finally found a fellow gay. Then he felt self-conscious and looked around the room. People were still dancing. Nobody was watching him.

'Nice suit,' the waiter said with a suggestive wiggle of his eyebrows.

'Hired, unfortunately,' replied Stephen.

'You've been hired?' The waiter did a pearl clutch. 'A genuine working girl. Who's the lucky millionaire? You look expensive.'

Stephen laughed, offended but also amused at how forward the waiter was, how confident he was in hitting up a wedding guest. It was reckless. He could get fired, but he probably did it all the time. Stephen stared him up and down again, reassessing what he was being offered. The guy was probably in his late thirties, and he had a coastal face with scrubbed skin that shone with sun. His nose was sharp and long. Stephen guessed at his heritage. Something from up there in northern Europe. Perhaps Scando or maybe Balkan.

'Actually, I'm going cheap,' Stephen said, holding out his glass, which he'd already emptied.

'I love a discount,' the waiter said, and his smile was a clear, unambiguous come-on.

The lingering at the end of the wedding almost did Stephen's head in, but the waiter was hard from the moment Stephen got in the taxi with him, heading back to Stephen's hotel. Stephen made him even harder by licking his neck and feeling inside the guy's shirt. The taxi driver remained nonplussed, professionally averting his gaze from the rear-view mirror.

As a hopeful precaution, Stephen had declined Carmel's offer of sharing their family suite and booked himself a separate room. The waiter pushed himself into Stephen's back as Stephen struggled with his key. Inside, Stephen undressed completely for him and stood naked before a fully dressed man. He wanted to feel he was in control. It was his room and he felt he had picked up the waiter, not the other way around. But after a while he ceded to what turned out to be a more dominant force.

The sex was urgent and satisfying. Getting laid at his sister's wedding felt like some kind of irony, Stephen thought. Afterwards, while they lay there in the dim light of dawn, Stephen settled into the waiter's armpit. He liked the way the waiter's body was hairier than his.

'I take it you were into it?' Stephen asked cautiously.

The waiter paused, as if he was deciding whether Stephen was worth the intimacy of a full disclosure. He confessed: 'It's the dark brown nipples that really do it for me.'

Stephen side-eyed the waiter, then looked down to compare nipples. The waiter's were pink. Stephen had never been a nipples person. Never really took notice. It seemed ridiculous that the colour of nipples could be different.

'I knew yours'd be brown though,' the waiter said.

'Could you tell through my suit?'

'Correct,' the waiter said. 'Are you part Asian?'

Stephen thought about that for a second, about why he asked. What that had to do with it, but of course he knew. He tried not to imagine his father's nipples. Or his mother's by comparison. He shook the thought out of his head.

'I suppose I've got my dad's nipples,' Stephen said, finally conceding that the conversation was what it was. 'But he just died, and he'd probably die again to hear another man was admiring his son's.' Stephen was sorry he had invoked his father like that. He'd wanted to keep the situation light but now he felt he was bringing the mood down.

'I'm sorry to hear about your dad,' the waiter said.

'It's okay,' Stephen replied, keen to move on.

'But I'm not sorry I'm into you,' the waiter said, flicking the sheet back to show he had another hard-on. Stephen shrugged. He faked a look of no-interest and remained silent. The waiter fumbled for a change of subject. 'Do you often pick up waiters?'

'Not often,' Stephen replied. 'Do you often pick up guests?'

'Only the cute ones,' the waiter replied, laughing, the movement shuffling the sheet down again, so his pubic hair was showing. 'Do you go out much?'

'Nah. I'm all about the chatrooms these days,' Stephen said. He'd tried and liked them because on there, he felt less like he was back home, less like he was back to a failed routine.

'Oh yeah, I'm on Instant Messenger,' the waiter said, playing along.

'We might already have chatted,' Stephen said, sure they hadn't. 'What do you call yourself?'

'Jiāngshī,' the waiter said.

'What's that mean?'

'You don't know what a jiāngshī is? Really?'

'No, I have no idea,' Stephen said, leaning back so he could have a clearer view of the waiter's face.

The waiter sat up. 'I'm obsessed by seventies and eighties Hong Kong ghost cinema,' he said. 'It's all crazy over-acted stuff. *The Eight Masters*, *The Spiritual Boxer*, *Encounters of the Spooky Kind*,

Fantasy Mission Force. You must know that one. It's got Jackie Chan?'

'You've lost me,' Stephen replied, wondering if he'd picked up a nerd. 'Is that where you go on IM? Into the Hong Kong cinema chats and talk about that stuff?'

'Sometimes, yeah.'

The waiter was painting over the picture Stephen had created in his head. He was becoming less and less sexy. Hong Kong cinema from the discount bin of the video store? Yuck. Stephen went to gay chatrooms to talk sex and to masturbate. Still, he found himself asking the waiter: 'So, what's Jiāngshī though?'

'Chinese vampires, my friend. Chinese hopping vampires.' Again, the waiter seemed to think this should be obvious to him.

'Does that mean you've come to suck my blood?' Stephen smirked.

'No, that's the Transylvanian vampire, the Bram Stoker invention. That's the European shit. The jiāngshī is much cooler. The Chinese hopping vampire. I can't believe you don't know about them.' The waiter was in full diatribe mode now. 'They're from one of the dynasties, maybe Qing dynasty. They believed that if you died far from your place of birth, it was your family's responsibility to walk your corpse back home so you could be buried. They'd have to walk with the corpse strung between bamboo poles. The dead person would hang there between them, hopping up and down as they walked. Weird, hey.'

The waiter reached over to graze his fingers along the crevice of Stephen's armpit, to show him where the bamboo would fit. It felt creepy and Stephen tensed. The waiter carried on.

'They walked mostly at night to avoid the heat of the day. It would have looked pretty weird and gross, and so the people who came across them made up stories about hopping vampires who stole the qì of the living. Their life force.' He stopped, as if he'd made his point. Then he added, 'Chinese hopping vampires! Cool, huh?'

Stephen shook his head. 'That's actually quite macabre.'

The waiter stood up on the bed to demonstrate, holding his hands out, bouncing up and down, his cock and balls in Stephen's face. He was hoping for a laugh, but Stephen was annoyed. Not because of the stupid story – he was remembering something about the way the guy had sex with him. He'd seen it before, that look. When they'd been fucking, the guy had seemed really turned on, but also fascinated. The way he treated Stephen's body parts. It was a bit like how a scientist would look at you, as if he was noting your properties rather than being lost in the electricity between you. And then the conversation about nipples and their colour. Stephen was developing a theory about him. Would it be rude to mention it? The guy was so sure of himself.

'So, I reckon you have a thing for Asian guys.'

The waiter shrugged. He stopped bouncing and threw himself back onto the bed. 'No shit.'

Stephen shifted his position. The waiter felt uncomfortably close now. 'I don't know. I suppose I'm just saying it sounds like a fetish.' He wondered if the waiter got off on chatting to young Hong Kong guys in the Hong Kong cinema chat rooms.

'So what if it is?' the waiter replied. 'Do you want me to feel bad about that?'

'I'm just saying it's problematic when you look at me and just see an Asian guy,' Stephen added.

'We're not getting married or anything. Take it as a compliment. Don't you have preferences of your own?'

Stephen thought about it. He did a quick count back. Maybe he did. They were usually tall.

'I bet you do.' The guy was grinning, unashamed.

'But why Asian guys? What is it you like about them?'

The waiter paused for a moment. 'Have you slept with any Asian guys?

Stephen couldn't think of any. 'Nope.'

'Why not?'

'It just hasn't happened.'

'Maybe you didn't want it to happen. Maybe in a way you're racist,' the waiter said, crossing his arms playfully.

Stephen had had enough. He got up to shower.

The waiter followed him in. 'I'm not trying to be rude,' he said.

'I'm not racist,' Stephen said, turning on the shower.

'Okay, good. But I'm not either, if that's what you were implying.'

Somehow, the water and the steam turned things around for Stephen, and he wanted to have sex one more time with the waiter. But afterwards, he felt used again. He dried himself quickly and left the bathroom.

As the waiter was getting ready to go, he leaned in to kiss Stephen, then pushed Stephen's hand onto his crotch as a kind of final word. He was hard again. Despite his misgivings, Stephen handed the guy the hotel notepad and a pencil.

'What's this for?'

'Write down your number.'

'What for, are we seeing each other again?'

'Maybe.'

The waiter smirked and wrote his number. Beside it he wrote *Jiāngshī*.

'Do I get to know what your real name is?' Stephen asked.

'I'll tell you if you decide to call me.'

Stephen convinced himself that the headaches would go away, but the pain continued to grow there under his skull, pushing out into the subarachnoid space, tenting the dura mater like a hard-on under a blanket. He had no time to worry about his own health. Somehow, he'd moved back in with his mother and become the chief coordinator of her medical appointments, and there were a lot of them. He'd gone from having sex under bridges in Edinburgh to walking his mother over a pedestrian bridge to a geriatric specialist. *Thanks a lot, Carmel,* he thought. *Thank you, Leanne.* Was this why they'd wanted him back?

Aileen took the seat to the left. Stephen took the one on the right. Above their heads, a television on the apricot-coloured masonry wall announced the Powerball results. Sets of orthopaedic sandals shuffled past, but neither Stephen nor his mother acknowledged those wearing them. It was uncomfortable being there, for the both of them. Aileen had been reluctant to come, and Stephen was still feeling guilty about his absence during his father's decline. He wondered if he had it in him to make up for it, but he was giving it a go. When they called her name, Aileen flinched as if she'd been poked in the ribs.

'You'll be okay,' Stephen said.

As Aileen and Stephen entered the examination room, they were greeted by a man in his early thirties.

'I didn't expect him to be Indian,' Aileen whispered to Stephen. He squirmed at her remark as they sat down.

'Good afternoon, Mrs Bolin,' said the specialist. 'My name is Ishaan Anand. So, I've been told that you've been having some memory problems.'

Aileen had placed her handbag protectively across her lap, and could not look any more disinclined to be there. 'Occasionally.'

'I was just wondering if I could ask you a couple of questions as a sort of a test to see how you might be going with it,' Ishaan said.

There were questions about what day of the week it was, and the date. Aileen's eyes went wild with panic when she couldn't remember the year. Ishaan asked her about the season. Stephen watched his mother's anxiety grow. She said 'March' again, then corrected herself. 'Autumn.'

'Next,' Ishaan said, 'I'm going to say three words to you, and I'm going ask you to repeat them after me. I will ask you at the end if you can recall the three words.'

'Alright,' said Aileen gloomily.

'The three words are ball, tree and flag.' Ishaan spelled them out too.

'Ball, tree and flag,' Aileen said sharply.

'Are you able to remember that?'

'Of course.'

'Okay, next I'm going to ask you to do a brief sort of calculation. I'm going to ask you to start from one hundred and I'd like you to subtract seven from that serially. Are you able to do that?'

'Serially?' Aileen asked. 'What does that mean?'

'Just take one hundred and minus seven,' Stephen said.

'Please let your mother do the work,' Ishaan told him. And then to Aileen he said, 'Just keep subtracting seven.'

'Eighty-three,' said Aileen quickly. Then, with her blood pressure rising, she corrected herself. 'No. Ninety-three.'

'Okay, just keep going.'

'Eighty-six.'

'Good.'

'Sixty … ah … sixty-nine … ah … seventy … seventy-nine.'

'And the next one?'

'Seventy-four? No. Seventy-two.'

'And the next?'

Stephen noticed a stain on Ishaan's shirt, beside his tie. It was like an island or a coral atoll on the blue of the fabric. Whatever caused the stain had to be oily, because it spread through the individual threads of the fabric and hadn't dried out. He wasn't sure how or when the interview ended, or if his mother remembered the three words, but all of a sudden Ishaan was standing up to shake hands with them. Fifteen minutes had passed without him noticing.

'So we'll start you on that medication, Mrs Bolin.'

'I'll try,' Aileen said.

'Here's a script,' Ishaan said, tearing a sheet from a pad and handing it to Stephen. And then they returned down the hall.

The receptionist gave them a disarming smile. 'How did you go?' she asked. The question, like the prescription, was directed to Stephen.

'I think alright.'

The receptionist slid a piece of paper across the desk, saying it was today's account, and then rattled off a spiel about a follow-up letter that would be sent to Aileen's GP. She also asked for Aileen's health insurance provider card. Aileen froze. Stephen couldn't work out why his mother wasn't responding.

'It's in your purse, Mum,' he said.

'Where's my purse?'

The receptionist, ever helpful, pointed to the bag that Aileen gripped tightly across her mid-section.

On the way out the door, his mother suddenly said, 'Flag. I remember now. Flag. I knew it would come to me as soon as I walked out.'

Stephen felt bitter that his sisters' lives were occupied with their husbands and families. Surely he was the wrong person for the job of looking after their mother. He wished he was that cliché again: the cast-out queer, disqualified from having any family responsibility. Even during his online masturbation sessions, the niggle of his mother was there in the room. She might wander in to ask where her specs were. Or come to tell him a story she'd already told him. Longing to be rescued for a weekend, he called Jiāngshī, only to be informed: *number not listed.* His situation was pitiable, and he didn't even have work as an excuse for having no social life.

When his old agency team asked him to lunch, he said yes. He didn't have to think about it. Though he was troubled by the thought of going back there, as if he'd never been overseas, he still hoped they were meeting to offer him a job. At the table he was nervous and found himself drinking heavily. When the alcohol took hold, he told himself he deserved the buzz. The wine was acidic and fruity. It burned the back of his throat, so he drank more of it to numb the sting, even though white wine was like avgas to him. He kept waiting for the job offer to come, but maybe they were wooing him slowly.

Too boozed up to go back to work, it was a fast-tracked, sugared-up race to dinner after that, where there were better wines, but by then he was drinking too fast to appreciate them. When the bill came, he threw his credit card at the waiter, wanting to beat his former workmates to the punch. He needed to look more magnanimous than them, like a big man just back from London. He didn't want be the loser who needed a job. With their meal paid for, his friends offered to buy him a drink at a different place. Somewhere in the Valley.

Before long, Stephen was looking around for the good haircuts in the room, for the tight pants and the tight shirts and the designer cologne. Growing desperate, he even followed someone into a urinal. The guy was hot. Stephen was hoping he would flop his cock out for him, then it would be on, but the guy was a prude. Stephen smiled through gritted teeth as he re-entered the club to continue his search.

He ordered another drink, had another shot that his workmates had ordered. He didn't care that he would have a huge hangover tomorrow.

The aneurysm didn't care either. It had bided its time under the protective helmet of Stephen's skull. Now, on the dance floor, it bounced around against his brain to the rhythm of some old-school house. The music reminded the aneurysm of its origins, of the dancing and drinking and drug-taking Stephen did to conceive the aneurysm in London and Edinburgh. And when he was least expecting it, when he was making eyes at a man off to the side of the dance floor, a man who was tearing his shirt open to show off his drug-fucked abs, the aneurysm popped. Stephen fell to the ground like a civil demolishment.

The bleed was sudden and catastrophic. The blood pressure to key parts of his brain plummeted. Stephen could still hear and think, but there was no denying his loss of muscle control. While he lay there, he could hear the panic in the voices of his old work friends, who were pleading to others for help. He heard the music stop. He heard the disappointment of the other punters when the house lights came on. He heard the paramedics arrive and felt their hands searching for his pulse. He felt them lift him to a gurney and then onto the ambulance.

There was no pain, just darkness. Within it, he could think. And Stephen thought immediately of his sisters. How they hardly knew him. How spectacularly they would fail to provide for him if he was dependent on them. They wouldn't know the first thing about how he liked to live. He imagined how they'd dress him in clothes that he hated. How they'd feed him food he disliked. How they'd play their terrible music while he lay paralysed on a bed somewhere. That would drive him insane. They would absorb him into their lives, and he would be wondering if it was his life anymore, if it was even worth living as part of their furniture.

Still, Stephen's consciousness wandered through the few functioning alleys of his brain, determined not to give up while the hospital worked frantically on him. He gave them all the assistance he could from within, pulling extension leads from faulty inputs, searching for live ones, rerouting connections like an operator in a disintegrating telephone exchange. And even when the doctors gave up, he kept going, haunting the unconscious halls of his skull, trying the broken light switches one by one.

It took him two days while his body lay in its coma. But then miraculously he was able to open his eyes in the hospital room, though nobody was with him to witness the miracle. As if guided by instinct or reflex, he reached across to his bedside table, where there was a notepad and pen. But what Stephen wrote came via a dark back channel of his brain. A memory leaked through into his pen, wetting the tissue of his awareness. *Jiāngshī*, he wrote. Signing off, he pulled the plugs from every makeshift connection he'd created, and he submitted his body to its fate.

In the hours after his heart stopped, as the stagnant blood drained from the front to the back of his head, Stephen regained some of his senses. Incredibly, he could hear movement in the room. There was no blood rushing through his ears to muffle the sound. He heard Carmel weeping by his bedside, which he thought was out of character for her. Then he felt a soft brushing on the skin of his hand, and heard his mother's voice whispering into his ear.

'Just try to keep going,' she said.

The words echoed through the empty husk of Stephen's body. Every cell communicated the words to the cells beside them and the cells beside those, and the message became something else, as each cell said its final words to the other. Hello from the cells of the son to the cells of the father, greetings from the cells of the father to the cells of the grandfather. There was brief recognition and microseconds of familiarity before the interconnectedness of Stephen's makeup began to melt and to lose its form and to say goodbye.

The fading was gentle. Like a slow leak in a blow-up pool. The sides of each cell began to sag, allowing the qì inside to escape over the lip, until the integrity of each structure was so compromised that the walls of Stephen dropped away and his qì was gone, all in one rush.

Jiāngshī

Waking through treacle and molasses after his third victim, Stephen's skin was more alive with sensitivity. The bugs crawling under his shirt were unhappy that he was stirring. He could feel the pin pricks of their legs. The minute clicking of their wings was like a thousand tiny alarm clocks. And in their nymph form deep in the dirt beneath him, ancient cicadas transmitted seductive messages.

Stephen listened to their song. He wished he could join them where they slept. Would he be forced to suffer another night of the demands that had been put on him? Couldn't the earth just consume him instead?

Infuriated, he rolled over and sat up, took a quick survey of his surrounds. Above his head, fruit bats circled, disturbed by his human form. He was in a furrow between trees that grew evenly spaced in rows, their tops forming a broken canopy over his head. When he stood up to get a better view, he realised that the trees were banana plants, tall and burdened with fruit. He had slept through the day in a plantation.

Disappearing into the distance were lines of white banana

bags, moonlit apparitions floating head height from the ground, protecting the fruit from the bats. Stephen tried to find his way to a road, but he could not get past the wire fencing that ran the entire perimeter of the plantation. He was unable to lift his stiffened knees over it. He tried lifting the wire over his head, but his shoulders wouldn't flex either.

He decided to keep going along the fence. There had to be a gate or an exit somewhere. At one point he saw a sign: *FARM QUARANTINE. NO ENTRY.* The nearest plants were dotted with blue and pink fluorescent paint. These were diseased, it seemed. Their leaves were burnt, shrivelled or dried. The weeds at his feet were trimmed low to the ground and the soil had been compacted recently. As he blundered along, the repetition of the plantings, the evenness of the trunks, all of it lulled Stephen into a kind of trance.

Suddenly there was the sound of something crashing through foliage, then animals running. An engine approaching from a distance. A motorbike or perhaps a quad bike. It was coming in quickly. The memory of the previous night made Stephen fear for whoever was on the bike. He couldn't trust himself. He was a danger to people. He cut across a gap in the plantings and waited. A mob of animals rushed past him, running deep into the plantation. They were mostly small and dark, but one or two were larger, more threatening, the size of Labradors. Feral pigs.

Wherever they were going, Stephen felt he should follow. He had an idea: if he threw himself to the ground in front of them, they might finish him off. He wondered if they would like his rotting flesh. Perhaps they would break him down into his various parts – legs one way, arms the other, head and body separated so he could do no further harm. He wondered what would happen to his soul. Maybe it would go to the pig that got his head. Maybe it would travel with the pig that won his heart. And what about the one that took his hips, where the ache was in control? Would his ache be transferred? Would the rest of him be at peace?

As he was thinking this, the opportunity presented itself. It burst through a wall of banana plants, an enormous boar. It was as shocked to see Stephen as he was to see it. The dry mud on its back was like pebblecrete, caked and baked stiff. The animal was quivering, coiled to react, but it was confused, unsure whether to attack or to back away.

Stephen wasted no time. He collapsed his legs and raised his arms, so that he was kneeling and beckoning. He gave a low, mournful moan from his unmoving mouth. But the engine, the motorbike or quadbike, was getting closer, and the pig panicked at the sound. Headlights sprayed through the plants. Would it ride right over the top of him?

'Hey!' a loud male voice called as the bike engine was cut. The pig bolted, and Stephen rose to flee with it, but the voice commanded him to stop. *Why am I so compliant?* he thought.

Although the moonlight was bright, he was standing under the shade of a tall banana plant. The shocking detail of his face and the state of his body was partially hidden. The man had a gun, probably for the pigs. Stephen hoped he would use it on him.

'What are you doing here, mate? This is a private farm. We are under quarantine.'

Stephen wanted to warn him. He wanted to tell the man to run. He wanted to tell him that he was in danger, like the three others before him. The old man who'd reminded Stephen of his father. The guy who'd only wanted a quiet smoke away from his family. The young woman at the wok in the food tent. Stephen wanted to tell the farmer to save himself, to fire his gun or to climb back on his bike.

But the bowing vacuum in Stephen's solar plexus pulled and heaved and once more he was springing forward, coming at the farmer like a slingshot. Stephen wanted to stop himself. But he was taken over by the urge that controlled him. He wanted what it wanted. He wanted to consume what this man had, what he couldn't get enough of. He wanted to eat the spirit that moved this man, to consume his energy, his vitality, to bring it into the dead heart at his own core. To revive the part of himself that had been deprived of nourishment his whole life.

The farmer fell backwards, and Stephen's body hung over him, immobilising him in the dirt as Stephen fed on the farmer's spirit. Stephen's body began to hiccup. He was drinking him in too fast. But he let those jerking movements happen, ugly as they were. He no longer tried to rein them in. He was no longer embarrassed or self-conscious. He was hungry for everything the farmer had. Everything he was. Stephen felt no shame or reluctance. It was what he needed. He would take him, and the farmer's energy would repossess the deprivation within.

2012

'Dad would have loved this. Stephen would have hated it.' Carmel handed the letter to Leanne. It was from their father's sister's grandchild.

Leanne tried to untangle their connection. 'She's our grand-cousin?' It seemed too lofty a term. In any case, the letter contained an open invitation to attend a family reunion in Townsville. A chance to reconnect with long-lost relatives, people who had only been names on their family tree.

A helpful copy of the tree came with the invitation. Someone who knew their way around a computer had designed it. The background was a bit overdone. It looked like the parchment of an ancient tome, when in fact most of the people on the tree were younger than Carmel and Leanne. Their respective families, the Taylors and the Seymours, had been helpfully highlighted. At the top of the tree, above their grandfather William, was a name neither of them recognised. Pan Bo Lin, their great-grandfather.

'Do you think Mum will be up for it?' Leanne asked.

Carmel sighed. 'Not really.'

Aileen had shown surprising resilience in the ten years since

Stephen had died. Despite a series of infections, despite a bowel operation she hadn't fully recovered from, she had stoically stuck around. But she was facing the cruel march of Alzheimer's. This morning was hard to remember. Yesterday, almost impossible. An event with this many relatives would overwhelm her.

Carmel mentioned the reunion during her Sunday visit to Aileen's retirement home. It gave them something to talk about, instead of just watching television together.

'Will Stephen be going?'

She's having a good day, Carmel thought. *She remembers him.* She rubbed her mother's arm as she leant in to check on a couple of sunspots she'd been watching on Aileen's face. Carmel made a swift calculation about how best to answer the question about Stephen. Should she remind Aileen gently that Stephen had died? Would it push her back into mourning? Better to lie.

'He's busy, Mum.'

Aileen nodded as if she was used to getting that answer. 'If he's not going, then I won't bother going either.'

Carmel thought it was tragic that her mother had even been considering it. She would bring a nice photo of Aileen to Townsville, she decided, maybe a framed one of Aileen and Willie. And she'd bring one of Stephen too. That way, they'd all be there together.

Carmel took a window seat on the plane, with Leanne next to her, their husbands across the aisle and the four children spread out all the way to the other window. Out of earshot of their husbands, the two sisters conspired to abandon their families. It was a fantasy they often joked about when they got together. 'We could go diving out on the reef,' Carmel said with a grin.

After they checked into their hotel accommodation the two families split up. From Carmel's family suite, she could see the Townsville marina on the other side of a baking, flat expanse of carpark. Little white boats lined up, moored to pontoons. A small red biplane sat on its own pontoon, advertising a mobile number.

In the room next door, Leanne observed the plane from her window. She thought it didn't look airworthy. Castle Hill, with its squat arse parked permanently on the ground, was more her style of adventure anyway. Maybe she could go for a run later, if it wasn't too sweaty today.

Leanne remembered Townsville to be just a stopover for when the family drove up to Innisfail to see their grandfather. Some cousins still lived in the town – they were the ones who'd organised the reunion. Most of those coming were North Queenslanders and Far North Queenslanders, some were from the Northern Territory, others from WA. They knew their Auntie Dorothy was still on the Gold Coast. Leanne and Carmel and their families were the only other branch from down south.

The next morning, the eight of them huddled together in the restaurant foyer waiting for a table. There was a hungry throng at the buffet but nobody looked familiar. When their families had been seated, Leanne did a scan of the faces around her. There was a table of Scandinavian backpacker types. They were clearly not part of the reunion. There was another table of tall Black men who weren't either. They seemed to be a sports team, wearing matching tracksuits and loping across the space with the sort of confidence that came with being an athlete. Leanne felt like a different species altogether.

She went to join Carmel at the hot food section. The bacon was running low, and the hash browns were looking tired, but the mushrooms had just been topped up. Leanne asked her if she recognised anyone.

'Not really.'

Carmel had been scanning the room too. Most of the people were from her husband's gene pool: Matthew was a tall man, and Sian and Jaydn had taken after him. Carmel decided to concentrate on those who were shorter, like her and Leanne. That narrowed the options dramatically. Below the shoulder height of the others, that's where she saw them. They had to be her aunties. Two of her father's sisters. They were older than most of the hotel guests too, silver-haired and stern.

Leanne had noticed the aunties too. With her hands holding her tray, she nudged Carmel on the elbow and whispered, 'I think that's our lot over there.'

'Do you think it's Vivian and Thelma? It's not Dorothy.'

'Oh God, I can't remember,' said Leanne. 'Let's go over.'

With a quick eye signal to their children, they made a train and weaved their way through the tables to introduce themselves. Vivian and Thelma smiled as they approached, and Vivian even attempted to stand, but Carmel rushed over so she wouldn't need to.

'Don't get up,' she said.

'We're Vivian and Thelma. It's wonderful that you could come. You are …?'

Carmel explained that she and Leanne were Willie's daughters, and then she introduced their children, who'd come over for a look.

There was sudden relief in Vivian's eyes. She flapped her hands about, as if she wanted a hug. Still holding her tray, Carmel unlocked one knee to lean in close enough so her aunt could at least run her hand over Carmel's back.

'We'll come back after breakfast and catch up properly,' Leanne promised.

Back at their own table, Carmel and Leanne relaxed. Hopefully things would be simpler down at the park now that they'd made themselves known. There would be less confusion about who belonged and who didn't.

There was a crowd gathering under the shade of a large banyan fig. Sunlight fell through the structure in shimmering shafts. Aerial roots plunged down along the outward spread of its limbs. They mirrored the circular walls of the historic rotunda that had been built around the same time the tree had been planted. But the tree had long ago exceeded the colonial structure in radius. It was a fertile allegory for the family they were celebrating.

Carmel, Matthew, Sian and Jaydn strode across the thick grass. Leanne and Timothy followed, with Joanna and Dinnika, who looked glum at the prospect of interacting with relatives. As the four cousins formed a quick clique, talking behind their hands and taking selfies, Matthew and Timothy hung back, feeling less obligated than Carmel and Leanne to make conversation with strangers.

The two sisters scanned the reunion group for their elders, deciding it would be easier to understand all the connections if they started at the very beginning. As well as Vivian and Thelma, who were sitting in fold-up chairs, there was a venerable-looking gent in a mobility buggy. Children were swinging off the back of it as if they were on a theme park ride, but the old man had parked it and was not going anywhere. People were coming to him.

Carmel excused her way through the unknowns until she and Leanne arrived at Vivian's side. In a surprisingly loud voice, the old woman announced them.

'Everyone, these are my brother Willie's girls. Please introduce yourselves.'

Carmel and Leanne said their full names aloud, as if they were at a seminar where everyone had to do it. But nobody else followed up with theirs. They just waved and smiled and left Carmel and Leanne to their embarrassment.

Vivian, who was wearing a knitted cardigan, was fanning herself in the heat. Carmel moved back to her side, figuring she was still the most likely person to connect them with other relatives.

'I'm having trouble recognising faces,' Carmel told her aunt.

Vivian smiled. 'Oh, don't worry about that, you'll get to know everyone.' She swivelled towards Carmel. 'Where's your mother?'

Carmel was suddenly embarrassed. She felt guilty that she hadn't found a way to bring Aileen along. The oldies were the whole point.

'She wasn't quite up for the trip,' she said.

Vivian nodded. 'My legs are not very good these days either. I have trouble walking.'

'You poor thing,' Carmel said, pulling Leanne by the hand into the conversation. Leanne obliged.

'Are you the oldest relative here?' she asked without any segue, not worried she might seem impolite.

Vivian waved in the direction of the old bloke in the mobility buggy. 'Except for Alexander over there. He's two years older and has been all his life.'

Carmel laughed at the unexpected mic drop. 'Who's Alexander to you?'

'He's my cousin. He's not a Bolin. He's a Lo. My mother's …' Vivian corrected herself, 'your grandmother Christina's brother, Georgie Lo's eldest son. They're all Los over there.'

She indicated a group of people that had split into two halves, with toddlers and primary school-aged children running from one to the other, rolling in the grass where they had space. Carmel couldn't quite follow the genealogy, but maybe it would become clearer.

'Can you give us a snapshot of who's here then?' she asked her aunt.

Vivian frowned. 'I'm not sure I know everybody myself. You might have better luck with someone from your generation to tell you who turned up. My memory is not as sharp. Were you saying your mother was unwell?'

'Oh, she's a bit like you. Worried about her memory.'

'Maybe she's happy to forget,' Vivian said. 'Life is too long sometimes to hold it all in your head.'

'That's true. She's sorry she couldn't make it.'

'What a shame your father spirited her away from us.'

Vivian smiled as she said it, but Carmel wondered if the statement might have carried an ancient barb. She didn't know how to respond.

To her relief, they were rescued by a woman in her fifties who had long dark hair and a tanned face as if she'd just come back from holiday. She inserted herself between Carmel and Vivian, who seemed delighted with the interruption.

'Oh, I know this person. This is your cousin. Hello, Katrina.'

'Hello, Auntie Vivian,' Katrina said, spinning around to give the older woman a kiss on the cheek.

'You probably don't recognise me,' she said, returning to Carmel and Leanne. 'Haven't seen you since we were all kids.'

'Katrina can tell you who's who,' Vivian chimed in, explaining to Katrina that the two of them were trying to work out the connections.

Their cousin looked grateful to be asked. She took Carmel and Leanne by the arm, one on each side, and spun them in an arc as she described what they were seeing.

'If you look over there on the left, those people are the Los.'

Vivian piped up that she'd already told them that much.

'Thank you, Auntie,' Katrina said. Then she continued: 'So, there are two people here from Grandad's sister's family. They're the Kennedys, who are the kids of Great-Aunt Mabel, who married Michael Kennedy. They still live in Townsville.'

'I didn't know we had a Great-Aunt Mabel,' Leanne said.

'Don't worry. I grew up in Townsville and I didn't know either. Mabel's mother was Bridget, who was married to Great-Grandad Pan. But he had two wives apparently, so Bridget got rid of him.'

Leanne looked baffled, but Carmel kept an open expression, hoping to be able to put all of that into some sort of order when they had some time to themselves. Katrina carried on.

'My lot over there are the Skarsgaards. My husband didn't come. We've separated, but that bunch of clowns are my kids. They still live with me.'

Three tall, honey-haired and handsome boys stood goofing around against the tree, not far from Carmel and Leanne's children. The two groups were eyeing each other off, trying to be cool about it, and Carmel felt a twinge of disappointment that her kids weren't being more friendly.

'Why aren't they talking to each other?' Carmel asked. 'When did young people get so aloof?'

'I don't know,' Katrina said. 'Mine are hopeless. I can't see them looking after me in my old age.' She winked at Vivian, who rolled her eyes and tutted.

'The Emersons are here too, that's Auntie Dorothy's clan. I don't think she could come though. There's the Robinsons, that's my sister Tina's family. Thelma's people are the Sandersons – look how many of them are here. And the Harvards, of course, which is Vivian's family with Uncle Keith, who passed away when we were kids. Do you remember?'

Leanne shook her head and Carmel shook hers as well, feeling a little shown-up.

Katrina changed tack and led them back towards the base of the tree. 'Let's get these cousins of cousins talking. We're not here for us. We're here for them, to make sure they carry on these family connections, eh.'

The three women crossed the sun-speckled grass to where Sian, Jaydn, Joanna and Dinnika were standing. Simultaneously the three clownish boys made their way to their mother, and before long the young people were all chatting in a group. Carmel was surprised to find that some of it was genuinely congenial, with a lot of laughing.

That was until Sian made a startling observation.

'I came expecting a lot more Asians.'

She said it innocently enough. Carmel wasn't even sure if she meant to say what she did, but there was an awkward silence. Realising she'd made the wrong type of comment at the wrong time, Sian pulled her phone from her pocket as if she was reacting to a notification.

The conversation went back to small talk, but soon everyone was being marshalled for a group photograph. As the photographer set up her kit, her assistant directed people to converge on a spot at the base of the tree where the light was good. Vivian, Thelma and Alexander were set in the middle, while others were moved around. Some of the adult children were taller than their parents so they had to stand behind them, and somebody made the comment that nutrition had improved in the last seventy years, with so many tall children there.

It took several minutes. The photographer climbed a stepladder so she could raise the camera to get a better angle. She shouted to the group to be ready and then she coaxed the Bolins, the Los, the Harvards, the Robinsons, the Sandersons, the Emersons, the Kennedys, the Taylors and the Seymours to give three cheers. On each of the hoorays, the camera flashed, and the photographer reset, reminding the group to smile. They all did as she asked, except for Sian. She couldn't smile. She couldn't reset.

The venue for the reunion dinner faced the water, which was the view that everyone wanted. Tables were lined up to accommodate the family groups. Inside there was a bar and a kitchen taking orders for food. Reunion guests were milling about between the two, ferrying supplies back to their groups.

As a waiter brought a round of drinks to her table, Carmel thought it was amazing that her children were now old enough to drink. It made the family reunion feel like a milestone, like they were showing them off as adults. She wondered if Leanne was feeling it too. It was as if she and her sister had survived something and were celebrating the fact. Condolences are a part of any reunion, of course, and Stephen and Willie were still present, looking out from their frames on the table. But people seemed to be there to celebrate the survivors, the remaining relatives – how far they'd come and how much they'd achieved. She kept the two photographs on the table just in case anyone asked.

A few relatives were still introducing themselves. The Kennedys were at the next table over and Jaydn had started a conversation with them. Katrina's family, the Skarsgaards, were still in orbit. But there remained some mystery about a few of the connections. Leanne slipped the family tree out of her bag on a couple of occasions so that the people she spoke to could identify themselves on the chart. Sian listened in from a distance.

Matthew and Timothy were watching a television that was broadcasting a sporting event. Several men from the group and a couple of the women were standing there with them, transfixed by the screen but laughing and chatting, losing themselves in the alcohol buzz and the noise.

Eventually, Sian came to sit with her mum, holding the family tree in her hand.

'This is amazing,' she said, pointing to the chart.

'Isn't it?' Carmel replied, happy to see her daughter in a better mood. But Sian was there to make a point, which she launched into as if she was presenting a thesis.

'Look at it,' she said, using her finger to trace the various branches that emanated from the relative at the top, Pan Bo Lin. 'Do you notice anything?'

Carmel gave her daughter a sideways glance. She took her spectacles out of her bag, holding the paper to the side, moving her head so that her shadow wasn't obscuring it. 'What do you mean?'

'I mean,' Sian said, 'don't you think the names on this tree are interesting?'

'In what way?'

Sian always had a unique take on the world, Carmel thought. She often marvelled at her daughter's mind, her critical thinking. But this was a party, not a time to go off on one of Sian's intellectual tangents. Sometimes she wished her daughter would lighten up.

'Well, I can see Grandad and his cousins, the Bolins and the Los. But after that,' she said, 'no more Bolins. No more Los.'

'Maybe everyone had daughters,' Carmel said. She took a closer look anyway. Even if just to prove Sian wrong.

Her Auntie Vivian Bolin, her father's oldest sister, had married Keith Harvard. Auntie Thelma Bolin had married Nick Sanderson. Auntie Dorothy Bolin had married Jonathon Emerson. The Emerson grandchildren were running around the tables, trying to scare each other with a rhinoceros beetle that had flown onto their table attracted there by the festoon lighting. Further down the chart, her father's brothers. Uncle Vernon Bolin had married Margie Tyler, but Uncle Thomas Bolin hadn't married at all. Carmel wondered if he'd been gay like Stephen. What a shame they hadn't been able to get to know each other, she thought.

Her grandfather's brothers, Alvin Bolin and Clarence Bolin, had also never married. But Mabel Bolin, her grandfather's sister, had married Michael Kennedy. And of course her grandfather had married her grandmother. William Bolin and Christina Lo. As Vivian had told her, the Los at the reunion were the descendants of her grandmother's brothers.

Carmel stopped to look up at Sian, who was peering into her face, hoping for a reaction. 'You'll have to explain it to me, darling,' she said. To her the family tree seemed fairly typical.

'Sanderson, Skarsgaard, Emerson, Harvard. Very white names, don't you think?'

'It's just a funny coincidence,' Carmel said, cringing at the word 'white', which young people seemed to be using a lot these days.

'And I feel sorry for Uncle Stephen,' Sian continued.

‘Why?’

‘I just think he must have felt some pressure to carry on the family name.’

‘Grandma and Grandad never made him feel that kind of pressure,’ Carmel said, although she couldn’t be sure. She’d never asked Stephen about it.

‘But also,’ Sian began, ‘why did you all marry white people? Apart from your grandad and grandma?’

Carmel sat back. Sian had used that word twice now. White. It was a pithy question but not the sort you expected from your daughter. And not something she’d thought about. She felt she was being criticised. ‘I’m sure we didn’t.’

Sian gave her mother a librarian stare. ‘Every marriage in a hundred years has been to someone of European or Anglo descent. Caucasian. Can you not see it? Nobody married anyone Chinese. Not even Asian, or First Nations or Pasifika or African, or … How can that be a coincidence?’

‘Never thought about it,’ Carmel said. She realised when she said it, though, that she sounded like she was defending her position. But she hadn’t consciously taken that position. Her daughter had made an observation and Carmel had made herself look defensive.

On the flight home, the cabin was filled with sunburned tourists. Everybody was heading back to real life. People were resting. Carmel was hoping to talk to her sister about the conversation she’d had with Sian, but Leanne was caught up telling a story about a massage she had in her room, on the sly, while the rest of them were off exploring. Carmel vaguely remembered Leanne excusing herself for a couple of hours after breakfast.

'What sort of massage was it?'

'Thai. Shiatsu.' Leanne told Carmel it was a form of deep tissue massage that targeted the lymph nodes.

'Oh, that's Japanese,' said Carmel.

Leanne was miffed to be corrected but tried not to show it. 'Anyway, when I was lying there face down on the table, do you know what he asked me?'

'Who?' asked Carmel.

'The masseuse. He asked me if I was part Asian.'

Carmel turned to look across at Sian, who was sitting on the far aisle seat beside her brother. She'd love this conversation.

'What did you tell him?' she asked Leanne.

'I told him that Dad was Chinese and Mum was Scottish. But then he asked me what I identified as.'

Carmel realised two totally separate conversations were converging. 'And?'

'I told him I identified as Scottish.'

Carmel pushed out her lower lip as she considered Leanne's answer, wondering if she would have said the same. A man in front of her stood up from his seat and began stretching his legs, rubbing his knees. Carmel was presented with a view of his rear, pushing closer and closer to her face as he bent over to touch his toes. The intrusion forced Carmel to lean in closer to her sister.

'I guess that makes sense,' she said. 'Mum had us eating porridge for breakfast and every time we heard bagpipes, she'd go all misty. Remember? Grandma's accent? I mean we talked about her background a lot. Not so much Dad's. And anyway, he wasn't the immigrant.'

'That's right,' Leanne said. 'And it gave me an am-not to fall back on at school.'

'A what?'

'An am-not. You know … when someone calls you a name and you say, "am not"?'

To their relief, the man had stopped doing his exercises and was taking his seat again.

'I can't believe the names we got called at school,' Carmel said.

'You mean ching-chong?' As Leanne said it, she palmed her forehead three times, making a gentle slapping sound, having a quiet laugh at herself.

'Am not,' Carmel said, laughing with her sister. 'Kids are horrible. I think Stephen copped it all the time as well.'

'Horrible,' echoed Leanne, shaking her head from side to side and making a hard line with her mouth.

Carmel turned again to look at Sian. She was sure Sian hadn't gone through that name-calling. They lived in Brisbane. It was the new millennium. But now she planned to ask her daughter.

'I don't think kids are like that anymore,' Carmel said.

Leanne noticed her sister had been staring down the row at their children. 'They're definitely more aware of that sort of stuff.'

'They sure are,' Carmel said, 'or they get called out for it. Our generation, on the other hand …'

Leanne arched an eyebrow.

Carmel decided she should segue to her topic. 'Sian pointed something out to me at the reunion. She said she noticed something odd about our family.'

'We have always been odd,' Leanne said.

'Right?' Carmel continued. 'Well, Sian said that all of us, like, every single one of us, all the cousins, all the aunties and uncles, all the grandparents, everybody from Dad and Mum's generation onwards, we all married Caucasian people.' The word felt foreign coming out of her mouth, but 'white' sounded worse, she thought.

Leanne wanted to make light of the situation, but she could see Carmel was troubled by it. While Leanne thought the statement was provocative, she didn't feel personally attacked, just uncomfortable with an idea that seemed to be an outrageous generalisation. Surely it was something that could be disproved. She pulled her copy of the family tree from her bag, unfolding it onto her tray table. The names were all there before her. But she'd never seen it from Sian's perspective. She'd never taken such a critical look at the names listed and considered what they pointed to. It seemed like such a strange way to think about your own family.

Carmel was relieved that Leanne was struggling with the idea as well. The two sisters looked at each other. For the first time in a long time, they looked at the structure of each other's faces. They were faces they'd taken for granted their whole lives, faces they thought they knew. But now they were analysing them for family traits. Carmel remembered pulling Chinese eyes. Remembered Stephen doing it to her, but it was just a joke. Just kids making fun.

Mostly she could see parts of Aileen in her sister, because they were both women, and Leanne was growing older too, following their mother into the inevitability of grey hair. But also, parts of Willie were there, and this was now her focus. She and her sister definitely had his eyes. Their mother's were blue. But they also had his heavy brow, the weight and colour of his lips, and his olive complexion, which they'd benefited from on the beach their whole lives. Their mother hadn't had their ability to tan. She had been the family member to burn at the mere touch of sun. Their hair, as well, was different to Aileen's. It was a different shade to hers; the hairs in between the whites were black. Aileen's hair was more auburn.

Neither Carmel nor Leanne wanted to look over at their husbands. They loved their men. If there was a new question being raised about the motivations behind their marriages, what did it say about their families? And if it was three or four generations deep, then what? It was too big a question to answer. Leanne couldn't fathom it, but because Carmel had been living with the question a few days longer than her sister, she had settled on one thing.

'I don't think it's been a conscious choice,' she said, finally.

Leanne shrugged. She felt confused, but confused about what? It seemed ridiculous for her to be upset. 'Of course it's not,' Leanne said, as if she was trying to convince herself of the fact.

The two families bid each other goodbye at the airport. Carmel, Matthew, Sian and Jaydn piled into the back of a maxi-taxi along with their luggage. Sian sat in the passenger seat beside the driver. Opportunely, at least for Sian, the driver's name was Michael Ling. She began an animated conversation with him, which was very unlike her. Carmel could tell that her daughter was doing it for show by the way Sian kept looking over her shoulder to see if Carmel was paying attention.

First Sian asked him if he drove taxis full time. He told her he only did it during the day. At night he looked after his kids while his wife did shift work. She asked what his wife's name was. He gave her a smile and said, 'Li Na. Like the tennis player.'

The taxi went down Kingsford Smith Drive. Sian pointed at the Enjoy Inn restaurant on the left and asked Michael if he had eaten there. He told her he hadn't, an answer that seemed to disappoint her. Then she asked him where he liked to eat.

'McDonald's,' he said, deadpan.

'Really?'

'Nooo,' he told her, his face breaking into a cheeky grin. 'Sunnybank is the only place for Chinese food in Brisbane.'

Grabbing onto Michael's statement as if it was about to fly out the window, Sian announced, 'We should go to Sunnybank one day.'

Carmel felt like Sian was somehow criticising her again. She squeezed Matthew's hand to bring him into the loop, but he didn't react. She decided she would just let Sian continue with the crusade she was on.

Despite his indifference, Matthew's hand felt solid around Carmel's. She would often reach for it in bed, and he would hold her hand like this, strong and secure. But when he fell asleep, his grip would relax and he'd end up rolling over, lost to her. Carmel would feel as if her own hand had been just a squatter in Matthew's, or a cuckoo chick in some other bird's nest. Not in the taxi though. There was nowhere for him to roll to and eventually he squeezed her hand in reply.

'That sounds like a plan,' he said to Sian, as if he'd been listening all along.

Carmel hadn't told Matthew about Sian and her theory. She didn't want to give it too much oxygen before she'd worked it out, but Sian was fixated. As they drove through the inner-city bypass Sian kept talking to Michael, and every question felt to Carmel like a search for weaponry.

'How long have you been in Australia?'

'Fifteen years.'

'Where did you live before coming here?'

'Hong Kong. My wife and I came here just before the handover to China.'

'How did you meet your wife?'

'Arranged marriage.'

Carmel smiled. If Sian was worried the Bolin marriages had been premeditated, that showed it could have been worse.

Sian's questions kept going. 'What does Ling mean in Chinese?'

'Refrigeration.'

'Refrigeration?' She looked defeated.

Michael laughed. 'I'm joking. It's a Zhou Dynasty name, after the people who were in charge of the emperor's ice. The Ling. Or as my kids like to say, Lingerators.'

'Haha,' Sian said, her mood restored. She paused to consider her next question. Again, she looked over her shoulder to check that her mother was still following. Satisfied, she turned back to the driver. 'Do you know what the Chinese name Bolin means?'

The driver repeated the name, saying it the way Sian had said it, like *bowling* without the 'g'. He said, 'I don't think that's a Chinese name.'

'Yes, it is,' Sian clapped back. She spelled out the five letters for him.

'Ah,' he said. 'That would be two separate characters in Chinese. Bo and Lin. Whose name is that? Yours?'

'It's my mother's maiden name,' Sian said, turning to Carmel, this time looking as if she had just done her a great service.

'Our name is Taylor now though,' Carmel added. She wasn't sure why she thought she needed to make that point. Perhaps she didn't want Matthew to feel left out. She squeezed his hand again as if he was the one who needed reassurance, although he was hardly listening to the conversation. She realised then that she needed to fill him in when they got home, even if that meant admitting to herself that Sian might be right. As much as she wanted to believe it was just a long history of coincidences, Carmel was struggling to write it off so easily.

★

That night, when they were lying in bed together, Carmel decided to broach the topic. She approached it from a different perspective, though, as if she was testing which one sat better with her.

'Did you notice how strong the Chinese gene is in our family? All that black hair still coming through after so many generations.'

'So wonderful,' Matthew said. 'I think those old birds would be proud to see their heritage in all those kids.'

'Do you think they all have similar features?'

'I suppose …' Matthew took Carmel's face in his hands. 'I can see Willie's features in you. Definitely. He would have been a beautiful woman.' He grinned, proud that he'd set up such a corny joke.

Carmel had a sudden flash of her father's face on the day he told her about his cancer. How he'd tried to hide how annoyed he was at his diagnosis, how disappointed he was. He told her at the time that it was okay. That she shouldn't be sad. He said he'd had a good run. But the look in his eyes told her something different: that he wanted more, that he wasn't ready to go. Carmel supposed everybody felt that way when they knew they were in life's departure lounge.

When tears began to roll down Carmel's face, Matthew regretted mentioning Willie. He knew she had a lot of unresolved feelings about his death, and the way her brother had followed so soon after. He'd only meant to say something supportive. He apologised and tried to comfort Carmel, who wiped away her tears, sniffing back all that emotion.

'I reckon I'll need a week to recover from that trip,' she said. 'Family is exhausting.'

Matthew gave her a smile. 'It was always going to be emotional, right?'

‘Right,’ she said, hoping to stave off another surge of tears. She was growing annoyed with herself. Maybe it was time to tell him what was bothering her.

‘Sian made an interesting observation about our family,’ Carmel said. ‘I mean my family.’

Matthew tried to tread carefully, not wanting to upset her again. ‘Yeah? What did our little activist discover?’

‘Exactly,’ Carmel said. ‘Our little activist. According to her, we’re a family with a thing for Caucasian people.’

‘Well, you’re only human,’ Matthew said, making sure Carmel could read his humour clearly. Hoping he could keep the conversation light this time.

‘I’m being serious,’ Carmel said. ‘She did a count back and pretty much every single relative on the Chinese side, including yours truly, has married someone Caucasian.’ She kept her face neutral, not wanting to give away any viewpoint.

‘So what?’

‘That’s what I thought when she told me,’ Carmel replied. ‘It does *look* bad though. From the outside.’

Matthew rocked his head from side to side, like he was weighing up a few options. ‘Why does it look bad? It’s not as if you all did it on purpose.’

‘Well, it can’t just be a coincidence. Although I agree that it wasn’t on purpose.’ She exhaled, steeling herself for the next part. It felt like she was confessing to a crime. ‘What I think is that we may have instinctually made some decisions, for reasons we might not have been aware of at the time. And those reasons may not be things we can be proud of, looking back.’

‘You’re not proud of bagging me?’ Matthew asked, pretending to be offended. ‘Seriously though, you know what people say – love is blind.’

'I think that's true,' said Carmel, 'but what if that blindness is blindness towards people who look like us? What if we don't have an eye for Chinese people?'

'So, you think there are people in your family who only want to marry a Caucasian person because they don't find Asian people attractive?'

Carmel considered this. It sounded base and ridiculous now that it had been said out loud. 'I think Sian is embarrassed about it.'

'Is that what she told you?'

'Not really. But maybe that's what she thinks.'

'So our daughter thinks your family is sexually racist, against their own people?'

Carmel blanched. She pulled her head back, so her chin disappeared into her neck. 'Who are *our* people? Who are *your* people?'

'I don't have a *people*,' Matthew said.

'Yes, you do,' Carmel countered.

'Yeah, but we don't call them *our* people,' Matthew said. Then he stopped and thought about it for a moment before correcting himself. 'Maybe we unconsciously think of them as our people. But anyway …'

'You see how tricky it is,' Carmel said, happy to see Matthew stumbling around the politics of it, just as she had.

'We might have to ask our activist daughter to help us navigate this one,' Matthew said. Then he asked what Leanne thought about it. Carmel told him she'd only just sprung it on her in the plane, and that they'd talked about being given a hard time at school by other kids because of their dad. Because they all knew he was Chinese.

'We all were given shit, actually,' Carmel said. 'Leanne, myself and Stephen.'

Matthew felt guilty that he'd never known about that. 'That's terrible,' he said. 'Maybe somewhere in your subconscious you decided then that you didn't want to put your own kids through the same thing.'

Carmel made a face. 'I mean, I feel self-conscious enough about our parenting without feeling bad about how and why I married to begin with. What genes I chose to blend with. Oh my god.'

It was getting late. They agreed they wouldn't be able to resolve anything that complicated and it was growing more so, even as they dug at it. Matthew kissed Carmel to calm her and then reached over to switch out the light.

In the dark, they held hands, and Carmel listened to Matthew breathing. When his cadence slowed and he drifted off, she gave his hand a squeeze. Matthew stirred, and he squeezed back, his breathing quickening. Then it slowed again and this time she let him fall asleep, let his hand stay open.

Jiāngshī

Stephen was marching, running, barrelling through the night. Since leaving the banana plantation, he'd moved with furious, energetic intent, faster than before. He cut through acres of sugarcane like a cyclonic gust, defoliating plants, removing their blossoms. Turning them to broken sticks.

Where he could, he met with the road again, but when it veered away in a direction that his internal compass didn't agree with, he went back to crossing fields, cutting off the curves, running as the crow flies except the crows were sleeping. Conceding to instinct, handing over to the force in his hips, he felt like he was facing the truth now.

He wanted to destroy the vehicle he was in, his loathsome corpse. He wanted to bruise it, tear it, end it. He wanted to remove his skin. There was no pain and no end to the energy he had for self-annihilation. But now, it was as if he was doing what he'd always known he should be doing, as unlikely as that was. He was running to Innisfail, the town of his birth, and he would not stop or be stopped. He remembered his dream, the one in which he had invited his sisters to carry his corpse north, strung between poles of bamboo. Was that a fantasy or a premonition? Either way, it was wildly inaccurate, for there was no bamboo and no sisters. On this journey he was alone.

What he was learning in death was superseding what he had understood in life. His death was his honesty, its motivations unadulterated. He couldn't control himself like he had in life, making excuses for his behaviour, rationalising his thoughts, avoiding them at times. His body was rotten in death; his skin was being flayed. But his actions and his destination, they were true. They were telling him who he really was and what he'd done all his life.

Up ahead, a bent sign had been pushed over by a recent storm or flood, or the impact of a vehicle. It bowed towards him as he emerged onto the verge of the highway. *Welcome to Innisfail*, it said, with a photograph of a day-lit town. Sailboats in a marina. Painted blue water reflecting the colour of the sky. The air around the sign buzzed with mosquitoes.

He passed another one at Mourilyan. A celebratory ribbon was painted across the top. *Welcome to Innisfail*, it said again. As if he would believe it now, having been welcomed twice. Further down the road, a truck with a double trailer drove in the opposite direction. As it flashed by, a shock wave of exhaust air pushed him off the road and into a ditch. He kept running until he could return to the road, where another truck did the same thing. Stephen caught a glimpse of its cargo: bug killer, crop spray, something called Movento from Bayer. The bugs on his skin crawled over his scalp to the opposite side.

WE'D LIKE TO MEAT YOU, a poster for a butcher's shop announced. It was a joke, but not to Stephen, who abhorred the meat he was born with and despised the skin he'd been given. He passed a house surrounded by a small oasis of ornamental plants, hydrangeas, oleanders, rain trees and tulip gardens. Such a pretty facade. But the crops around them were razed to the ground by a harvester.

He crossed the Johnstone River and found his way to a footpath in Mighell, a concrete strip that ran alongside the highway. A cemetery appeared unannounced on the other side of the path. Mildewed tombstones and concrete-bordered plots appeared, surrounded by lawn as if they were garden beds in a park. But this was not his resting place: the names on the graves were Italian, German, Irish, English. Stephen didn't belong with them. His hips ached for a different destination. If anyone had seen him pass, he thought, they might have imagined they'd seen a soul escaping from a grave.

The morning was coming. He saw cars on the highway, carrying tradesmen and farm workers off to the morning shift, or travellers getting an early start. The ache in his hips was only growing more intense. The path merged back with the highway and Stephen found himself suddenly at a large roundabout where the highway merged with a street. He passed by some shops, and then a McDonald's drive-thru, which was lit up like a runway.

This street. This thoroughfare. His heart, the black stone that it had become, began to burn in his chest. It was something he hadn't felt before, and it drove him to run quicker. This place was familiar to him, to his heart. He passed a fuel station, an electrical shop. Soon, the road arrived at a set of lights. Ahead, Stephen could see the awning of an ancient hotel on the corner. Above him on the light post, a street sign that read *Ernest Street*.

And then, as if a string had been cut from the body of a puppet, he fell through a galvanised grate into a drainage pit under the road.

Suddenly there was nothing to feel. Nothing to think. The ache that had haunted him all these nights had evaporated from his nervous system. Darkness and anaesthesia finally enveloped his head.

In the end, for Stephen, it was just as his letter to his sisters had described. He knew when he got there. He knew where to stop.

As Stephen's body came to rest, his decomposition, a process that had been fantastically delayed, went into hyperdrive. The microbes he'd attempted to wash off went to work. Tendons detached and bones fell loose of their flesh.

The tag from his toe was freed, floating off into the stormwater drain. It sailed two hundred metres in the dark, away from the pit that his corpse had fallen into. It travelled beneath the bitumen surface of the road, below the lip of a concrete kerb, and under the awning of the Crown Hotel, which sat opposite the pit. The rising sun would soon light up a shower of hose water that came from the morning cleaning. It would flow down into the drain, washing Stephen's tag further along.

It went beneath the next building, a bottle shop that used to be a mechanic's shop, and then it turned right. It travelled down a pipe that followed a narrow lane and made its way below a series of warehouses. Stormwater had run from their downpipes into gutters where Stephen's father had once played, barefoot in the deluge.

It went that way, Stephen's tag, as if it was being sailed. It took a short cut through to Owen Street. And as it drew closer to its destination, it floated out of the drain and onto the footpath, returning Stephen's name to the foundations of a building that had been built to outlast his grandfather's family, his father's family, his sisters' families.

The walls of the building had been recently repainted red. Not just any red. Those who had chosen the colour, those who had restored this particular place and rebuilt it with money donated by the families who revered it, who may once have been ashamed of it, whose patriarchs, after falling from favour, might have been left to die in it, surrounded by a cloud of opium and joss – they would have seen that red as something to celebrate. Something to own. Something to love. Not the colour of embarrassment but the colour of good fortune. The colour of lacquerware. The colour of vermillion. The colour of cinnabar powder. The colour of a lantern. The colour of a firecracker. The colour of a money envelope and a bead made from coral. The colour of the silk shéng, two cords joined together, tied into a Pan Chang knot to hang on the door of a much-loved ancestor's home. A knot with no beginning. A knot with no apparent end.

That red. The colour of blood.

Acknowledgements

This work is a fictional minestrone of lives. But also, books. I first read about jiāngshī in *The Shadow Book of Ji Yun, Imperial Librarian and Investigator of the Strange* (edited and translated by Yi Izzy Yu and John Yu Branscum) and had the idea then that my protagonist could be dead and walking. I drew a lot on a published family history written by relatives Joanna Olsen and Keith Shang. Their historical work, titled *With His Gold in a Little Velvet Bag: the story of a Chinaman and a bonnie lassie from Edinburgh* helped me understand how a family like the Bolins could happen in real life. As well, my own father's journal and the stories of my grandmother and mother helped me tell this Australian jiāngshī story with personal authenticity.

I have many people to thank for the motive force behind this work. Dr Michael Mohammed Ahmad from Sweatshop Literacy Movement offered me an incredible, empathetic mentorship. A distant relative, the photographer and gay icon William Yang, inspired me with his line, 'I came out as Chinese.' The 2023 Queensland Literary Awards Glendower judging panel of Mirandi Riwoe, Ronnie Scott and Melanie Myers gave me the golden sticker sponsored by Jenny Summerson, through the Queensland Library Foundation. My power publisher, Madonna Duffy, has lifted from the front end of the bamboo. My wonderful editor, Ian See, has lifted from the back. The energetic people at UQP have been cheering us all the way, as has my wonderful agent, Martin Shaw. The State Library of Queensland, the Queensland Writers Centre, the Brisbane Writing Crew. Garth Jones, Poppy Gee, Michelle Upton, Lara Cain Gray, Laura Elvery and Benjamin Law, as well as Noelle Jones, Wendy George and Julie Guy all figured in this journey. Siang Lu has shown me the way. Mirandi, Mohammed and Lech Blaine have made me blush with their praise. The photographers Chris Crawford and Skeet Booth took my shots. Josh Durham delivered a paranormal design. This is a dark story that I wrote lit by the thousand-watt smile of my partner, the beautiful Jonny Ng, with Falkor the Snow Monkey on watch.